ACCLAIM FOR BETH WISEMAN

"*A Beautiful Arrangement* has everything you want in an escape novel."
—AMISH HEARTLAND

"*A Beautiful Arrangement* has so much heart, you won't want to put it down until you've read the last page. I love second-chance love stories, and Lydia and Samuel's story is heartbreaking and sweet with unexpected twists and turns that make their journey to love all the more satisfying. Beth's fans will cherish this book."
—JENNIFER BECKSTRAND, AUTHOR OF THE
PETERSHEIM BROTHERS SERIES

"Wiseman's delightful third installment of the Amish Journey series (*A Beautiful Arrangement*) centers on the struggles and unexpected joys of a marriage of convenience . . . Series devotees and newcomers alike will find this engrossing romance hard to put down."
—PUBLISHERS WEEKLY

"Wiseman is at her best in this surprising tale of love and faith."
—PUBLISHERS WEEKLY ON LISTENING TO LOVE

"*Listening to Love* is vintage Beth Wiseman . . . Clear your calendar because you're going to want to read this one in a single setting."
—VANNETTA CHAPMAN, AUTHOR OF THE
SHIPSHEWANA AMISH MYSTERY SERIES

"I always find Beth Wiseman's books to be both tenderly romantic and thought provoking. She has a way of setting a scene that makes me feel like I'm part of an Amish community and visiting for supper.

I loved the title of this book, the message about faith and God, and the heartfelt romance between Lucas and Natalie. *Listening to Love* has everything I love in a Beth Wiseman novel—a strong faith message, a touching romance, and a beautiful sense of place. Beth is such an incredibly gifted storyteller."

—SHELLEY SHEPARD GRAY, BESTSELLING AUTHOR
OF THE SEASONS OF SUGARCREEK SERIES

"This is a sweet story, not only of romance, but of older generations and younger generations coming together in friendship. It's a tear-jerker as well as an uplifting story."

—PARKERSBURG NEWS & SENTINEL ON HEARTS IN HARMONY

"Beth Wiseman has penned a poignant story of friendship, faith, and love that is sure to touch readers' hearts."

—KATHLEEN FULLER, AUTHOR OF THE MIDDLEFIELD
FAMILY NOVELS, ON HEARTS IN HARMONY

"Beth Wiseman's *Hearts in Harmony* is a lyrical hymn. Mary and Levi are heartwarming, lovable characters who instantly feel like dear friends. Once readers open this book, they won't put it down until they've reached the last page."

—AMY CLIPSTON, BESTSELLING AUTHOR OF A GIFT OF GRACE

"*Plain Promise* is Beth Wiseman's masterpiece. It's the story of two unlikely friends' journey toward faith and love. This heart-warming novel brings readers hope and paints a beautiful, authentic portrait of Lancaster County, Pennsylvania. Her characters are so real that they feel like old friends."

—AMY CLIPSTON, BESTSELLING AUTHOR OF A GIFT OF GRACE

"Beth Wiseman's *Plain Pursuit* is a charming work of fiction that beautifully paints the quaint picture of the simple ways of the Amish lifestyle. This novel, like its predecessor, *Plain Perfect*, really brings home a message of family devotion. This is wholesome entertainment that I can effortlessly recommend without any reservation. What a sweet, romantic story."

—WORD-UP-STUDIES.BLOGSPOT.COM

"Wiseman's Christian romance novel is just 'plain' good."

—FAYETTE COUNTY RECORD, LA GRANGE,
TEXAS, ON *PLAIN PERFECT*

"*Plain Pursuit*'s storyline will hit you in the heart almost from page 1. As you keep going deeper into the story, it ceases being a 'story' and begins to feel like you are an active participant in a group of people's lives. Learning the history of shunning in the Amish world is contrasted by your world, where anything would be done to save a child's life. When you witness where these two worlds collide, there is frustration, awe, and tears. [It] will take you from the thrills of a new love as Noah and Carley explore each other's pasts together, to the bottom of despair as the life of a child hangs by a thread."

—*THE ROMANCE READERS CONNECTION*

"I was kind of dreading reading yet another Amish novel as not too many of the more recently published ones measure up to Beverly Lewis or Wanda Brunstetter. However, *Plain Perfect* is the exception rather than the rule. And I couldn't help but keep reading the well-crafted story. The characters could be real, with real life struggles, and even the Amish had issues to work through."

—LAURA V. HILTON, LIGHTHOUSE-ACADEMY.BLOGSPOT.COM

"Beth Wiseman gives the reader a delightful glimpse into the life of [the] Amish [in *Plain Perfect*]. [Her] writing is truly inspired."

—SCHULENBURG STICKER, SCHULENBURG, TEXAS

"The importance of finding peace and acceptance, especially within oneself, is a central theme in this book, the second in Wiseman's Daughters of the Promise series. Well-defined characters and story make for an enjoyable read."

—ROMANTIC TIMES ON PLAIN PURSUIT

"[A] touching, heartwarming story. Wiseman does a particularly great job of dealing with shunning, a controversial Amish practice that seems cruel and unnecessary to outsiders . . . If you're a fan of Amish fiction, don't miss *Plain Pursuit*!"

—KATHLEEN FULLER, AUTHOR OF THE
MIDDLEFIELD FAMILY NOVELS

"[*Plain Pursuit* is] a well-crafted story with fully drawn characters and has nice pacing."

—LIBRARYTHING.COM

"Wiseman's (Amish Secrets) collection of timeless stories of love and loss among the Plain people will delight fans of the author's heartfelt story lines and flowing prose."

—LIBRARY JOURNAL ON AMISH CELEBRATIONS

"Beth Wiseman's novel will find a permanent home in every reader's heart as she spins comfort and prose into a stellar read of grace."

—KELLY LONG, AUTHOR OF THE PATCH OF
HEAVEN SERIES, ON HOME ALL ALONG

"Suggest to those seeking a more truthful, less saccharine portrayal of the trials of human life and the transformative growth and redemption that may occur as a result."

—LIBRARY JOURNAL ON LOVE BEARS ALL THINGS

"Wiseman has created a series in which the readers have a chance to peel back all the layers of the Amish secrets."

—ROMANTIC TIMES, 4 ½ STARS AND JULY 2015
TOP PICK! ON HER BROTHER'S KEEPER

"Wiseman's new launch is edgier, taking on the tough issues of mental illness and suicide. Amish fiction fans seeking something a bit more thought-provoking and challenging than the usual fare will find this series debut a solid choice."

—LIBRARY JOURNAL ON HER BROTHER'S KEEPER

"Wiseman's voice is consistently compassionate and her words flow smoothly."

—PUBLISHERS WEEKLY REVIEW OF SEEK ME WITH ALL YOUR HEART

"Wiseman's third Land of Canaan novel overflows with romance, broken promises, a modern knight in shining armor, and hope at the end of the rainbow."

—ROMANTIC TIMES ON SEEK ME WITH ALL YOUR HEART

"In Seek Me with All Your Heart, Beth Wiseman offers readers a heart-warming story filled with complex characters and deep emotion. I instantly loved Emily, and eagerly turned each page, anxious to learn more about her past—and what future the Lord had in store for her."

—SHELLEY SHEPARD GRAY, BESTSELLING AUTHOR
OF THE SEASONS OF SUGARCREEK SERIES

A BEAUTIFUL
ARRANGEMENT

OTHER BOOKS BY BETH WISEMAN

THE AMISH INN NOVELS

A Picture of Love
An Unlikely Match (available June 2021)

THE AMISH JOURNEY NOVELS

Hearts in Harmony
Listening to Love
A Beautiful Arrangement

THE AMISH SECRETS NOVELS

Her Brother's Keeper
Love Bears All Things
Home All Along

THE DAUGHTERS OF THE PROMISE SERIES

Plain Perfect
Plain Pursuit
Plain Promise
Plain Paradise
Plain Proposal
Plain Peace

In His Father's Arms included in *An Amish Cradle*
A Cup Half Full included in *An Amish Home*
The Cedar Chest included in *An Amish Heirloom*
When Love Returns included in *Amish Homecoming*
A Reunion of Hearts included in *An Amish Reunion*
Loaves of Love included in *An Amish Christmas Bakery*

A BEAUTIFUL ARRANGEMENT

AN AMISH JOURNEY NOVEL

Beth Wiseman

ZONDERVAN®

ZONDERVAN

A Beautiful Arrangement

Copyright © 2020 by Elizabeth Wiseman Mackey

Requests for information should be addressed to:
Zondervan, *3900 Sparks Dr. SE, Grand Rapids, Michigan 49546*

ISBN 978-0-310-36092-6 (library edition)
ISBN 978-0-310-35717-9 (softcover)
ISBN 978-0-310-35719-3 (downloadable audio)
ISBN 978-0-310-35718-6 (ebook)
ISBN 978-0-310-36394-1 (mass market)

Library of Congress Cataloging-in-Publication Data
CIP data is available upon request.

Zondervan titles may be purchased in bulk for educational, business, fund-raising, or
sales promotional use. For information, please email SpecialMarkets@Zondervan.com.

Printed in the United States of America

21 22 23 24 25 LSC 10 9 8 7 6 5 4 3 2 1

To Linda Crane

GLOSS

ab im kopp: crazy, off in the head
ach: oh
aenti: aunt
boppli: baby
bruder: brother
daed: dad
danki: thank you
Deutsch: Dutch
dochder: daughter
Englisch: those who are not Amish; the English language
fraa: wife
Gott: God
grossmudder: grandmother
gut: good
haus: house
kapp: prayer covering worn by Amish women
kinner: children
lieb: love
maedel/maeds: girl/girls
mamm: mom
mammi: grandmother
mei: my
mudder: mother
nee: no

GLOSSARY

...nge: "running around"; the period of time when ...sh youth experience life in the Englisch world before ...king the decision to be baptized and commit to Amish ...fe

...hweschder: sister

sohn: son

Wie bischt?: Hello; how are you?

ya: yes

CHAPTER 1

Lydia closed her eyes and pretended to be asleep as Samuel entered their bedroom. Then she could feel him ease back the single white sheet on their bed before he extinguished the lantern on his nightstand and lay down. It was still hard for her to believe she was Mrs. Samuel Bontrager.

Her husband would be asleep within a few minutes, snoring lightly. He'd missed supper for the second night in a row. Lydia had left him a plate filled with glazed ham, roasted potatoes, and pinto beans on the stove—a few of his favorites. She tried to prepare a special supper on the nights he knew he'd work late. Employees at the furniture store were required to work overtime during inventory.

A gentle breeze floated on moonbeams through the screen of the opened window as she waited. Combined with the two battery-operated fans in the room, it made the August heat bearable at night.

After Samuel drifted off, Lydia gingerly lifted the sheet, dropped one leg slowly to the wood floor, and lifted herself from the bed. She tiptoed into the living room and felt her way around in the dark until she stepped over the threshold of their daughter's room. A small nightlight, also operated by batteries, dimly illuminated the area, and two fans similar to the ones in her and Samuel's bedroom cooled the space. She watched the baby's chest rise and fall in peaceful slumber.

At seventeen, Lydia was not only married but raising a six-month-old. Mattie was the light of her life, but recently she'd begun to wail for what seemed like no reason. Lydia would pace with her, gently rocking her child in her arms, often for as long as an hour. By the end of the day, Lydia was exhausted, but sleep still didn't come easily.

"You are the most beautiful person in the world," Lydia whispered as she gently stroked Mattie's head, combing back a cap of golden tresses, wondering if her daughter's hair color would change over time. Her eye color had stayed the same so far, the royal blue Lydia imagined the deepest parts of the ocean would be. Set against her porcelain skin, Mattie's eyes made her look like the china dolls Lydia had seen in *Englisch* stores—perfect in every way. Although in her tranquil sleep, she was a far cry from the red-faced, screaming child Lydia had tried to console earlier in the day.

Lydia kissed her finger and pressed it to Mattie's forehead. Then she closed her eyes and prayed, asking the Lord to heal whatever was causing her daughter to have so many crying spells. She also asked Him to help her be a better mother. She must be doing something wrong for her baby to cry so much.

She stared at her little bundle and wondered if babies dreamed.

Lydia used to dream she would fall in love, then marry and have a big family. But she and Samuel had fallen in lust, made a baby, and then married. They knew nothing about being in love. Lydia was married to a good man, three years her senior, who'd fathered their child. But their attraction to each other had floundered following the hurried wedding their parents arranged—forced—in an effort to alleviate some of the shame they'd brought to their families.

It seemed to have worked. Everyone was in love with Mattie, her grandparents on both sides completely smitten. Over time, what Lydia and Samuel had done to make their marriage necessary had become less a burden for everyone.

Yet Lydia longed for the excitement of falling in love, for the dizzy feeling and passion she'd read about in books. She and Samuel had missed that entire phase, dating and falling in love. She would never experience those emotions. She was married to a kind man she'd known her entire life, but in a relationship with no romance. And she and Samuel hadn't been intimate since the day Mattie was conceived.

They'd made a few awkward moves toward consummating their marriage, but Lydia had been in the throes of morning sickness. She'd also resented their forced wedding, and that sentiment had carried over to Samuel. Then when her belly began to expand, she'd felt unattractive. And after Mattie was born, her attention was solely on her daughter, and she was always exhausted.

Samuel finally stopped trying to rekindle a physical relationship, and they slipped into a kind of companionship, a relationship of convenience, even though they shared a bed.

But that wasn't what Lydia believed marriage should be. They'd married only because they'd gone against God, exploring a territory reserved for married couples. Now they were raising a child together, but all they had in common was their love for Mattie.

Samuel adored their daughter. Lydia longed for him to feel that way about her—and vice versa.

. . .

Samuel came home to the farmhouse he and Lydia rented. He was grateful the Yoders' rental property had become available at just the right time, a week before he and Lydia married. It wasn't his dream house, and he hoped to own his own home someday, but it was close to the furniture store.

This was his third night in a row to work late. Hopefully, they would finish taking inventory tomorrow so he could be home at a normal hour. He missed seeing Mattie before she went to sleep. When he didn't work late, he and Lydia both tucked her into bed—after small talk during supper and their evening devotions.

Time with Lydia was often strained and uncomfortable, though. Neither of them knew how to tame the huge elephant in the room—the fact that they still didn't really know each other.

It was hard to love a woman when you didn't know her. At least not the way a man should know his wife.

Once he'd settled his horse in the barn, he trudged up the front porch steps, then into the house, yawning. After he hung his hat on the rack and kicked off his shoes by the door, he lowered his suspenders. Then he lit the lantern on the hutch before picking it up and walking into the kitchen. He slowed his stride when he saw Lydia sitting at the kitchen table in the dark.

Usually by now, she was in bed pretending to be asleep while Samuel slipped into the shower. He slept lightly, but he felt the bed move each night when she got up. A wooden slat in the hallway also groaned right before she stepped into Mattie's room. Most nights, he didn't know when she came back to bed or how long she stayed in their daughter's room, but every morning, she was up before he was, cooking breakfast.

"*Wie bischt?* Is everything okay? Is the *boppli* all right?" He ran his hand the length of his short beard as his pulse picked up. "Are you all right?"

"*Ya*, we're both fine."

His heart rate slowed, but Lydia sounded defeated. Samuel held the light closer to his wife's face. "Have you been crying?" The whites of her eyes were red, and he could see dark circles under her eyes even in the dimly lit room.

"Mattie cried off and on, all day long, even more than she has been." Her bottom lip trembled. "I don't know what I'm doing wrong." Pleading eyes sought comfort from him, which was unusual. Lydia never wept or showed much emotion in front of him. He knew Mattie had cried a lot lately—he'd seen it on the weekends—but Lydia rarely commented on it.

"Maybe she's sick." He set the lantern on the table and sat down across from her. He could smell his supper on a plate atop the stove, but even though his stomach rumbled, concern for his daughter dulled his appetite. He was also eager to comfort his wife. She didn't give him that opportunity very often.

Lydia sighed as she blinked back tears. "I've taken her temperature, and it's normal. She doesn't seem to have a cough or cold, and she's soiling her diaper in a normal manner." She shrugged as she gazed at him from the other side of the table. His wife was as beautiful today as the day they'd made love in the barn. At least, they'd thought it was love. It had seemed the best way to justify their physical longing for each other.

"Should you take her to the doctor?" Samuel cut his eyes slightly to the left when a gust of warm wind blew through the open window, sending the aroma of his supper wafting up his nose.

Lydia stood, walked to the stove, and returned with the plate of food. She set it in front of him and then took a fork from the drawer and gave it to him. "What would I tell the doctor?" she asked as she sat down again. "That she cries a lot? A *mudder* should be able to figure out why her *boppli* is crying."

His wife sounded fragile, and her vulnerability tugged at his heart. He kept his eyes on her as he forked a small chunk of ham, but he didn't put it in his mouth. He wanted to say something to help her, but the words weren't coming. He knew even less about raising babies than she did. He ate the bite of ham. "'Tis *gut*," he said after he swallowed, then cringed at his failure to offer an inkling of solace.

"*Danki*." She pushed back her chair and yawned. Samuel wasn't sure if that was a genuine show of exhaustion or if she was just eager to avoid further conversation with him. Not that he blamed her. She'd opened up to him, and he hadn't had anything constructive to say.

"Good night." She slid her chair under the table and then started to leave the kitchen, her shoulders slouched as if she carried the weight of the world on them.

Samuel searched his mind for something to make her feel better. "Lydia?"

She slowly turned around. "*Ya?*"

"You're a *gut mudder*." He meant it. Miles of emotional distance stretched between him and Lydia, but she tended to Mattie's every need and loved her as much as he did.

She offered a weak smile before she again turned to go.

Samuel did love Lydia, even though he'd never told her so. The emotion seemed to have grown when he wasn't paying attention. Maybe *I love you* were the words he'd been searching for. He stood and took a few steps, but then his throat seemed to close. *What if she doesn't love me back?*

. . .

Lydia rolled onto her side, ready to close her eyes when Samuel came out of the bathroom. She wasn't even sure why. He hadn't tried to be intimate with her since well before Mattie was born. But lately, she longed to be held—especially tonight when she was so worried about her baby. It had just been so long that she didn't know what to do. And even if she initiated physical contact, what if he rejected her?

She positioned the sheet so she could see her husband out of one eye when he came in. He wouldn't be able to see her face at this angle.

In only a towel, he entered the room and wound his way around the bed and out of view, but the glance was enough to remind her why she'd been attracted to him physically in the first place. He was tall, handsome, and perfectly proportioned with a broad chest and muscular arms. His smile was what had originally caught her eye, though—the way it crooked up on one side and gave him a mysterious aura. She tried to recall the last time she'd seen him smile. Maybe when he was with his parents. Before he'd grown a beard, the shadows on his face matched the dark hair on his head, which lent him a rugged, boyish look she found attractive.

But Samuel probably hadn't had a chance to grow into the man he was meant to be emotionally. That's how she felt about herself as a woman. And he, too, must feel like they'd been forced into a life they weren't ready for.

She rolled onto her back and opened her eyes just as he was getting into bed, then she turned her head his way, letting him know she was awake. Catching sight of her opened eyes, he hesitated but eventually fluffed his pillow and lay down on his back.

Lydia waited, wondering if Samuel would reach for her, even if it were only to hold her in his arms. But when he extinguished the flame in the lantern and turned away from her, Lydia's hope went as dark as their bedroom.

. . .

Samuel wanted to pull his wife into his arms and make love to her. It was a physical longing, but he also thought it might bring them closer emotionally. He'd tried one too many times when they were first married, though, and the rejection stung a little more each time. Yet Lydia was uncharacteristically ensuring he knew she was awake. Did she share his desire for a physical relationship?

Yawning, he decided not to chance another rejection. She would be up soon to check on Mattie. Every couple had a routine, and Samuel and Lydia had settled into theirs. Marrying before he was ready wasn't his first choice, but he'd made his bed, and he had to sleep in it. He just wished he didn't have to sleep in it alone.

. . .

The next morning, Samuel didn't know when he'd dozed off, and if Lydia got up to check on Mattie, he hadn't heard her. As he breathed in the aroma of bacon sizzling in the kitchen, he remembered he was supposed to ask his wife a question on behalf of a coworker.

Sometimes he only had enough time to grab toast, but that was because he stayed in bed to avoid talking with Lydia. Unless he heard Mattie up. He enjoyed her giggles and bright eyes in the mornings. But their baby slept through the night and often didn't wake up until after Samuel had left for work.

Today he hurriedly dressed, cared for the horses—thankful Lydia cared for their chickens—and then went straight to the kitchen to allow enough time for conversation.

"*Wie bischt*," Lydia said as he sat down at the table. She poured a cup of coffee and handed it to him. His wife didn't drink coffee very much, but she always had a pot percolated for him as well as a packed meal for work. For a moment, he thought about how the furniture store was a good place for him. Samuel had worked for Lydia's father, Henry, building furniture in his barn. Yet not only had his new father-in-law scowled at him a lot but that barn was where he and Lydia had committed their sin. Samuel didn't want to be reminded of that. Besides, his job at the furniture store paid more, and he needed the money.

"Do you have time for eggs?" Lydia nodded toward the skillet in front of her, and when Samuel told her he did, she cracked open two eggs and slipped them into the bacon grease.

He waited a couple of minutes before making the request. He didn't know if Lydia would see it as a good thing or a burden. "I need to ask you something," he said. Then he drew in a deep breath when she looked over her shoulder and lifted an eyebrow. "Do you remember Joseph? He works with me at the store."

Lydia slid the fried eggs onto a plate and then placed them in front of Samuel. They were runny, the way he liked them. "I remember. Joseph has worked there only a short time, *ya*?"

Samuel nodded. Joseph's family had moved to Montgomery a few months ago. "He wants to be formally introduced to your friend, Beverly. She was with you when you brought me *mei* dinner last week."

"Beverly Schrock?"

"*Ya*. I guess that's her last name. He was wondering if maybe they could meet here for supper one night, but I know you're tired a lot, and if you don't want to do that, I—"

"*Nee, nee*. It's fine, but I don't really know Beverly. She's more of an acquaintance, and she lives in Odon, in a different district. I've been around her only a couple of times. Once at a quilting party a long time ago, and she might have been at Levi and Mary's wedding, but I'm not sure." She paused. "Actually, she just needed to use the restroom that day we saw each other on the sidewalk. We exchanged pleasantries, and she followed me into the store. After I introduced her to you and Joseph, I pointed her to the restroom."

"I guess you don't know if she's seeing anyone?" Samuel reached for another slice of toast. This was the most conversation he'd had with Lydia in a long while that wasn't about Mattie.

"I saw her working at the bakery in Odon one time. I can go by there and find out if she's interested in being introduced to Joseph, assuming she still works there." Lydia poured the bacon grease into a jar before she lowered the skillet into some soapy dishwater.

"Are you sure it would be okay?" Samuel stood, the piece of toast still in his hand. He'd eaten both eggs. "I know it's extra work for you."

"*Ya*, I'm sure, if Beverly is agreeable. We haven't had anyone to supper except our families. It might be fun." She glanced at him and smiled.

Samuel pushed in his chair and walked to where Lydia was standing at the sink. She jumped when he touched her back, and then she turned to face him.

"I-I just want to tell you to have a *gut* day." Then he leaned down to kiss her, something he never did. Maybe a small gesture of affection would remind her of the spark they'd once felt for each other. But when she offered him her cheek, he was reminded why he stopped trying to get close to her.

After a quick peck, he stepped into the living room, took his hat from the rack, and slipped into his shoes. He didn't mean to slam the door behind him. Or maybe he did.

. . .

Lydia leaned back against the counter and squeezed her eyes closed. *Why did I do that?* Samuel had made an effort to kiss her, on the lips. And she'd turned away from him.

Mattie started to cry before she had time to further analyze what had happened. She grabbed the bottle she'd already warmed from the counter and went to her daughter's room. Maybe Mattie missed breast milk. Lydia had to quit nursing when she stopped producing enough milk a couple of months ago.

"*Wie bischt, mei* precious *maedel.*" She placed the bottle in her child's outstretched hands as she pulled a diaper from the changing table next to the crib. When she'd changed her, she scooped Mattie into her arms and held the baby close to her as she made her way back to the kitchen.

She settled into a kitchen chair, crossed one leg over the other, and gently rocked Mattie in her lap. When she'd finished half the bottle, Lydia put her over her shoulder until she let out a hearty burp, which she almost always did. That ruled out gas as Mattie's cause for crying.

Lydia let her thoughts drift back to Samuel's attempt to kiss her. After they'd settled into this way of life almost a year ago, she wondered what had prompted him to do so. She wished she wouldn't have turned away from him, but he'd caught her off guard.

For the hundredth time, she tried to envision what dating would have looked like for them. Would he have brought her flowers? That wasn't typical of her people, but Lydia knew some Amish women who'd received flowers when they were courted. Would they have gone to see a movie together since they'd both been in their running-around time? But that period was cut short, followed by a hurried baptism and wedding.

Now they were living like mere companions. Could the pattern be changed? She hoped so. But it would take effort from both of them—and turning away from Samuel this morning sent a message she hadn't intended.

CHAPTER 2

Lydia set the table with the bone china her grandmother had given her before she died. She'd used the fragile dishes only once before, when her parents came for supper for the first time. She'd had a week to plan this evening, and she wanted it to go well. Lydia might be inexperienced as a wife and mother, but she was a decent cook, and she wanted Samuel to be proud of her.

Mattie was eating Honey Nut Cheerios in her high chair, and Samuel was tidying up the living room. Lydia was grateful for his help. In all the years she'd lived at home, she couldn't recall her father doing any type of housework, but Samuel had. His mother, Fannie, had been confined to a wheelchair since he was five, after she'd been thrown from a horse.

He was still helping them. His father, Herman, had a heart attack a couple of years ago, which limited what he could do physically. Samuel not only helped his folks financially but he checked on them almost daily. Lydia admired his commitment to them. It was a trait she'd known about long before she and Mattie became part of his family.

"*Danki*," she said as she joined him in the living room.

Holding a stack of mail Lydia had left on the coffee table, Samuel bent over to pick up a pacifier that had slipped out of Mattie's mouth earlier.

"For what?" He stared at her as though he really didn't know what she meant.

"For picking up in here. I-I was going to get to it, but I just didn't have time." Mattie had cried a lot today, but Lydia should have managed her time better. She couldn't blame her daughter.

"It's no problem." He shrugged, then held up the mail. "I'm going to put this on our dresser. I'll go through it later." Samuel paid the bills, so unless it was from one of her out-of-town relatives, mail was seldom addressed to her.

She was standing in the same spot when he returned.

"What's wrong?" Samuel ran a sleeve across his sweaty forehead. It was always warmer in the house when the oven was in use.

"Nothing is wrong." Lydia cast her eyes down and bit her bottom lip before she looked at him. "I just want everything to go well."

Samuel picked up a baby rattle. "All we can do is make the introduction. You can't make people fall in love. It either happens or it doesn't."

That wasn't what Lydia meant, but she swallowed back the knot trying to form in her throat. Then she went to the window when she heard a buggy pulling into the driveway. It was Joseph.

"*Danki* for having me," he said as Lydia and Samuel welcomed him into their home. He handed her a heavy paper bag. "It's cantaloupes. We've got more than we can eat, and *Mamm* said you might enjoy them."

"*Ach*, wonderful. *Danki*." Lydia motioned to the couch. "Please have a seat. You two can chat while I finish up our meal. Beverly should be here soon."

Lydia scurried back to the kitchen, her stomach churning with anticipation. She'd been worried about the meal, her presentation, and being the perfect hostess for this matchmaking event. Now she wondered if it would be awkward and uncomfortable.

Beverly hadn't remembered meeting Joseph, but since she wasn't seeing anyone, she'd been happy to accept the invitation to supper. Lydia must not have been paying much attention when she met Joseph either. Beverly was a beautiful woman with dark hair, huge brown eyes, and a flawless smile, and Lydia hoped she could be objective and not place her entire opinion on Joseph's looks. Twenty like Samuel, he was tall and thin, which wasn't bad, but he had bushy eyebrows that almost met in the middle of his forehead, ears that seemed unusually large, and a toothy grin.

Lydia didn't know how old Beverly was, but she suspected she was eighteen or nineteen. And the few times she'd been around her, she seemed very sweet.

Lydia recalled what Samuel said. *You can't make people fall in love. It either happens or it doesn't.* When he said that, Lydia could have sworn she heard an edge to his voice, perhaps referencing their own relationship. Either way, he was right.

Lydia gave the table another once-over, pleased with the setup. She checked her apron for spillage and brushed out the wrinkles. Taking a deep breath, she lifted Mattie from her high chair and prayed she wouldn't scream through the entire meal. Then she bounced the baby on her hip as she strode into the living room, just as Samuel was opening the door and motioning for Beverly to come in.

Lydia watched Beverly's face closely, but the woman's expression didn't give anything away when she was reintroduced to Joseph. She smiled, shook his hand, and thanked Lydia and Samuel for having her.

After their guests fussed over Mattie for a few minutes,

saying how cute she was and even getting her to giggle, Mattie was back in her high chair, and everyone was seated at the table. Following the blessing, Joseph looked at Lydia and grinned. Something about his quirky smile and crooked teeth was rather cute, and that seemed to make his big ears and bushy eyebrows stand out a little less.

"Lydia, how did you know roast, potatoes, and carrots is *mei* favorite meal?" he asked.

"And everything is so pretty." Beverly glanced at Joseph before turning to Lydia. "These dishes are lovely." She tapped a finger on the corner of her plate.

Lydia tried not to swell with pride as she felt herself blushing. "*Danki.* They were *mei grossmudder*'s." She looked across the table at Samuel, but he was busy cutting his meat.

The roast was tender and seasoned just right, and Joseph and Beverly settled into a comfortable conversation about their jobs.

"I work only part-time at the bakery, but I enjoy interacting with other people." Beverly chuckled. "Although the temptation to overindulge on pastries and pretzels gets the best of me sometimes."

Joseph laughed. "I can't think of a better job to have, one with an unlimited amount of food." He glanced at Samuel. "Our jobs are okay, but can you imagine if one of the shelves at the furniture store was lined with nothing but baked goods?"

Samuel nodded, grinning slightly through a bite of food.

Lydia wondered what it would be like to have a part-time job, to be around other people, to have a break from motherhood if only for a short while. A flood of guilt rushed through her as soon as she had the thought. Her job as Mattie's mother was important.

Then out of nowhere, Mattie got that look on her face, the one Lydia had learned to recognize. Her tiny lips drew into a pout as she sucked in her chubby cheeks, and then her mouth opened wide and the wailing began.

"I'm so sorry." Lydia almost knocked over her chair as she hastily lifted Mattie from the high chair, sure she would miss most of the meal and conversation from here on. Pacing the living room might quiet her daughter, but silence wouldn't come quickly.

"Oh dear. That was sudden." Beverly stood. "Poor *boppli*."

"*Ach*, please." Lydia bounced Mattie on her hip. "Finish your supper. I'll just walk her around in the living room for a few minutes."

"She's probably teething, isn't she?" Beverly gently touched the tip of Mattie's nose. "Is that what it is, little one?"

Teething was the one thing Lydia hadn't thought of. Neither had her mother mentioned the possibility when she'd last visited her.

"*Mei schweschder*'s *boppli* was about this age when she started teething. The pain usually came on at mealtimes. Sometimes Susan—my niece—would just start screaming as though it had suddenly kicked in."

Lydia cut her eyes in Samuel's direction, hoping he wasn't paying much attention. The man liked to eat and had a way of disengaging himself during a meal. But he stared at her intently, leaving Lydia to wonder if, in truth, he doubted her mothering skills, no matter what he'd said last week.

"I-I thought she'd be a little older before she cut a tooth." Lydia put a finger in Mattie's mouth and rubbed along her gums. "I don't feel anything."

"Don't feel bad. Susan is a little older than Mattie, and *mei schweschder*, Anna, didn't realize she was teething. She couldn't feel anything either. But now Anna makes a paste with ground cloves and some other ingredients to rub on her gums. It works. I'll get the exact recipe and get it to you." Beverly smiled.

Mattie shrieked so loudly that Lydia cringed, apologizing again as she took her baby into the living room to pace with her. She certainly hoped the salve Beverly mentioned would work.

Beverly joined her a few minutes later. "Will she come to me so you can finish your supper?" She held out her arms.

"*Nee*, I can't let you do that. I'm sure she'll be fine soon." Lydia was fairly certain that wasn't true.

"Oh, she's so precious, and I don't mind at all. I've kept Susan occupied lots of times so *mei schweschder* could finish a meal."

Mattie went willingly to Beverly, and the baby's crying hushed, leaving only a whimper coming out of her mouth.

Lydia had lost her appetite, but she went back into the kitchen, planning to apologize to Joseph for the interruption. But Joseph was already standing. "It was a *wunderbaar* meal, Lydia. But since I'm done, I'll help Beverly with the *boppli*. You two enjoy some quiet time while you finish your supper." He winked at her.

Now Mattie was completely quiet. Lydia wanted to burst into tears as she wondered if the problem wasn't teething but her. She had never managed to get her daughter to stop crying that quickly. Someone else was comforting her child when she couldn't.

"He likes her," Samuel whispered once Joseph was in the other room.

Lydia tried to smile, but she wished supper hadn't been interrupted. Yet Joseph had clearly been eager to spend time with

Beverly, so maybe it worked out okay. Beverly seemed like the type of person who was nice to everyone, though, so Lydia couldn't tell how she felt about Joseph so far. She also wondered if she and Beverly might become friends. How nice it would be to have a friend her age to talk to again. Beverly might be someone she could not only trust but who wouldn't judge her.

"I like her too," Lydia responded softly before she sat down across from Samuel. But her appetite hadn't returned. After a few minutes of shifting food around on her plate, she decided to serve dessert in the living room.

. . .

Samuel set his plate on the coffee table and covered his mouth so he wouldn't spew food everywhere. He'd worked with Joseph for only a couple of months, but all he really knew about him was that he was a hard worker, he was almost always happy, and he smiled a lot. He also had an endless supply of jokes, and he could tell them in an animated way that set him apart from the average joke teller.

"What did the blanket say to the bed?" Joseph raised his eyebrows up and down, grinning. "Don't worry, I've got you covered." He laughed as if he'd just told the funniest joke in the world, which made everyone chuckle. Joseph held up a finger and led right into another one. "Why did the robber take a bath? So he could make a clean getaway."

Then Joseph pressed his lips together and drew in his eyebrows as he shook his head. "I got fired from *mei* job at the furniture store today." He glanced at Samuel, who stopped laughing.

"What? *Nee*, you didn't." Samuel would have known about this.

"*Ya, ya,* I did." Joseph held on to his sober expression. "A little old lady came in to check her balance, so I pushed her over."

Samuel laughed so hard his stomach ached. When he looked at his wife, Lydia was in stitches, too, and so was Beverly.

"Stop!" Beverly was almost crying. "I can't breathe."

Mattie had gone to sleep an hour ago, and Samuel couldn't remember the last time he'd stayed up this late. Nor could he remember this much laughter filling his house. Ever.

Lydia's spirits had lifted, and Samuel was happy to see her enjoying herself. Earlier he could tell it upset her when Mattie started crying during the meal, and she'd seemed embarrassed when Beverly was able to calm their daughter right away. He'd considered offering to help with Mattie, but he worried that might embarrass his wife even more. Men generally left childrearing to the mothers, but Samuel tried to help out with Mattie as often as he could.

Samuel knew how hard it was to get their daughter to stop crying when she had one of her spells. He hoped Beverly was right, that the cause was teeth fighting their way in. Lydia was a good mother, just inexperienced and learning, the same way Samuel was growing into his role as a father. He wished growing as a couple came as naturally as parenting.

"This has been such a fun night." Beverly stood, her face still flushed from laughing. "But I better go home before *mei* neighbor thinks someone's kidnapped me. She's a widow who lives alone, and she keeps a pretty close eye on me."

The way Beverly tipped her chin and batted her eyes at Joseph, Samuel was sure this had been a good matchmaking effort.

"Maybe I'll kidnap you." Joseph stood and tried to keep a straight face, but that toothy grin of his appeared and then spread into a smile.

"*Ach*, well, you'd be the funniest kidnapper ever." Beverly lifted her small black purse from the couch, then hugged Lydia. "*Danki* for a *wunderbaar* meal and"—she looked over her shoulder at Joseph and grinned before she turned back to Lydia—"For the hilarious entertainment."

"I assure you I don't deserve credit for the entertainment." Lydia laughed, which was nice to hear. A reminder of the way she used to be.

Samuel thought back on his history with Lydia. They'd played together as children, but Samuel hit his *rumschpringe* three years ahead of her, and they grew apart. He hadn't sowed any real oats, but he'd done his share of running around and even gone out with a few girls. Then Lydia matured and reached dating age, and before long Samuel's physical attraction to her peaked. She often came into the barn to watch him and her father working. Samuel noticed how she mostly watched him, and it became apparent she was attracted to him too.

Three years had lapsed since they'd spent much time together, and in reality, they hadn't known each other anymore.

Samuel snapped back to the present and saw Beverly touch Lydia's arm. "I'll be sure to get you some of *mei schweschder*'s salve. And the recipe for it."

After everyone had said their goodbyes and the door was closed, Samuel and Lydia both rushed to the window.

"Do you think he'll kiss her good night?" Samuel pressed his face closer to the pane of glass.

"*Nee*, of course not. It's only their first time together."

Samuel didn't look at her as he recalled the first few times he and Lydia had kissed, before their physical desire had escalated. Was Lydia thinking back on those times too? When she leaned near to him to have a better look, her arm rubbed against his. Then she moved even closer, and he tried to discern if she was intentionally brushing up against him.

Visions of that fateful day in the barn flooded his mind. They'd worried about getting caught, but he could still remember the passion he'd felt. Then what they did was over in a matter of minutes and left them both regretful. As the man—and older than Lydia—he shouldered most of the responsibility for their poor judgment. But every time he looked at Mattie, he couldn't imagine his life without her. It was confusing to him. Why would God gift them with someone to love in such a special way when they'd gone against Him?

The feel of his wife so close to him brought back a whirlwind of feelings and desire. Now they could be together in an intimate way without feeling guilty, but they were down a rabbit hole and couldn't seem to find their way out.

Lydia grabbed his arm. "Look," she said in a loud whisper.

Samuel was already looking, and as Beverly kissed Joseph on the cheek, Samuel's arm found its way around Lydia. "*Ya*, I know." He turned to face her, smiling, his arm still loosely around her waist. "We did *gut*."

Lydia smiled, but the smile quickly faded, replaced by an expression Samuel didn't recognize. He wasn't sure if it was desire . . . or fear. Her eyes shone with purpose, and he wanted to believe it was longing. But when he inched closer to her, she eased away. Just like she always did.

. . .

Lydia wanted to call out to Samuel after he abruptly excused himself and said he was going to bed, but her voice had left her. It had probably fled with her nerve, which had also forsaken her. This time her husband had clearly made his intentions known, and she'd pushed him away even though she longed to be close to him in every way. *Why did I do that again?*

Her thoughts went back to that day in the barn. Their behavior in those secret meetings, when her father was in town, had quickly turned to more than kissing. On the day they went too far, everything was over before Lydia even had time to process what they were doing. She couldn't blame Samuel. She'd been a willing participant, but the intimacy hadn't been anything like she expected.

Was that because it was awkward and rushed? Or maybe it was because, deep down, she'd known they were going against God. Whatever was holding her back now, she wanted to talk to her husband about it, to see if they could work through it. Seeing the way Beverly and Joseph looked at each other throughout the evening made Lydia want to recapture the excitement she'd once had with Samuel.

After she cleaned the kitchen, she took a deep breath and marched to the bedroom. They were a married couple with a child. Surely they could have a conversation about the way they were living and why.

She crossed the threshold of their bedroom, and then she stepped to her husband's side of the bed. His eyes were closed.

"Samuel?" she said in a whisper.

When he didn't answer, Lydia blinked back tears. Samuel always snored lightly when he was asleep, but he wasn't snoring now. She took a step back. He opened one eye but then quickly closed it.

Her husband was doing to her exactly what she'd been doing to him. He just wasn't as good at it.

CHAPTER 3

Beverly had her midday meal with Anna the following Monday, eager to tell her sister about the evening with Joseph. They were eating in the restaurant at Gasthof Amish Village. It was a touristy place frequented by the *Englisch*, but since Anna worked there, she got a discount. And the buffet was always good.

"I haven't laughed so hard in a long time." Beverly smiled as she recalled the jokes Joseph told. "And you know how I feel about a man who can tickle *mei* funny bone."

Anna handed eight-month-old Susan a cookie from the buffet. The baby hadn't eaten much, but she'd been quiet, and both women were thankful for that. Beverly reminded herself she needed to take Lydia the salve she'd made for her. Maybe she'd go to Lydia's house later. She might even know what Joseph thought about meeting her.

"It's *gut* to see you so happy. It sounds like Joseph made quite an impression on you, *ya*?" Anna grinned from across the table. Lydia's older sister was also her best friend. Only two years apart, they'd grown up in a houseful of boys. Anna would be twenty-one in a week, and she and her husband, Emanuel, had been married for two years.

Beverly longed to have the kind of relationship Anna and Emanuel had. She'd had it with Enos, but not for very long. The Lord had taken her husband much too soon. It was hard to believe it had been over a year since he died. Beverly feared she would miss him every day for the rest of her life, but she prayed God would give her a second chance at love. She'd dated only one man since her husband's death, and that hadn't gone well.

"All men won't be like Chriss." Her sister locked eyes with her. "You know that, *ya*?"

She nodded as she recalled the short courtship she'd had with a friend of her cousin's. "I know, but I still want to move slowly. *Mamm* and *Daed*—and everyone else—hope I'll remarry soon, but I want to marry the right man. I'm worried I won't love anyone the way I loved Enos." She sighed, but recalling Joseph's animated storytelling, she couldn't help but smile. "I feel encouraged after meeting Joseph, though."

"I'll be praying things go well with him." Anna winked at her before she turned to Susan. "She's being a little angel today."

Beverly touched the tip of the baby's nose. "You're such a *gut* girl." She turned back to her sister. "I need to take Lydia that salve, and I'm hoping to hear what Joseph thought about meeting me."

"Let me know what she says." Anna's eyes twinkled with an excitement Beverly felt. "I hope he's the one."

Beverly smiled. She'd had only one supper with Joseph, but she was already mildly smitten. "Me too."

. . .

Joseph had been helping the store's van driver deliver furniture all morning. But now he hoped to catch up with Samuel in the break room over dinner. He was breathless by the time he rounded the corner and found his coworker sitting alone at the table.

"What did Beverly have to say about me?" Joseph's heart pounded, his mind a crazy mixture of hope and fear. He'd dated plenty of women back in his hometown, but he hadn't found anyone he was really interested in since moving to Montgomery a couple of months ago.

"Slow down, fella." Samuel chuckled. "We're not in eighth grade."

Joseph pulled a container from the refrigerator and sat down across from his friend, soaking in the air-conditioning, a perk of working for an *Englisch* family. "I know." He bit into a ham-and-cheese sandwich but couldn't help but eye Samuel's food. After he'd downed the bite, he said, "I can't wait to be married if it means someone will pack me a dinner like that. *Mei mamm*'s great, but I rarely get to bring that kind of meal to work."

"Lydia is a *gut* cook." Samuel forked one of two pork chops on his plate and plopped it down next to Joseph's partially eaten sandwich.

"And you're a *gut* friend." Joseph lifted the pork chop and took a big bite, closing his eyes to savor the flavor. "I remember *Mamm* sending dinners like this when I was in school. She'd put in a little icepack. We didn't mind eating it cold." He tipped his head to one side. "I don't exactly remember when sandwiches started showing up instead." Smiling, he nodded at the microwave. "Dinner is even better when it's hot."

He gave his friend time to offer up any information, then grunted. "So. What did she say?"

"I don't think Lydia has talked to Beverly." Samuel laughed again. "It's only been three days."

Joseph groaned. "I know, but I really want to see her, and I'm anxious to know if she's interested in going out with me."

He sat taller. "Hey, *mei* friend. Why don't we all go on a picnic Saturday, when I get off work at noon? It won't exactly be a double date, just friends hanging out."

"I'll talk to Lydia and see what she thinks. It might be too hot for Mattie." Samuel scooped up the last of the peas on his paper plate.

"*Ya*, you're right." Joseph raised his eyebrows several times, grinning. "Maybe we could go later in the afternoon."

Samuel smiled as he stood and tossed his empty plate in the trash can. "Maybe so." He turned to Joseph and chuckled. "You act like this was love at first sight."

Joseph leaned back in his chair and considered the possibility. "Maybe it was."

. . .

Lydia paced with Mattie, battling tears of her own as her little one cried. She'd tried freezing teething rings and some over-the-counter medication for babies cutting teeth, but neither seemed to be working.

When a buggy rolled onto the driveway, Lydia prayed it was her mother and that she could leave Mattie with her for just thirty minutes—so she could go for a walk or do anything to escape her daughter's crying.

Her mother wasn't who stepped out of the buggy, but it might be someone even better—for two reasons. Beverly was carrying a baby on her hip, and she had a paper bag in her hand that Lydia prayed held the salve she mentioned.

Lydia met her at the door. "This must be your niece, Susan." She was a beautiful little girl with blond hair the same color as Mattie's. It just wasn't as curly.

"Forgive the unannounced visit, but I thought you might need this." She handed the bag to Lydia. Mattie had stopped crying and was focused on the small person with Beverly. "And I also thought Susan might be a nice distraction. She's a couple of months older than Mattie, but maybe they'll take a liking to each other."

Lydia sat Mattie on the floor near a pile of toys. Her daughter had been sitting up by herself for only a couple of weeks, and after one good tumble and hitting her head on the wood floor, now there was a rug in the play area.

Beverly placed her niece across from Mattie.

"She's a beautiful little girl," Lydia said as they watched the babies eyeing each other.

"I think babies just like being around other babies." Beverly pulled her eyes from the little ones. "But if this is a bad time, please don't let us keep you from anything."

"*Nee*, this is a great time, and I'm so relieved Mattie isn't crying at the moment." She held up the bag. "And this is?" *Please let it be the miracle medicine.*

"It's the salve I told you about. *Mei schweschder* gave me the recipe, and I went ahead and made some for you in case you didn't have all the ingredients." Beverly folded her hands in front of her. Lydia wanted to rush over and hug her, but she thanked her instead. They didn't really know each other that well.

"Please, sit." Lydia motioned to the couch. "I just took some apple turnovers out of the oven, and I can percolate some coffee if you have time."

"*Ya*, that would be great."

When Lydia returned a few minutes later, Beverly was down on the floor with Mattie and Susan. "They seem to like each other," she said as she stood and accepted the coffee and a turn-over from Lydia. "I didn't know if little Mattie had cousins to play with."

Lydia shook her head. "*Nee, mei* only *schweschder*, Mary, doesn't have any *kinner*. She and her husband, Levi, hope to soon, but it just hasn't happened yet. And Samuel is an only child." Not only were Samuel's parents older than most of their friends' parents, but he'd been born in their forties.

"Susan is an only child too." Beverly took a sip of the coffee before taking a bite of the warm turnover. "This is delicious."

"*Danki.* It's *mei mudder*'s recipe."

Beverly cleared her throat. "Um . . . I have something to ask you." A flush crept across her cheeks as the corners of her mouth curled upward. "I know it's going to sound juvenile, but I was wondering if Joseph said anything about me to Samuel." She momentarily cringed, but the smile quickly returned.

"You liked him?" Lydia recalled how she judged Joseph by his looks when she'd first met him, a reminder that beauty truly was in the eyes of the beholder. Although being around Joseph had surely made him more attractive. He smiled a lot, he was funny, and he seemed to have a kind heart. Babies could tell those things, and Mattie had warmed up to him right away, just like she did with Beverly.

"*Ya*, he's handsome and funny, and I'd like to get to know him better." Beverly's face turned even redder as her smile broadened.

Lydia held up a finger when her cell phone rang from the kitchen. "Excuse me. We use our phones only if it's important, so I better get that."

Once in the kitchen, she was surprised—and a little concerned—to see it was Samuel calling. But he'd just forgotten his wallet and wanted to confirm that he'd left it on the kitchen counter, which he had. He also asked her about going on a picnic Saturday with Joseph and Beverly. Could she ask Beverly if she wanted to go?

"If you think she'll be interested," Samuel said in a whisper. He was probably at the far end of the store where he got the best cell service, but there might be customers around.

Lydia peeked into the living room. Beverly was back on the floor playing with Mattie and Susan again. "*Ach*, I'm pretty sure she'll be interested, although she might have to work at the bakery. She's here right now, so if you can hold on a minute, I'll ask her."

Beverly's face lit up when Lydia asked about the picnic, and she nodded right away.

"*Ya*, looks like it's a go," Lydia told her husband. "Beverly and I can discuss a time, but we probably need to go later in the afternoon, so Mattie doesn't get too hot."

Samuel agreed, and as Lydia ended the call, she realized she'd never been on a picnic with Samuel.

"Apparently, Joseph took a liking to you, because this was his idea." Lydia lowered herself to the floor with Beverly and the babies, soaking up the silence. Maybe she needed to have another baby so they could entertain each other. The thought caused her stomach to swirl as she questioned again why she was nervous about being intimate with Samuel. She'd always wanted a big family.

"This will be so fun." Beverly clapped her hands a couple of times.

The woman was simply gorgeous. How had she remained single this long? "Have you, um . . . dated a lot? I'm only seventeen, so Samuel has been my only, um . . ." She couldn't really call him her boyfriend before they married. "He's been the only one," she finally said.

Beverly's joyous expression faded as her eyes darkened. "I'm twenty, and I've dated a little." She paused as she picked up a toy block and fumbled with it. "I got married right before *mei* seventeenth birthday."

She had? Lydia couldn't help but wonder if her new friend had been in a family way, too, since she'd also been young when she married. But if Beverly was single now, that had to mean she was a widow, and she hadn't mentioned children.

Now Beverly looked enchanted. "We were so in love, and we didn't want to wait to get married." She paused as she looked somewhere over Lydia's shoulder. "Maybe *Gott* nudged us to get married young since He knew He would call Enos home soon. *Mei* husband died of an infection that developed after a tonsillectomy. We were married only two years."

Lydia brought a hand to her chest. She couldn't imagine losing Samuel, and the moment she had the thought, she realized that she did love her husband—even though it wasn't the kind of love she wanted. She shook her head. "I'm so sorry."

"Enos died almost a year ago." She rolled her eyes and finally grinned. "Everyone, especially *mei* parents, hope I find someone special and remarry soon."

"Maybe Joseph will be that person." Lydia hoped Beverly and Joseph would find true love. And maybe living vicariously through them would help Lydia understand how a real romantic relationship was supposed to be.

"I did date one man after Enos died." She shrugged as her lips turned under. "But it didn't work out."

Lydia wanted to ask why, but sometimes people just weren't meant to be together, and she didn't want to pry.

"Where should we have the picnic?" Lydia handed Mattie her pacifier when she reached for it, amazed at how well the two girls seemed to entertain each other, even at such young ages. Mattie mostly watched Susan reaching for toys, studying them, and then moving on to whatever else was in reach.

"What about one of the schoolhouses? No *kinner* will be there since school isn't in session." Beverly's contemplative expression bubbled with childlike enthusiasm. It was hard not to share in her excitement.

Lydia agreed. From there, they planned the menu. When they were done, Lydia said, "I'll bring all the food, but maybe you can bring Susan since she and Mattie seem to entertain each other."

"I'll check with *mei schweschder*, but that's a lovely idea. Are you sure I can't bring some of the food, though?"

"*Nee*. Let this be *mei* treat."

Lydia couldn't recall ever going on a picnic except with her family when she was younger. This would be the first outing where she planned the menu and prepared the food herself. This would be her first picnic with Samuel.

. . .

After devotions that evening, Samuel struck up a conversation about Joseph and Beverly. "He's excited to see her again." He closed his Bible and put it back on the end table beside the couch.

"She's excited, too, although . . ." His wife twitched her mouth back and forth before she went on. "I was a little surprised."

Samuel grinned. "Because he's a little goofy-looking?" He snickered, even though he felt bad about the comment afterward.

Lydia pressed a hand over her mouth, but Samuel was sure she was stifling a grin of her own. Finally, she said, "Beauty is in the eye of the beholder, and Beverly clearly likes Joseph."

Samuel was enjoying having a conversation with Lydia, one where they laughed and talked about someone other than Mattie. It was interesting how easily they could delve into other people's lives and find humor but not know how to build a relationship for themselves, one that included laughter. Samuel decided to stay on course. He liked seeing Lydia smiling and laughing.

"Joseph is a *gut* man. He volunteers at a men's shelter once a month, and on most Tuesdays, he takes his *grossmudder* to supper. She likes pizza, and she can't drive a buggy anymore. His parents brought her along when they moved here from Ohio, along with Joseph's *bruder* and *schweschdere*." Samuel shrugged. "I just like the way he's happy all the time."

"Maybe that's why he and Beverly hit it off. She's like that, too, always smiling and seemingly happy." She paused. "But today, for the first time, I saw a part of her I hadn't seen in the short time I've known her. I didn't know she'd been married."

Samuel's eyes widened. "She's a widow?"

"*Ya.* Her husband died from an infection less than a year ago. When she spoke about it, she got a faraway look in her eyes, and for a few moments, I thought she might cry. But then we started talking about Joseph again, and her happy mood returned."

He shook his head, frowning. "That would be horrible to go through. I can't imagine anything happening to you." The words slipped out so easily, yet he couldn't seem to communicate with Lydia about their relationship. When he looked at her, she was staring at him, intently, as though she had something important to say. He wanted her to tell him what kept them so distant. Maybe if they talked about it, they could fix it.

Then Mattie began to scream. Lydia didn't move at first. She just kept gazing into his eyes. Finally, she jumped up, picked up the salve she'd been given earlier, and scurried to their daughter's bedroom.

And the moment was lost.

CHAPTER 4

S amuel tried to stop by his parents' house most days. Not only was it on his way home from work but he worried about them. With his mother in a wheelchair and his father's weak heart, they didn't get out much.

But when Samuel stopped there Thursday evening, he knew something wasn't right.

"What's wrong?" He stood rigid in the entryway of the house he'd grown up in, his heart hammering. His parents were creatures of habit. They always sat in the same places, the blinds were always raised, and one of them always greeted him with a welcoming "*Wie bischt*."

But now it was dark in the room, and neither of them said a word. His father was on the couch, half sitting and half lying down, propped up with pillows and covered with a yellow-and-brown afghan. And even in the low light, he could tell his mother's face was pale and that her shoulders drooped forward.

His father slowly looked up at Samuel with a dazed expression. "What's wrong?" Samuel asked again as he looked back and forth between them.

His mother straightened in her wheelchair and took a deep breath. "Your father had an episode today." She paused as she raised her chin, but her bottom lip trembled. "We didn't know what was happening, so we called nine-one-one. We haven't charged the mobile phone lately, and it went dead before I could tell the operator much. But I managed to tell her I thought your *daed* might be having another heart attack. An ambulance arrived not long after I made the call, and they took him to the hospital. They helped me into the ambulance and stowed *mei* wheelchair."

Samuel pushed back the brim of his hat, his heart still beating wildly. "Why didn't you call me at work?"

His father closed his eyes, appearing to drift off to sleep. His mother cleared her throat. "We didn't want to worry you until we knew what was happening."

"And?" Samuel wished his heart would stop beating so fast. "Did he have another heart attack?"

"*Nee*," his father said, opening his eyes. "Something called atrial fibrillation."

"What's that?" Samuel didn't take his shoes off before he made his way to the recliner in the corner. He sank into the chair, lowered his hat in his lap, and held his breath.

"It happens after heart surgery sometimes." His mother's hands shook in her lap. "Sometimes it goes away on its own, which it did today." She clasped her hands together when she saw Samuel's eyes homing in on her lap. "But he's fine."

He wanted to tell her his father didn't look fine. He hadn't looked this frail since he'd had heart surgery two years ago. He hung his head for a few moments before he looked back at his mother. "I think you need someone to come and stay, a caregiver. Or *someone* who can help you."

Samuel had suggested this in the past and received a strong no from both his parents. Their home had been made wheelchair-friendly when his mother was injured, but now he feared neither of them had the energy to take care of themselves properly. Even though he made sure there was always food in the house, he often wondered how much they ate. And it broke his heart when he could tell they hadn't bathed recently.

"We take care of each other just fine." His father spoke with the authority Samuel remembered from his childhood. Usually Samuel would back away from an argument when his father spoke so sternly, but today he had to speak up.

"I disagree. I really believe you need help." Samuel tried to match the authority of his father's voice, but his delivery failed when his voice cracked at the end of his statement.

"*Mei sohn . . .*" His mother smiled at him as if he were a small child again. "I promise to let you know if we need help, but we really are okay right now."

Samuel didn't think it was a promise his mother would keep. They had always worried about the financial strain their health issues caused. Even though they were able to draw from a community health-care fund, they were reluctant to do so for fear of draining the account. Instead, they'd gone through almost all of the money they'd saved over the years. Samuel gave them all the money he could spare. He'd been doing that since he was old enough to earn money, but now he had a family, and formula and diapers weren't cheap. He also knew a full-time caregiver would be expensive.

"This is only a temporary setback," his father said, struggling to sit up all the way. His disheveled gray hair jetted to one side, and when he reached up to comb it down with his hand, Samuel saw the hospital bracelet still on his wrist.

"I'm going to stay for supper." He stood. "I'll cook."

His father chuckled. "Please don't."

Samuel smiled. He was glad his father could still find humor in life. "*Ach, Daed*, I know *Mamm* is a *gut* cook, but I'm craving some meat loaf, and it's the one thing I know how to make—as long as you haven't used the fresh meat I brought you last night." *And because you both look exhausted.*

"Sammy, that isn't necessary." His mother still called him Sammy sometimes, the way she did when he was a boy. He found the nickname just as endearing as he had years ago.

"It's not necessary, but I want to." Samuel stood, forced a smile, and then stepped into the kitchen to make their meal. He also needed some time alone to think, and he reviewed the situation as he gathered the ingredients he needed.

His and Lydia's rental house wasn't big enough to move his parents in with them, nor would it accommodate a wheelchair. Besides, Samuel hoped to own a home someday. If his family moved in here to care for them, Mattie wouldn't have her own bedroom, and Lydia would probably be overworked. And if he and his wife had little privacy, how would they ever grow closer? Last, bringing someone in to help would require more money than he had to spare, and he knew his parents wouldn't accept that type of help from members of the community for free.

He didn't know what to do. But tonight, he could prepare them a meal, make sure they had their medicines in stock, and snoop just enough to see if they were going without anything they needed.

. . .

Lydia stepped back and eyed the table she'd just set. She'd brought out the bone china again, deciding it didn't need to be reserved for company, and tonight she'd serve her husband a delicious meal. She'd baked two Cornish game hens, mashed sweet potatoes and lathered them with butter and brown sugar, and made a cucumber salad. For dessert, she'd baked a key lime pie.

The salve Beverly had given her worked wonders, and Mattie was already fed, bathed, and tucked into bed. Maybe this supper, this time alone, would help her and Samuel find their way into a romantic relationship, even if it was only a baby step in that direction. She wanted to connect with him on a more romantic level, but she'd rejected her husband so much that she wasn't sure if romance was even important to him. She recalled the kiss on the cheek, a small offering of intimacy she'd turned away from. And the night she'd clearly seen desire in his eyes but had pulled away. Later, she'd tried to tell him she wanted them to be closer, but he'd pretended to be asleep.

She had to let him know how she really felt.

She placed two sterling silver candleholders in the middle of the table, ready to be lit when she heard Samuel pulling in, usually within the next thirty minutes. She'd already bathed and even spritzed herself with a light vanilla body spray. Her hair was washed and still drying as it stretched down her back and past her waist. She was self-conscious about the baby weight she still carried, but she wouldn't think about that this evening. She had to fight past her nervousness.

An hour later, she placed the food in the oven to stay warm and stowed the cucumber salad in the refrigerator. After another hour went by, she lit the lanterns throughout the living room and kitchen, then slumped into a kitchen chair holding a box of matches. She stared at the unlit candles as anger built, the emotion quickly replaced by hurt. Samuel could have called to say he would be late. *And where is he?*

The hurt lingered for a while, but by the time Samuel walked into the house, two and a half hours later than normal, Lydia was seething with anger. She stood, leaned against the kitchen counter, and clenched her fists at her sides.

. . .

Samuel left his shoes by the door and hung his hat on the rack. He wanted to bypass a shower and crawl into bed, but he breathed in the aroma of food coming from the kitchen. Even though he wasn't hungry, he would force a few bites so he wouldn't hurt Lydia's feelings. She'd probably been wondering where he was. He couldn't call her because his cell phone was dead, and so was his parents'. Twice, his father asked if Lydia would be worried or angry, and both times Samuel assured him she wouldn't be. She'd probably left food on the stove for him, like when he had to work late doing inventory.

But when he walked into the kitchen, he had no doubt she was mad. Samuel could feel the daggers she threw at him with her eyes, and her face was so red that she looked like she might combust. He eyed the fancy table she'd set, and a sinking anguish settled in the pit of his stomach. He held up both palms.

"I'm sorry I'm so late." He lowered his hands and walked toward his wife. She gritted her teeth, resembling some sort of wildcat, as her expression grew even tighter with strain. It was almost comical, but he didn't dare smile. He didn't think he'd seen her like this since they'd found out she was pregnant, when they'd both acted out of character in a situation that warranted it. They'd both matured since Mattie was born, yet it wasn't hard to see that Lydia was about to lose her composure now. This wasn't the routine haze they walked through each day.

He rubbed his forehead and braced for the lashing that was sure to come. They'd had words before, but nothing that wasn't quickly brushed off or forgotten. Maybe that's what they needed, to fight a little. It might be better than pretending they lived a normal life, complacent and quiet, tiptoeing around each other. *Avoiding each other.*

"I'm sorry," he said again as he inched closer to her. He knew better than to touch her. She'd just distance herself.

Her bottom lip trembled as she stared at him, long and hard, her eyes blazing. Then she sidestepped around him and marched out of the kitchen without looking back. A moment later, he heard her slam what he was sure was their bedroom door. They'd always slept in their bed together despite their emotional distance, but now he assumed he'd be sleeping on the couch.

Mattie began to wail. Samuel waited for Lydia to emerge from the bedroom, but when she didn't, he shuffled through the living room and went to his daughter. As he picked her up and held her against him, tears burned his own eyes. He swayed from side to side with Mattie, and to his surprise, she stopped crying. Samuel held on to her, though, needing to feel her close.

He wouldn't have been home so late if his father hadn't thrown up at the kitchen table. Hurled was more like it. Then he began to choke, and Samuel and his mother were frantic. His father recovered, but he was filled with embarrassment, and there was a big mess. His mother had fought tears, and Samuel told them repeatedly it was okay. After he helped his father get cleaned up, he'd helped him into bed. Then his mother had broken down and sobbed, saying she didn't know what she'd do if anything happened to his father.

His people believed everything that happened was God's will, but when it came to the possibility of losing his father, Samuel didn't want to rely on God's will. He wanted God to heal him, and that's what he silently prayed for.

Mattie started to cry again, and this time Samuel cried along with her. What he wouldn't do to be held right now.

He didn't know Lydia had come into the room until she whispered his name. Mattie twisted to face her mother, but Samuel couldn't look at his wife. He was a grown man with tears running down his cheeks, his shoulders lifting up and down as he tried to bounce Mattie on his hip.

Lydia wound around him. "Give her to me," she said softly as she held out her hands.

Samuel eased Mattie into his wife's arms, but there was no hiding his tears. He dropped one arm to his side and covered his face with his other hand.

A few minutes later, he realized Lydia must have applied some of that salve to Mattie's gums, because when he uncovered his face, their daughter was back in her crib, asleep. Samuel wanted to disappear as humiliation wrapped around him and his pulse pounded in his temples, but instead he met Lydia's eyes.

. . .

Lydia gazed into her husband's watery eyes. She'd never seen him cry, and whatever anger and hurt she'd felt earlier was gone. Something far more serious than her disappointment was going on with Samuel, but as she waited for him to explain, he hung his head. After a few seconds, he found her inquiring eyes. "I'm sorry," he said again in a whisper, his voice shaky as he quickly looked away from her.

"It's okay." She reached out and touched his arm, and he flinched, the way Lydia had so many times.

He squared his shoulders, ran a hand the length of his short beard, then inched around her. "I'll sleep on the couch tonight," he said on his way out.

Lydia stood in their daughter's room, her feet rooted to the floor, unsure what to do or say. They'd lived like roommates for so long, time void of much emotion, that Samuel's display upset Lydia on several levels. She longed to go to him, to hold him, to tell him everything would be all right. Maybe that desire was based on a maternal instinct she'd developed since Mattie was born. But it could have always been there, hidden beneath other feelings that had stolen space in her heart.

Either way, she loved her husband, and she thought again about how she'd feel if she lost him. His announcement that he would sleep on the couch seemed to say a lot, but she didn't know how to decipher what it meant. Was he just feeling overwhelmed? Or did he want to put more distance between them?

Finally, her feet moved toward the crib. She kissed her finger and planted the kiss on Mattie's forehead.

Maybe Samuel was so unhappy with her that he just couldn't take it anymore. Or had something happened at work? Or with his parents? She wanted to ask him and decided she would, but when she tiptoed into the living room, he was curled up on the couch, still in his clothes with his eyes shut.

Lydia suspected he wasn't asleep. She watched him for a long while, but he never opened his eyes. He'd either mastered the art of faking sleep, or he really was in a deep slumber, exhausted by whatever had upset him.

She prayed for her husband, asking God to take care of whatever had caused him to break down like this. Then she squatted beside him and kissed him lightly on the cheek, halfway expecting him to startle. When he didn't, she whispered, "I love you." Then she went to bed.

CHAPTER 5

The next day, Lydia was scheduled to meet her mother and sister. They tried to get together for the noon meal a couple of times a month. Her parents lived near Lydia, so her mother dropped by fairly often, but she didn't get to see her sister as often because she lived in Shoals.

Since Mary was always the one who journeyed to Montgomery, they usually let her select where they would meet. Today she'd asked if they could eat at Fat Boys Pizza. After tethering her horse, Lydia unhooked the car seat in her buggy. Lots of Amish mothers held their babies in their laps when traveling by buggy, but Lydia wasn't comfortable doing so when she traveled alone with Mattie. Samuel had purchased a used car seat and made some adjustments to the buggy so it would accommodate Mattie comfortably.

Samuel. He'd been on her mind until late into the night, and when she got up to make breakfast, he was already gone. Maybe their picnic with Beverly and Joseph tomorrow would lift his spirits. Joseph was a funny man, and she hoped his humor would be enough to distract Samuel from whatever had upset him.

She lifted Mattie onto her hip and reached for the diaper bag. She'd dropped her wallet into the tote, but her mother always paid for their meal.

As she opened the door to the restaurant, she took a deep breath and prepared to put on a happy face, the way she always did. It was exhausting sometimes. When she was with her family, she didn't let on that her life wasn't as perfect as she pretended it was. Everyone knew Lydia and Samuel had a rocky start to their marriage, but these days, they all believed they lived in marital bliss. It was what everyone expected, and over time, she stopped saying anything to anyone about her marriage, leaving the assumption that she'd slid into her role as mother and wife. Her mother had even told her how proud she was of her and Samuel for turning their lives around and living the way God wanted them to.

Besides, her mother would only lecture her even though several times she'd mentioned how much more mature Lydia had become. That part was probably true since becoming a mother made a seventeen-year-old grow up rather quickly. And because Mary tended to take on other people's problems, empathetic almost to a fault, Lydia didn't want to burden her at a time in her life when she seemed so happy married to Levi.

She found them at a table toward the back of the pizzeria, and they already had a high chair pulled up to the table. Mary stood and hugged her and Mattie. Then their mother reached for Mattie and began baby talking to her before she said, "I'm sure she's grown since I last saw her." After sufficiently smothering her granddaughter in kisses, she got her settled in the high chair.

"Mattie shouldn't cry from teething as much as she did at our last restaurant." Lydia slid into a chair and put the diaper bag on the seat next to her. "A friend gave me a homemade salve for her gums, and it really seems to be helping." She paused to hand Mattie a couple of small toys from the diaper bag. "You might know the woman, Mary. I thought I saw her at your wedding. Her name is Beverly Schrock."

"Hmm . . . I don't recall the name." Mary unfolded her napkin and placed it on her lap. "I didn't know a lot of the people there, ones from Levi's district."

"I'd run into her a couple of times before we spent any time together," Lydia said. "Samuel forgot his dinner one day, and since I had errands to run in town, I dropped it off. Just as I was going into the furniture store, Beverly came up beside me and we chatted. Then she went inside with me, asking to use the restroom. But first I introduced her to Samuel and Joseph, a man Samuel works with. I almost didn't remember her last name. Joseph took a liking to Beverly, and they both came to our *haus* for supper last Friday night. Tomorrow Samuel and I—and Mattie—are going on a picnic with them."

"That's *gut* you and Samuel are doing things with another couple." Her mother smiled as she picked up her menu.

"I'm not sure if they're a couple yet, and, like I said, I don't know Beverly well, but I really like her." She straightened her prayer covering after her mother cleared her throat and pointed to it. The wind had been brutal on the way there. "But her *schweschder* has a *boppli* a couple of months older than Mattie and used the salve when she was teething. It worked."

"I remember Mattie being fussy the last time I was at your *haus*, and *ya*, the last time we all met." Her mother shook her head, frowning. "I don't know why I didn't think her gums might be hurting." She shrugged. "But it's been a long time since either of you were *bopplis*."

When the waitress came for drink orders, they all decided to order the buffet. Mary and Lydia waited until their mother returned with her plate before they got their food.

"So how is everything with you and Samuel?" Mary asked as they selected slices of pizza. Her sister's question was purely a polite inquiry.

"*Gut.* Everything is *gut.* And you and Levi are well?" Lydia returned the courtesy question, and her sister nodded.

They slid into their chairs back at the table, where Mattie gnawed on some pizza crust. Mary began talking about the flowers she'd recently planted, but Lydia's mind drifted back to Samuel, the way it had all morning. Her husband had been upset before, mostly about work or his parents' failing health, but seeing him break down the way he had last night affected her more than she would have thought. Her heart hurt for him, so much so that she'd been willing to push past her fears to comfort him.

Lydia would be with Samuel for the rest of her life, and it had been easy to tell him she loved him when she thought he was asleep. *Why?* Over time, the bitterness about being pushed into marriage had faded. Maybe they needed to go backward before they could move forward.

. . .

Samuel slunk around in a haze all day Friday. He'd gone into the break room twice to call his parents, but they hadn't answered. His folks believed phones were only for emergencies, but Samuel had asked them to please keep theirs on so he could check on them. Then he recalled how his mother said her phone went dead when she'd called the ambulance. He'd doubted his father had the strength to go anywhere to charge the phone today. He should have thought to take care of that himself.

Around four o'clock, he called Lydia. They weren't as strict about cell phone usage as his parents were, but they did try to limit their calls to a minimum.

"I-I'm going to be late again tonight," he said when she answered. "And I'm sorry I didn't call to tell you I wouldn't be home on time last night. *Mei* parents . . ." He paused when he feared his voice would crack, so he cleared his throat. "*Mei daed* had an episode with his heart yesterday. He's okay, but I need to drop off a few things they were out of, and I might try to help them straighten things up, so if I'm later than—"

"Samuel, it's fine." Lydia spoke softly, and Samuel could hear noise in the background. "Stay as long as you need to."

"Where are you?" He rubbed his forehead as his temples began to pound, something that happened more and more.

"After we ate, *Mamm,* Mary, and I decided to do a little shopping. We're at the Bargain Center right now."

Samuel wanted to tell her he heard her say she loved him. He wanted to tell her he loved her, too, but he hadn't given them time to *fall* in love before they got married. He wondered if falling in love could still be a possibility.

"I'm sorry, too, Samuel, for being so upset that you weren't home on time. I just wanted supper to be . . . special, I guess."

"*Nee.* Don't apologize. I should have called, but the phones . . ." He leaned his head back and closed his eyes. His wife had made a true effort to do something special for him, and he'd been too consumed with his parents to find a way to call her. Maybe he could have checked with the neighbors. "And, Lydia . . . I really appreciate that you went to so much trouble to make us such a nice supper."

"You're welcome," she said. "I probably should have told you what I had planned, but I wanted it to be a surprise, and I didn't know about your parents, and—"

"I'll call from now on if I'm going to be late, whatever the reason." This felt like they'd had a fight and made up, which Samuel supposed they had. Oddly, it also felt good to have any kind of emotional connection with Lydia. Stemming from a fight wouldn't have been his first choice, yet he was glad they'd pushed through it and seemed to be in a better place. "But I'll try not to be too late tonight."

"Take as long as you need," Lydia told him again, her voice gentle and soothing. He was embarrassed about the way he'd let himself fall apart the night before. Hearing her talk to him in such a nurturing manner caused a surge of affection for her. He fought to keep his raw emotions in check.

"Do you want me to check on your folks after we're done here?"

"*Nee*, I'm sure they'll be fine until I get there." Lydia wasn't close to his parents, but that was his fault. He didn't want her to see how bad things were, so he often downplayed their situation, encouraging her to visit them with Mattie only when they seemed to be doing well. He'd made up excuses for her not to visit when the house was an awful mess or when they were in a bad place like they were now. His parents might be embarrassed, and Samuel didn't want that.

After they ended the call, he went back to a table he'd been working on in the back of the store, wishing the noise from the electric sander would drown out the worries spinning in his mind. He didn't go more than five minutes without looking at the clock on the wall, and right at five, he clocked out and rushed to his horse and buggy.

When he arrived at his parents' house, he knocked twice, then opened the door. "It's me." As he walked into the living room, all was quiet, which made his stomach lurch. His mother was always in her wheelchair in the corner where she kept her knitting basket on the floor, books she was reading on an end table, and a glass of meadow tea. His father was usually on the couch reading or napping.

"It's me!" he said louder, but it was still quiet. Their buggy was outside, and the horse was in the barn, so they were home. He tossed the bag with the few items he'd brought onto the couch.

After finding the kitchen and mudroom empty, he finally knocked on their closed bedroom door. "*Mamm, Daed*, are you in there?"

"*Ya*, we're okay. Just napping," his mother said from inside the room.

"Why are you napping this late in the day?" Normally, his mother would have a meal on the table, or they would have already eaten.

"We had an early supper. We're fine, dear."

Samuel sniffed the air. "What did you eat?"

Silence.

"*Mamm*, what did you eat?" he asked again, louder this time.

"Sandwiches."

Samuel scratched his cheek. They weren't napping anymore, so why hadn't they come out of the bedroom? He put a hand on the doorknob, but he didn't want to walk in uninvited.

"I'm just doing a little knitting, and your father is reading. We're just fine." She paused. "See you in a few days, *ya*?"

Samuel didn't move. Something was wrong, and that feeling in his gut intensified. He was reaching for the doorknob when heavy footsteps came from the other side of the door. His father opened it, still in his pajamas. Samuel looked past him at his mother, who was tucked under the covers on their bed, her head down. When she looked up, his jaw dropped, and he strode to her.

"*Mamm*, what happened?" He squatted by the bed and studied her black eye and bruised cheek.

She touched his arm. "It looks much worse than it is, Sammy. I had a bit of a tumble in *mei* wheelchair. I was reaching for something, and . . ." She shrugged. "I just lost *mei* balance."

His father groaned. "Tell him the truth, Fannie. The Lord won't appreciate the lying just to keep your *sohn* from worrying." He turned to Samuel. "Your *mamm* was reaching for me. I tripped on that stupid rug in the kitchen, which is now rolled up and out of the way. When I fell, it scared her, and when she reached for me to make sure I was all right, she fell out of her wheelchair and hit her face on one of the kitchen chairs." His father shook his head. "A silly course of events that left your *mudder* with a bruised face and me with a sore knee. But we're fine, *sohn*."

Samuel's gaze ping-ponged back and forth between his parents. "*Ya*, well, now that everyone is on board with the truth, did you really eat sandwiches?"

His mother tried to grin but flinched. "*Ya*, we did."

"*Daed*, I really think you and *Mamm* need some help around here." Samuel took off his hat, ran an arm against his damp forehead, and faced off with his father. As head of the household, his dad would be the one to make the final call. But now that his wife had fallen out of her wheelchair, maybe he would consider help.

"We're fine." His father set his chin in a stubborn line as a muscle quivered at his jaw.

"I know you don't want to take money from the community fund for home care, but I'm sure the members of our community could work up a schedule so someone can be here with you for a few hours each day."

"Sammy." His mother touched his arm again. "It's one thing for family to visit, but we don't want other people in and out of here. Your *daed* and I enjoy our quiet time. And you visit us almost every day." Smiling, she reached up and pinched his cheek as if he were a child. "And you really don't need to do that. We enjoy your visits, but you have your own family now."

This wasn't an argument Samuel could win right now, but it was his responsibility to ensure his parents were well cared for.

"I left a bag on the couch. You were out of coffee and a couple of other things, so I picked them up on *mei* way here." He tipped his head to one side and got a closer look at his mother's bruised face.

"It's not as bad as it looks," she repeated before attempting a slow and shaky smile that caused her to flinch again.

Samuel wanted to stay with these people who loved him more than anyone in the world. He wanted to take care of them. But his mother was right. He had a family to take care of. Samuel had never confided in his parents about the state of his marriage. They had enough on their plates. Sometimes, though, he suspected they knew he and Lydia struggled.

After he told them goodbye and left, his thoughts were all over the place, scrambled like overdone eggs in a skillet. He'd thought about every possible option, and his parents would reject them all.

When he pulled into his driveway, he saw Lydia giving Mattie a bottle in a rocking chair on the front porch of their small house. As he crossed the yard, he took in Lydia and how beautiful she was—even prettier as a mother holding their child. He recalled, again, the way she whispered *I love you* in his ear the night before when she thought he was sleeping. He might have told her he loved her, too, if he hadn't been sure he'd start to cry again.

He'd never known if Lydia loved him, but he was feeling closer to her lately, and maybe if he opened up more, she'd feel comfortable doing the same. Maybe he would talk to her more about his parents and let her into the world he kept secret from her.

. . .

Lydia gently rocked Mattie in her arms as Samuel came toward them.

"*Wie bischt?*" she said as he climbed the porch steps. Lydia was reminded of what a handsome man she was married to. But despite his confident stance, she knew he was hurting inside. "How are your parents?"

He leaned over and kissed Mattie on the forehead, then awkwardly kissed Lydia on hers. "Not *gut.*"

This was the first time Samuel had admitted this to her so bluntly. She should have known his heartache was about his parents. She'd suspected their situation was worse than Samuel let on. But hearing him say it hurt her heart. "I thought maybe their health had declined even more." She bit her bottom lip, waited until he sat down in the other rocking chair, and hoped her husband might open up to her more than he had in the past.

"*Mei daed* tripped on a rug and fell, then *Mamm* reached for him and fell out of her wheelchair. She's got a black eye and her cheek is bruised." He rested his elbows on his knees, then lowered his head to his hands. "I don't know what to do. They don't want to accept help, but they need to."

She held Mattie up to her shoulder and gently rubbed her back until she let out a healthy burp. "I can go over there during the day to check on them."

Samuel shook his head but didn't look up. "*Nee*, you have plenty to do around here."

Lydia was quiet for a few seconds, pondering if she should let this go. If she said what was on her mind, it might lead to an unpleasant conversation. She decided to be truthful. "Samuel, I've made plenty of visits to your parents unannounced." His head came up, but as quickly as he found her eyes, he looked down again. "They're Mattie's grandparents, and especially after your father's heart attack, I know it's even more difficult for them to get around. Seeing Mattie always brightens their day."

"Then you know how they live." He still didn't look at her.

"*Ya*, I know sometimes the *haus* isn't in order. Other times, they look a bit unkempt. But up until now, they've seemed to be doing all right." Mattie had fallen asleep on Lydia's shoulder, and she had a cramp in her neck. But if she left to lay their daughter down, Samuel would probably go take a shower. She wanted to talk to him about this.

He finally straightened and turned her way. "Why did you never mention this before?"

"Because you always discouraged me from dropping by to see them. At first, I thought maybe they didn't like me."

"They've always liked you," he was quick to say.

"*Ach*, well, as I got to know them, I felt like they did, so I assumed the way they live embarrasses *you*, because it doesn't seem to bother them." She held her breath and waited for a reaction. Samuel wasn't one to have an outburst, but Lydia was touching upon a sensitive subject.

He shook his head. "Your parents have a beautiful home, and it's always in perfect condition. You could eat off the floors. And Mary and Levi have a great *haus*." When he found her gaze, Lydia saw an emotion in his eyes she couldn't quite identify. "You've made a beautiful home for us too."

It warmed her heart to hear the compliment, and she smiled. "*Mei mamm, mei schweschder*, nor I are confined to a wheelchair and also tending to a sick husband. Don't be embarrassed about your parents, Samuel."

"They don't want to admit they need help." Samuel stared at his feet again.

"I'm the person to go check on your parents and spend time with them. They love seeing Mattie, and I'll subtly start offering to do things for them." Lydia had always liked Herman and Fannie. She'd hadn't known them well until Mattie came along, but Herman liked to tell stories, and he particularly enjoyed making people laugh. Lydia briefly thought about Joseph and the laughter he'd brought into their home. Maybe that's one of the reasons she liked spending time with Samuel's parents—the laughter.

Samuel shook his head. "*Nee*, it's not your responsibility, and I know you have enough to do."

Lydia tried to shift Mattie to the other shoulder without waking her up, and she gasped a little when the crick in her neck sent a shock to her nerve endings.

Samuel stood and lifted Mattie off Lydia's shoulder. Surprisingly, the baby didn't wake up. "I'll go lay her down."

Lydia assumed that was the end of the conversation until Samuel turned around and stared at her. "*Danki* for offering to check on *mei* parents." Pausing, he got a far away look in his eyes. "I-I'd be appreciative."

"I would have been going more often if I'd known they were having such a difficult time lately." She expected him to turn and go inside the house, but he held her gaze.

"Between work and taking care of *mei* parents, there just wasn't much time for anything else when I was younger. It was always just the three of us, and I knew they'd get old long before other parents who had children my age. But for the first time, I'm seeing them as old people, and I don't know what I'd do if something happened to them." He blinked a couple of times, and it was impossible not to see the torment in his expression.

"Something will happen to *all* of us someday. Our time here on earth is up to *Gott*. But I understand what you're saying." Lydia couldn't stand the thought of losing her parents, but it would happen at some point, hopefully far in the future. Samuel seemed to have stumbled upon that reality suddenly. She also recalled how her husband recently said he didn't know what he'd do if anything happened to her.

"I'll go lay her down," he said again.

A while later, they ate supper and went through their devotions, and then Samuel left to take a shower. When Lydia climbed into bed, she didn't roll to her side or pretend to be asleep; her eyes were wide open. When Samuel emerged from the shower, he locked eyes with her. Maybe this would be the night they made love. Maybe not. But as Samuel slipped into bed and pulled her into his arms, Lydia knew they were moving into new territory. A place where love, trust, and faith in each other might slowly grow into the marriage she believed they both wanted.

CHAPTER 6

W hen Joseph contacted Beverly about riding with him to their picnic today, she asked him to pick up her and Susan at Gasthof Village, where her sister worked. The restaurant wouldn't open for another thirty minutes, but the buffet was already laid out, and she and the baby were keeping Anna company while she ate.

"That looks so *gut*." Beverly eyed Anna's plate. Even the remainder of the German potato salad and battered fish fillet her sister had selected made her mouth water as she breathed in the aroma. "But Joseph will be here soon, and I don't want to spoil *mei* appetite." Grinning, she offered Susan some applesauce, and the baby smiled. "I'm excited for you to meet him."

Anna laid her napkin across her plate. "*Ya*, I'm eager to meet him too. I haven't seen you like this since you first started dating Chriss."

Beverly didn't like to think about the only man she'd dated since her husband died. Chriss had broken up with her and left her shattered for a while. "It's only *mei* second time to be around Joseph, but I liked him right away. Not only is he cute and funny but he was so good with Mattie. He clearly likes *kinner*."

"I'm happy you've taken an interest in someone." Anna frowned, and Beverly knew what was coming. "But you have to tell him what happened with Chriss, and you need to be truthful about everything."

"I know. But not until I know him better." Beverly sat taller when she saw Joseph in the already-open gift shop and waved him inside the restaurant. "Here he is now." She stood, and Anna did too.

"Joseph, this is *mei schweschder*, Anna." She nodded to the baby. "And this is Susan." Then she lifted her from the high chair and grabbed the diaper bag.

Anna shook Joseph's hand. "*Wie bischt.* It's very nice to meet you." She glanced at Beverly, then back at Joseph. "I wish I could stay and chat, but the restaurant opens soon, and I need to make sure everything's ready." She kissed Susan on the cheek. "You three have fun."

Joseph took the diaper bag from Beverly, and they left. Once they were in the parking lot, Beverly said, "*Danki* for meeting me here. It's closer for you than going to *mei haus*. And Anna will keep an eye on Rusty." She propped Susan on her hip and nodded toward her buggy. "That's *mei* horse, Rusty."

"He's a fine-looking animal. And by the way, you look really pretty." Joseph had the cutest toothy grin, and Beverly knew she was blushing as he opened the door of his buggy.

"*Danki.*" She looked down at her maroon dress. Her husband and Chriss had both told her the dark color brought out her brown eyes. She shook the thought. Today she didn't want to think about either of those men. She'd loved Enos with all her heart, and she'd even loved Chriss for a while—until he showed his true colors. But today was about Joseph.

He stowed the diaper bag in the back seat, then waited for Beverly to get comfortable with Susan before he clicked his tongue and set the horse in motion. It was a warm day, there wasn't a cloud in the sky, and Beverly's heart was light. And hopeful.

. . .

Joseph's eyes kept drifting in Beverly's direction. They'd had some small talk about the weather, but so far, he couldn't think of anything intelligent to say. How did he get lucky enough to spend time with the most beautiful woman in the world?

"Why do you keep looking at me like that?" Beverly raised an eyebrow as she grinned.

Joseph shook his head, sighing. "Your beauty overwhelms me. You literally distract me from you." It was the dumbest thing he'd ever said, but when Beverly burst out laughing, Joseph chuckled too. Even the baby smiled in between chewing on a teething ring.

"*Ach*, well . . . I would tell you to close your eyes, but since you're driving, that might not be a *gut* idea." Joy bubbled in her laugh and shone in her eyes.

His moronic comment hadn't lost her. "Maybe after I look at you a whole bunch, I'll get used to how pretty you are and won't have to stare at you so often." He laughed at his own silliness. "This will probably be our last date." He glanced in her direction as her expression stilled, hoping she was okay with calling the picnic a date. "I mean, are you even hearing the dumb things coming out of *mei* mouth?" He laughed, but then he stopped when she still wasn't smiling.

"I-I'm going to hope it isn't our last date, if that's all right with you." She lowered her eyes as she ran a hand through her niece's blond curls.

Joseph stared at her and then chuckled. "If it's all right with me? Ha! Be careful what you wish for. You might not be able to get rid of me."

"That might be okay." She paused as she batted her dark lashes. "I guess we'll see."

Joseph exhaled a long sigh of contentment. He'd dated a few girls over the past four years, since he'd turned sixteen, but none of them had seemed to appreciate his bluntness. Beverly did. At least Joseph hadn't run her off yet. And although she was a widow—Samuel had told him about that—Beverly didn't seem at all hesitant to spend time with him. Maybe she was ready to love again.

"There they are." He nodded to a buggy in front of the school. Samuel was unloading an ice chest from the back seat, and Lydia was holding Mattie, along with another tote she had swung over her shoulder.

"I offered to bring some of the food, but Lydia insisted she'd bring everything." Beverly waved when Lydia did, then she turned to Joseph. "I've been looking forward to this, and *Gott* certainly blessed us with a beautiful day."

"*Ya*, He did indeed." He slowed his pace and held out his arms. "May I? Will she come to me?"

Joseph couldn't wait to be a father. He'd grown up in a big family.

Susan went willingly to Joseph and even smiled at him.

"What made your family want to move to Montgomery?" Beverly stayed in step with him as they crossed the schoolyard to where their friends were waiting.

"*Mamm* and *Daed* wanted out of the hustle and bustle where we were in Ohio. We lived in a real touristy area, and they wanted that small-town feeling. They also wanted to make the move now so when all *mei* siblings and I marry and move out, we'll still be close together. I'm the oldest."

"You picked a *gut* place to avoid hustle and bustle. Montgomery is small. We get some tourists, but I'm sure it's nothing like the larger communities here in Indiana. I have an Odon address, but I'm closer to Montgomery."

Joseph liked the feel of a baby on his hip. He touched his nose to Susan's, and the little one grinned. "You're as beautiful as your *aenti*."

When he glanced at Beverly, she smiled.

"That's a *gut* look for you." Samuel stuck out his hand to Joseph. "A *boppli* on your hip."

"She even seems to like me." Joseph nodded at Lydia as she handed Mattie to Samuel and began arranging a blanket on the ground. "*Wie bischt*, Lydia."

"*Wie bischt*. We have a beautiful day for a picnic." Lydia smiled. She and Samuel made a cute couple. Joseph hoped for that with a woman someday. As he glanced at Beverly, he couldn't help but be hopeful. But he still had plenty of time to blow his chances.

A few minutes later, they were all seated around the babies and a generous offering of food. Life is *gut*, he thought as they bowed in prayer.

. . .

Lydia tried to stay focused when Beverly told her about a new recipe she'd tried recently, but her mind kept going back to the night before. She and Samuel had held each other all night long, but they hadn't made love even though her heart raced at the feel of her husband's body pressed against hers. It seemed they had an unspoken understanding that they weren't ready to be more intimate. But holding each other at night felt like the start of something they both wanted—to be closer to each other emotionally.

She'd seen how vulnerable her husband could be, and she wanted to be the one he clung to during the good times and the bad. It was what they'd vowed to each other when they married. Lydia could barely recall saying the words because she'd been fighting tears throughout the entire ceremony, but now she longed to make good on those vows, to fulfill their promise to God and to each other. For the first time since their wedding, Lydia could sense the elephant in the room growing smaller.

"Look how well these babies get along." Beverly pressed her palms together as she turned to Joseph. "Aren't they cute together?"

"*Ya*, like little mini people getting to know each other." Joseph grinned, and Lydia did too.

Beverly had seemed smitten from the moment she'd laid eyes on Joseph, and she could hardly keep from staring at him now. He was constantly looking at her too. Their blossoming romance led Lydia's thoughts back to her and Samuel, and her insides warmed with hope.

Lydia laughed when Mattie let out a high-pitched squeal. Then Susan did the same, and everyone chuckled.

"Maybe you girls need to feed these babies." Joseph rubbed his clean-shaven chin and grinned. Then he caught Mattie with one hand when she almost tumbled over.

"*Ach, gut* catch," Lydia said. "She's still wobbly since she hasn't been sitting up on her own very long."

"The food is so *gut*, Lydia." Beverly pointed toward the bowl of chicken salad, homemade bread, chow chow, crackers, sliced cheese, and bags of chips. Lydia had also brought a gallon of sweet tea and the buttermilk pie she'd made that morning.

"*Mei fraa* is a *gut* cook." Samuel winked at her, and Lydia felt herself blushing as she waved off the comment. But the smile on her face remained.

"It's just chicken salad," she said as she handed Mattie a cracker. Then she turned to Beverly. "That salve you brought me for Mattie's gums has restored our sanity."

"I'm so glad it helped her. I remember so clearly when Susan was teething. She still is, but she doesn't seem to be having as much pain. I think that's partly because of the salve, but *bopplis* also seem to have more trouble cutting their first tooth."

Lydia swallowed a bite of her sandwich and offered Mattie a spoonful of applesauce. "You must spend a lot of time with your niece."

"Every chance I get." Her eyes cut to Joseph. "I hope to have lots of *kinner* someday."

Joseph had already finished everything on his plate. "Everyone put your hands behind your back and extend your fingers to show how many *kinner* you want. Then we'll all hold our hands out at the same time."

Beverly laughed but did as Joseph asked. Lydia did too.

Samuel rolled his eyes, grinning. "Are you serious, *mei* friend?"

"*Ach*, just play along, Samuel." Lydia was eager to see how many fingers her husband would hold up. *Husband*. That word was feeling more comfortable in her mind today.

"On the count of three, show us your hands." Joseph paused, glancing at each of them. "Ready? One ... two ... three!"

Lydia had known how many children she'd wanted since she was a child herself, but a flicker of apprehension coursed through her. How had she and Samuel never discussed how many children they wanted to have? The answer seemed obvious. Intimacy and having babies went hand in hand. She might not have been expecting Mattie to come along so early, but her situation hadn't deterred her from her childhood wish. Now that the moment was upon them, her stomach twisted with nervous curiosity. She held out both hands, but it was a couple of seconds before she could look Samuel's way. When she finally did, he was holding up six fingers too. She exhaled the breath she'd been holding and smiled at him. He was quick to grin back at her.

When she looked at Beverly and Joseph, each had ten fingers spread wide.

Everyone laughed.

"What are the odds?" Scratching his cheek, Joseph clicked his tongue a couple of times before he turned to Beverly. "We better hurry up and get hitched. We've got work to do."

Beverly's face turned red as she playfully slapped Joseph on the arm. "Shame on you."

Lydia glanced at Samuel, who caught her gaze. Their friends didn't know Mattie had been conceived before wedding vows were made. Lydia wanted to tell them to be careful, to take things slowly. She wondered if Samuel was thinking the same thing.

Joseph stood and reached out a hand to Beverly. When she was on her feet, he said, "Any chance you two could watch Beverly's niece while we take a walk? We've got a lot to talk about—our future wedding and those ten *kinner* we're going to have."

Beverly shook loose of Joseph's grip and slammed her hands to her hips. "Joseph Wengard, you are *ab im kopp*."

"You ain't seen nothin' yet." He flashed his toothy grin, pushed back the brim of his straw hat, and held out his hand again. "Can you handle it?"

Beverly turned to Lydia, her eyes sparkling in a way that made Lydia envious. "Do you mind watching Susan while I take a walk with this crazy man?"

Lydia grinned as she shook her head. "*Nee*, I don't mind at all."

As they walked off, Joseph looked over his shoulder and winked at Samuel and Lydia. Then he turned to Beverly as they started across the schoolyard. "I'm thinking a fall wedding, then we get right to work on that family we'll have."

Joseph laughed when Beverly shook loose of his hand again. "*Ach*, come on," he said. "I know I still need to allow enough time for you to fall in love with me." Once again, he held out his hand, but this time his expression stilled, and he looked serious. "Don't be afraid. I won't bite."

"I'm not so sure about that." Beverly's smile couldn't have been any broader as she took his hand again.

Soon Lydia couldn't hear what they were saying anymore. She turned to Samuel and chuckled. "Your friend really is *ab im kopp*."

Her husband nodded. "*Ya*, he's one crazy fellow."

Lydia watched in awe as Beverly and Joseph sauntered to the back of the school property. "But somehow, I think things might work out for them."

"*Gott* always has a plan." Samuel handed Mattie her teething ring when she reached for it and almost toppled over.

"I never knew you wanted six *kinner*." Lydia held a hand to her forehead and squinted against the sun's glare.

Samuel smiled. "You never asked."

Lydia was quiet as she thought about what else she'd never asked her husband. She turned to him and grinned. "Favorite color?"

"Blue."

She raised an eyebrow. "Favorite dish I cook for you?"

"Trick question. It's all *gut*." He grinned as he winked at her again.

"Okay." She stretched out her legs on the blanket and crossed her ankles as she leaned back on her palms. "Something you'd like to do that you've never done before?"

"Go to the Indianapolis Zoo."

Lydia straightened and blinked her eyes a few times. "That's on my list too. Why did you never mention that?"

"You never—"

"Asked. I never asked." She laughed. Maybe it was time she got to know her husband. She knew his sleeping habits—what time he went to bed, how he snored lightly—and that he was allergic to feather pillows, but she hadn't even known his favorite color.

"And what about you? What's your favorite color?" An easy smile played at the corners of his mouth.

Lydia thought for a couple of seconds. "Yellow." His gaze met hers, and she was strangely flattered by his interest. "It's bright and cheerful."

"Favorite food?"

Such simple questions, but Lydia's insides swirled with a sense of wonderment. "Pizza."

Samuel nodded, but his smile faded as his mouth took on an unpleasant twist. "Uh-oh." He held his nose and pointed to Mattie and Susan. "Somebody has done their business."

"*Ya*, for sure." Lydia took a peek in Mattie's diaper just as

Susan whimpered a little. Lydia checked Susan as well. "Double uh-oh."

Samuel cringed. Lydia couldn't recall her husband changing a diaper unless she'd left him alone with Mattie. Every time, the diaper had been put on poorly. But when both babies began to grow increasingly unhappy, Samuel reached for the baby wipes and moved Mattie closer to him.

"She's smaller, so maybe less . . ." He shrugged, then backed away a little after he saw what was in their daughter's diaper. "Maybe we can switch babies?"

Lydia's eyes crinkled in the corners as she laid Susan on her back. "Too late. Now, watch and learn."

Samuel had surely drawn the short straw on the diaper changing, and Lydia laughed as he put a hand over his mouth, like he might vomit.

"Welcome to *mei* world," she said as her smile deepened into laughter.

Her statement could have a dual meaning—not just about diapers but about her life. Maybe if she invited Samuel into her world more often, he would invite her more into his. Like he'd done when he told her how worried he was about his parents.

"Lydia?" Samuel's tone was so serious that Lydia paused and looked at him.

"*Ya?*"

"Do you want to know what *mei* favorite thing is to watch?" He was holding up Mattie's little legs as he spoke.

"You mean like when we were in our *rumschpringe* and saw a movie or . . ." She resumed cleaning Susan, unsure what he was asking.

"*Mei* favorite thing to watch is you being a *mudder* to our *dochder.* When you feed her, burp her, cuddle her, and even change her diapers."

She looked up and gazed into his eyes. "I-I always worry if I'm being a *gut* enough *mudder.*"

"You're a great *mudder.* I've told you that before, and I always mean it."

"*Danki* for saying so." Lydia went back to the task at hand. Samuel still had Mattie's chubby little legs up in the air, one in each hand. And their daughter had a whole lot of business in her diaper.

Samuel raised his eyebrows several times as he looked back and forth between Lydia and Mattie, who was growing impatient. "Actually, you're most beautiful when you're changing diapers."

Lydia shook with laughter as she finished diapering Susan. "No deal. Mattie is all yours." She sat Susan up on the blanket as she caught her breath. After she'd moved some toys closer to the baby, she turned her attention back to Samuel and Mattie just as their daughter began to scream.

"Poor *boppli.*" She scooched closer to her husband and took over the diapering. It didn't take long for Mattie to get quiet again.

Samuel leaned back and held his nose. "That's a lot for such a tiny person, isn't it?"

Lydia shook her head as she cleaned Mattie. "Not really, and I should have made you suffer through it." Mattie had poop all over both her legs, and Lydia started to laugh again before she spoke to her. "*Daed* isn't a very *gut* diaper changer, is he, *mei maedel*?"

"We have company," Samuel said in a sobering voice.

Lydia turned in the direction he was looking, her eyes

landing on an old blue truck. The vehicle was rusted on every side, had no hubcaps, and had enough dents to bear witness to the rough life it had suffered. Lydia shivered every time she saw the truck and its driver.

"Should we leave?" Lydia glanced at the two babies before she looked back at Samuel.

As the door of the truck creaked open, a thick leg pounded against the ground of the small parking lot with a bare foot that was dirty—and large. The horses whinnied, and both babies began to cry.

"*Ya*, we need to leave."

Lydia's stomach clenched as fear knotted inside her.

CHAPTER 7

Beverly was wrapped in a cocoon of euphoria as she sat in the grass with Joseph. So far, he appeared to be everything she wanted in a spouse. It was too soon to be having those thoughts, but she was excited about the possibility of finding true love again.

They'd been chatting for only a few minutes when their conversation was interrupted by crying babies, horse whinnies, and lots of movement at their picnic area.

Joseph hurried to his feet. "We need to go." He didn't wait for Beverly to stand before he started walking, looking back only once to make sure she was following him.

Sensing his urgency, Beverly jogged to catch up with him. "What's wrong?" In the distance, Lydia scurried to gather their belongings while Samuel held both babies. Even farther away was an old blue truck in the parking lot of the small school. Beverly didn't remember seeing the vehicle when they arrived, and that caused her to pick up her pace, putting her ahead of Joseph.

They were both breathless by the time they reached Samuel, Lydia, and the children. Beverly reached for Susan and held her close as she moved closer to Lydia. "What's happening?"

Everyone was looking at a large woman who was using the school's water pump to wash her hands. She wasn't fat but big-boned and tall. Gray hair spilled past her waist in knotted masses. Her bare feet looked like two hams beneath discolored calves. She wore a blue dress similar in style to what Beverly and Lydia were wearing but no prayer covering.

"She's homeless." Lydia held Mattie close, the same way Beverly protectively pressed Susan against her.

Beverly had assumed that much. "Is that a tomato plant growing out of the back of her truck?" Her eyes widened as she studied the contents in the truck's bed—lots of black plastic bags, a rocking chair that was tilted almost upside down, a mattress from a baby crib, a rusted barbecue pit, and a host of other unsightly items stuffed together.

"Follow us to our *haus*," Samuel said as he ushered Lydia and Mattie to his buggy.

Joseph followed suit and grabbed Beverly by the arm as she clung to Susan.

As both buggies pulled out of the parking lot, the old woman turned around and watched them leaving. Beverly didn't want to be rude and gawk, but she couldn't help it. The woman stared at them with coal-black eyes unlike anything Beverly had ever seen. Then she smiled, revealing her yellowed teeth that appeared to have never seen a toothbrush. Beverly was taught to never judge a person by their looks, but when the woman's eyes met hers, Beverly shuddered.

"Some folks say she's a witch," Joseph said as he put the horse in a steady trot behind Samuel's buggy. "And others say she used to practice powwowing."

Beverly was from a different district, so she'd never seen the woman. But she'd heard of powwowing, a type of Amish folk magic she didn't know existed anymore. "She's Amish?"

Joseph shrugged. "I don't know. She doesn't wear a *kapp*, but some say she used to be Amish."

"How often do you see her?" Beverly held Susan and gently rubbed her back as the baby yawned, resting her head on Beverly's shoulder.

"Well, I've only been here a couple of months, but that was *mei* second time." He glanced at Beverly and Susan before he turned his eyes back to the road. "The first time I saw her, she was parked outside the Bargain Center, but three women came outside and yelled at her to leave."

"If she's homeless, she obviously lives out of that truck." Beverly sighed. "That's so sad."

"Samuel said she's been around for as long as he can re-member, but folks avoid her." He turned to her and pushed up the brim of his hat, his eyes widening again. "Samuel also said she used to have two dogs with her. Fierce animals. They'd bark if anyone got near them. But one day they were gone, and supposedly she keeps their carcasses in the truck, just skeletons now." He shook his head. "But Samuel said buz-zards followed her around for two weeks after the dogs went missing."

Beverly squeezed her eyes closed and held Susan tighter. "*Ach*, that's horrible."

"I'm real sorry our picnic got cut short, but we can visit for a while with Samuel and Lydia at their *haus*, then I can take you to Gasthof Village whenever you're ready." Joseph smiled, and Beverly nodded, but her mind was still on the woman they'd seen.

"Has anyone tried to help her?" Beverly gently rocked Susan, who was sleeping now.

Joseph shrugged. "I don't know. I don't think anyone even knows her name. But I'm sure Samuel and Lydia know a lot more about her than I do."

• • •

Samuel was glad to be home. He had no idea if the stories he'd heard about the old woman were true, but he wasn't going to take any chances when Lydia and Mattie were with him. He'd called his parents on the way home. They'd answered the phone and insisted they were fine, so he decided to wait until the following day to visit them.

"Until today, I hadn't seen the old woman in months." Lydia sliced the buttermilk pie they hadn't had time to eat. "Someone said they thought she'd finally moved on."

Samuel took four plates from a cabinet and placed them on the kitchen table. "People always say she's moved on when she goes unseen for months at a time. But then she shows up again. I'd forgotten Joseph said he saw her once not long after he moved here."

He walked into the living room just in time to push open the screen door to let Beverly inside. She was tiptoeing as she held a sleeping Susan against her shoulder. Samuel pointed to their bedroom, then whispered, "You can lay her on our bed. Mattie fell asleep, too, and she's in her crib."

A few minutes later, they were all settled around the kitchen table having pie and coffee.

"I just think it's sad and horrible." Beverly blew out a puff of air, shuddered, then shook her head. "And no one even knows her name. Very sad."

"Her name is Margaret," Lydia said before taking a sip of coffee.

Samuel's jaw dropped. They'd both lived here all their lives, and he'd never heard a name attached to the old woman. "I didn't know you knew her name."

Grinning, his wife winked at him. "You never asked."

Samuel smiled back at her before putting a bite of pie in his mouth. He wanted to tell her she looked beautiful and that her spunky attitude was cute, but he didn't want to embarrass her.

"Do you know her last name?" Beverly's voice rose with anticipation.

"*Nee.*" Lydia looked down, grimacing. "People call her all kinds of things." She raised her head. "They call her the old woman, the truck lady, the witch . . ." She cringed. "And some people call her the dog killer."

"I wonder how she survives." Joseph reached for a second slice of pie. "I mean, no one can live on tomatoes and dogs alone."

"Joseph!" Beverly slapped him lightly on the arm. "That's terrible."

Samuel stifled a grin. It was an awful thing to say, but Joseph's delivery and the expression on his face made it comical. Samuel could have sworn his ears wiggled in unison. He had to agree with Lydia. Joseph was a goofy fellow, but he was as good-hearted as a guy could be. Samuel was glad Beverly seemed to like him.

Joseph straightened. "You're right. It was a horrible thing to say."

Samuel waited for a follow-up, expecting Joseph to add to his statement, but he didn't.

"It always makes me sad to see a homeless person." Beverly seemed to be the most affected by their sighting. "I always wonder how someone gets that way." She dabbed her mouth with her napkin as she squinted her eyes. "I mean, where is her family? If she doesn't have anyone, don't the *Englisch* run places where she could live?"

"The community seems divided," Lydia said. "Some people have tried to help her, but she won't accept help. Others have banned her from their businesses. When I was a little girl, I saw her at the Bargain Center sometimes, but they apparently ran her off the property after she stole a few things." Lydia shrugged. "At least, that's what I heard."

"Joseph said he saw her run off from the Bargain Center recently. She was probably just hungry." Beverly ran a finger around the rim of her coffee cup as she frowned, seemingly lost in thought about the woman Samuel and Lydia had grown up around.

A baby cried in the distance, and both Lydia and Beverly sat taller, each with an ear cocked.

"It's Susan." Beverly eased her chair back, stood, and left to retrieve her niece. When she came back with her, she told Joseph it was probably time for them to go. After the three of them left, Samuel helped Lydia clear the table, then they both sat down to finish their coffee.

. . .

Lydia hadn't given much thought to Margaret in a long time. She'd just always been a fixture in Montgomery. Lydia hadn't felt as threatened by her in the past, but Mattie's birth had also given life to an emotion Lydia hadn't known before—a driving force to protect the one person in the world she loved more than herself or anyone else. But back in her own home, she felt safe, and that was largely because of Samuel. He was also fiercely protective of Mattie.

Beverly had been visibly bothered about the old woman's situation and homelessness.

"Do you think seeing Margaret today was a sign from *Gott*?" Lydia glanced around her kitchen, eyeing all that she had. She and Samuel lived simply, but compared to Margaret, they lived a life of luxury.

Samuel grinned a little. "I still can't believe you know her name."

They'd had a playful attitude between them today, almost like flirting. She smiled, but something in her gut gnawed at her. "Maybe we should try to do something for her."

Her husband stiffened. "Stay away from her."

Lydia blinked her eyes a few times as she stared at him. She resented his harsh tone.

"I'm sorry." Samuel lowered his gaze, then sighed and looked back at her. "We don't know how much is true about her, but I think she's dangerous."

"We don't know that." Lydia left the table, refreshed her coffee, and sat down again. "I've heard so many rumors over the years. I remember asking *mei mamm* about her when I was little. She told me the same thing, to just stay away from her. But as Christians, shouldn't we be trying to help her?"

Samuel shook his head. "She won't accept help, and you can't force that on a person."

Lydia couldn't shake the questions tumbling around in her mind. Beverly had seemed so interested in Margaret's story. Most people weren't. The old woman blended into the scenery like black fog that never lifted.

"I want to find out more about Margaret."

Samuel scowled as he ran a hand through his beard.

"I won't go near her, but I want to know her history, how she became the way she is." Lydia wasn't sure if the little voice in her head was God, her conscience, or plain old curiosity.

"Do you think anyone at the furniture store would know her last name?"

"Maybe." Samuel yawned. "I'm going to take a nap." He stood and headed toward the bedroom, but then he turned around. "Do you, uh . . . want to take a nap too?"

Lydia wasn't sure if he was asking her to lie beside him and sleep—or something else. Either way, she and Samuel seemed to be pushing through a wall they had laid brick by brick. She was about to say yes even though her husband's intent wasn't clear, but a tiny voice in the background broke through her scattered thoughts.

"Mattie is awake," she said as she stood. *Another moment lost.* At least they were having moments.

. . .

Joseph hadn't had such a good day in a long time, despite the interruption from Margaret. He gave his horse a gentle flick of the reins.

"Uh, I want to apologize again about the dog comment." He turned to Beverly briefly. She had her cheek pressed against Susan's, then gave her niece a quick kiss.

"It's okay." She repositioned the baby in her lap.

"I mean, who eats dogs, right?" Joseph cringed, wishing he'd learn when to shut up. "No one, of course."

Beverly smiled, but it didn't last long. Joseph was blowing it.

"I wish we knew more about Margaret," she said. "It bothers me that someone lives like that. I wish I could do something to help her."

Joseph turned to her. "You can't save the world."

She smiled. "But sometimes you can save one person."

Beverly had no idea the one person who needed saving was him. He would die if this woman didn't fall madly in love with him and become his wife.

When they pulled into the parking lot at Gasthof Village, Joseph reached behind them for Susan's diaper bag, then he held Susan while Beverly got out of the buggy. He kissed the baby on the cheek before he handed her back to her aunt.

"Today was a *gut* day." He reminded himself not to say anything dumb. "I enjoyed spending time with you and Susan. I hope we can do it again soon."

Joseph thought he saw a gleam of interest in Beverly's eyes as she smiled. Or did he imagine it?

"Well, as you said, our picnic was cut short." She shifted the baby to her other hip. "Um, maybe we should do it again?" Biting her bottom lip, she lifted an eyebrow.

Joseph would need to do triple duty during devotions this evening. The Lord was blessing him far more than he deserved. "Next Saturday?"

She nodded. "I always have Saturday afternoons off from the bakery. Meet here again?"

He started to object and say he'd pick her up at her house, but then he decided not to. Beverly had lived in her home with her husband. She would invite him to her house on her time frame, when she felt comfortable enough.

"I best let *mei schweschder* know we're back."

Joseph ran a finger along the baby's cheek. "It was *gut* to meet you, Susan." Then, as if by reflex, his hand found Beverly's cheek. He cupped it gently before he leaned over and kissed the spot where his hand had been. He half expected her to take off running, but she didn't move. Instead, she smiled.

"See you Saturday," she said as she walked away, looking back over her shoulder twice before she entered the gift shop.

Joseph put a hand to his chest, looked toward heaven, and said, "*Danki, Gott.* I won't let you—or Beverly—down."

He wondered if it was possible to be in love with a woman after spending time with her only twice. He decided it was.

CHAPTER 8

Sunday morning, Samuel eyed his parents' yard as he and Lydia pulled into the driveway. It needed mowing, and the flower beds could use some attention. He made a mental note to take care of that soon.

He and Lydia had left church right after the worship service, opting not to stay for the meal. Instead, they picked up fish sandwiches from Stop N Sea. Samuel's father loved that place, but he hadn't been getting out much lately. And when his mother went with him, someone always had to help them now. His father couldn't get her in and out of the wheelchair by himself anymore.

Samuel knocked twice on the door as Lydia stood beside him holding Mattie. When his father hollered for them to come in, Samuel pushed the door open and slowly entered. It was uncomfortably dark, and it took his eyes a few seconds to adjust.

"We brought fish sandwiches." He held up the two bags he'd carried in as he blinked his eyes a few times. "Why is it so dark in here?"

His parents looked at each other and shrugged. "It doesn't seem dark to us," his father said.

Samuel drew up the blinds that faced the front yard, letting in a stream of sunshine, and then he opened the window. He did the same thing with the window across the room, which brought through a nice cross breeze. But a breeze wasn't all that blew into the room as a cloud of dust met with the sunrays, traveling the length of the room.

Lydia walked straight to his mother and handed her Mattie. "Come here *mei* little bundle of joy."

Mattie opened her mouth as her eyes widened. She looked like she might scream as she stared at Samuel's mother.

"I promise I won't bite, Mattie." She spoke softly to the baby. "I look a mess, but your *mammi* loves you very much."

"Does it hurt?" Lydia squatted next to the wheelchair and leaned closer, taking in her black eye and swollen cheek.

"Nee." She kissed Mattie, then turned her around and sat her on her lap. Mattie reached for her mother right away. "It's okay, dear. You can take her. I know I don't look like myself right now." When Lydia had the baby again, his mother folded her hands in her lap and smiled. "I'm just so happy to see you all. It seems either you're here with Mattie or Samuel is here alone. It's nice to have you all here at the same time."

Samuel glanced at Lydia, who looked up at him too.

After he and Lydia had cleared the coffee table of magazines, coffee cups, and other odds and ends, they all bowed their heads in prayer. Lydia held Mattie and spread out the food while Samuel brought out plates, then glasses of tea.

After they'd all had a good chuckle over his father's two new jokes, Samuel filled them in about Margaret.

"I didn't even know that woman was still around," his father said. "She's got to be getting up in age." He lifted the remainder of his sandwich from the plate on his lap. "And I doubt she's in *gut* health. Living out of that old truck can't be good for her."

"I think her situation is sad." Lydia glanced at Samuel before turning to his father. "Samuel seems to think she's dangerous."

His father lifted one shoulder, then dropped it slowly as he finished chewing a bite. "I don't think she lets anyone get close enough to her to know if she's dangerous."

"I told Lydia she should stay away from the woman." Samuel was seeing his wife in a new light today. They'd held each other again the night before, and after all this time, they both seemed to be finding a comfort zone. Samuel wanted more from Lydia, but he'd learned not to push her. Rebuilding a marriage that had been based on emotional detachment and resentment would take time. Baby steps, he reminded himself.

"It must be miserable to live the way she does, to be alone all your life." Lydia gave Mattie a bottle as she worked in bites of her sandwich.

Samuel's mother cleared her throat. "*Ya*, she's been alone for decades, but up until she was sixteen or seventeen, she had a family."

Lydia's eyes widened. "Really? I wonder why *mei* parents never mentioned that."

This was news to Samuel, too, but he'd never really taken an interest in the old woman.

His mother chuckled. "We're quite a bit older than your parents, dear. They were probably young *kinner* when Margaret lived with her parents and only *schweschder*."

"She had a normal life?" Samuel scooted closer to Lydia from where he was sitting near the coffee table. He eased Mattie from her arms, along with the bottle, so his wife could eat. "That's hard to imagine."

"And some folks say she's got a bunch of money buried on that property." Samuel's father shook his head. "The *haus* probably needs to be torn down. Last time I drove by the old place, it was engulfed in vines and weeds, the windows were busted out, and it had clearly been abandoned for a long time. I only happened by it one day because it was storming. I took a back road to avoid an area that floods down by the railroad tracks." Sighing, he shook his head. "That was a couple of years ago, and I'd forgotten Margaret used to live not far from the Troyers' place."

Heavy dark lashes that shadowed Lydia's cheeks flew up as her eyes widened. "I just assumed everything she owned was in the back of her truck. What else do you know about her?"

Samuel wished he could think of a way to change the conversation. His wife—and Beverly—had an unhealthy curiosity about Margaret. Bless their hearts for wanting to help the woman, but some situations needed to be left alone. Lydia had taken running into Margaret as a sign from God. Samuel had taken it as a reminder from God to keep his family safe.

His father set his empty plate on the coffee table and wiped his mouth with his napkin. "We used to see them at worship service every other Sunday. The *maeds* were identical twins. I never could tell them apart."

"And Margaret's *mudder* was active in the community," his mother said. "She attended Sister's Day and was known for her baking abilities, which seemed to rise above the rest of ours."

Lydia's mouth was agape.

His mother sighed. "But after the girls' parents were killed in an accident, things began to get odd. It didn't happen all at once. First, they both quit going to church. Then they distanced themselves from everyone in the community. And over time, we saw less and less of both girls." She turned to Samuel's father. "Then we found out Margaret's *schweschder* just up and disappeared one day, right, Herman? I don't even remember her name."

His father nodded. "*Ya*, I believe so. It was a long time ago, but I believe that's what happened."

Lydia hung her head. She hadn't touched any of her sandwich since Samuel's parents started talking about the old woman. "Margaret's heart must have been broken when her parents died. Then when her *schweschder* left, she must have just stopped living her life."

Samuel's father glanced at Samuel, frowning, then cast his eyes in Lydia's direction. "I'm going to have to agree with Samuel. Margaret Keim should be left alone." He waved a hand in the air. "Whatever her reasons for choosing to live the way she does, it's not normal. I'd just let her be."

Samuel's gaze drifted to Lydia, whose eyes gleamed with satisfaction. Samuel's father had just provided her with a missing piece of the puzzle—Margaret's last name.

· · ·

On Wednesday, Lydia's heart thumped wildly as she paid her driver and hurried up the steps to where Beverly was waiting. Lydia was meeting her at the library in Bedford, and they'd each had to hire drivers to get there.

"Samuel highly discouraged this trip," she told her new friend. "But I'm so eager to learn more about Margaret and how she ended up where she is." Lydia bounced up on her toes. "And *mei mamm* was both available and happy to keep Mattie this afternoon." She paused. "Even though she didn't think this was a *gut* idea either."

"I'm so glad you learned Margaret's last name and a bit

more information about her. I just can't accept that she's a lost cause." Beverly touched her arm, and her enthusiastic smile faded. "Do you know how to use the internet?"

"*Nee.* But surely it can't be that hard." Lydia had begun to second-guess her motives as she wondered if they were somehow going against God in their pursuit to help Margaret. Either way, she couldn't wait to get into the air-conditioned building, which added a layer of guilt.

After they found the computers, it took about thirty minutes and brief instruction from the librarian to know how to do searches on Google. The older woman seemed confused about why two Amish women needed to use the computers, but she'd been willing to assist them when she'd learned why—a background check on someone they wanted to help. Even though the librarian didn't know who Margaret Keim was, she seemed to respect their quest.

"I'll be over by the children's books," Joan, as she'd introduced herself, said. "The little ones don't tend to put the books back where they belong. Just come find me if you need help."

Lydia and Margaret thanked her and then started navigating this new and interesting world.

"I thought you could find anything you need on a computer." Beverly was the one doing the typing, which was slow.

"That's what I've heard, but we're not finding anything about Margaret Keim. And I wish we knew her sister's name."

They tried searching all the ways Joan had suggested. *Margaret Keim Montgomery Indiana. Margaret Keim Indiana. Margaret Keim birth announcement. Margaret Keim Montgomery Indiana birth record.* After several other combinations, they still didn't have a match.

"Now that I think about it, if she was born Amish like

Samuel's parents told you she was, it's unlikely there would be anything here." Beverly stopped typing and leaned back in her chair. "They might have published a birth announcement in an Amish newspaper, but I don't think our newspapers are archived that far back, if they're even archived at all."

"And we don't really know how far back to go. I should have asked Herman and Fannie how old they think Margaret is." Lydia slouched in her chair also, drumming her fingers on the small table.

Both women were quiet for a while. Lydia wasn't sure what they'd do with any information they found anyway, but Beverly was as interested in Margaret's background as she was. Growing up, Lydia had just accepted Margaret as she was, and she'd stayed away from her as told. But something had changed, and this new interest in Margaret Keim's past was niggling at her to not give up.

Lydia felt a ripple of hope as an idea came to mind. "Herman said Margaret's old *haus* isn't far from the Troyers' place and that the last time he'd seen it, he'd taken a back road to avoid an area that floods. I know where the Troyers live. I wonder if we could find Margaret's *haus*?"

Beverly gasped. "Do you think we could?"

Lydia looked at the clock on the computer. "Maybe. But I can't go today. It's almost two, and I told *mei mamm* I'd pick up Mattie by three. *Mei* driver will be back in about thirty minutes. What about Saturday?"

Beverly shook her head as she grinned. "I can't on Saturday. I have a date with Joseph." She lowered her eyes for a few moments, then looked back at Lydia all dreamy-eyed. "We're going to have another picnic since the last one was cut short."

Lydia recalled when she'd been smitten with Samuel. As she

tried to see through Beverly's eyes, her own relationship came into view. For the first time since she'd married Samuel, the spark she'd felt for him initially had rekindled.

"You really like Joseph, *ya*?" Lydia smiled as she wondered what it would be like to have a romantic picnic with Samuel, just the two of them flirting and kissing, without changing diapers or distractions.

"*Ya*, I do. Like I told you, though, I've dated only one other person since Enos died, and it didn't work out." Beverly's expression took on a faraway look. "He wasn't the man I thought he was." Pausing, she met Lydia's eyes. "You're so lucky to have such a *gut* marriage with Samuel. It's so easy to see how much you love each other."

Lydia almost said *That's because we're masters at faking it.* But she just smiled. She liked Beverly and enjoyed having a friend who saw her and Samuel the way Lydia wished they were. Those who knew her well thought she and Samuel had settled into a good life, but they were still aware of how they'd started their marriage. So far, Beverly saw them as a happily married couple who had done things the right way and in the right order. She wasn't ready to confess that she and Samuel had to close a distance they'd created a long time ago. At least, Lydia hoped Samuel's goal was the same as hers.

Maybe in time she would confide in Beverly. Their friendship was growing, and it would be nice to have someone to talk to about her marriage. But Lydia wasn't ready to get off the pedestal Beverly had her and Samuel on just yet.

"Joseph seems like a very nice person." Lydia glanced at the clock on the computer again, knowing her outing would be coming to an end soon.

"And he's *so* handsome." Beverly blinked her eyes a few

times. "I never believed in love at first sight, but he might make a believer out of me." She giggled softly. "And he's so funny."

Lydia smiled. Beverly had stunning looks, and Lydia assumed she could probably have any man she wanted. But Joseph was the one stealing her heart. Lydia sensed a warm glow inside as she listened to Beverly. It gave her hope about her and Samuel.

They decided to meet at Lydia's house a week from today, then take a ride down by the Troyers' place.

"I hope your date with Joseph goes well Saturday," Lydia said as they stood outside the library waiting for their drivers.

Beverly hugged Lydia. "*Danki* so much for introducing us."

Lydia wished she and Samuel would be accompanying them on another picnic. But Joseph and Beverly obviously wanted to spend some time alone. Maybe there was some way for her and Samuel to have a date with just the two of them.

For now, though, she prayed Joseph and Beverly's time together would go well.

· · ·

Joseph held the fence post steady while his father poured cement around the wooden pole. It was the last thing he felt like doing after working all day at the furniture store, but Joseph's only brother, John, had broken his ankle and wasn't much help with anything at the moment. His three sisters helped his mother prepare the meals, take care of the laundry, and all the other stuff girls were supposed to do.

"I'll be glad when fall gets here." His father tipped the wheelbarrow level again and took a handkerchief from his tool belt. After he took off his hat, he cleared the pooling sweat from his forehead.

"*Ya*, me too." Joseph removed his own hat and emptied what was left of his ice water on his head.

"We can probably get one more post in the ground before your *mamm* calls us. I asked her to serve supper a little later than usual, so we'd have more time to work on this fence."

Joseph grumbled in protest as he put his hat back on and they moved to the next spot. He didn't care if his old work hat got wet.

The north segment of the fence had needed repair ever since they moved in two months ago, but they'd had to make other repairs before tackling it. Joseph, John, and his father had already replaced leaking water lines that ran to the troughs, repaired a section of the barn that was about to collapse, and cared for a host of other jobs inside the house. Joseph would be glad when his brother had recovered enough to work again.

"Your *mamm* said you're seeing someone, a girl from a neighboring district." His father stirred the liquid cement before he tipped the wheelbarrow.

Joseph held firmly to the post. "*Ya*. Her name is Beverly."

Normally, Joseph wouldn't discuss his love life—or lack thereof—with his parents, but he wanted to scream to the world that he was courting Beverly Schrock.

"We're going on a picnic tomorrow." Joseph blinked as sweat trailed from his forehead and into his eyes.

"I'd consider taking the woman to a restaurant to avoid this heat." His father set the wheelbarrow level again and reached for his glass of water on a nearby tree stump.

Joseph should have thought about that. It was supposed to be a lot hotter tomorrow than it was last Saturday. "Maybe I'll see if she'd like to go eat somewhere."

"Keep in mind it's Labor Day weekend. There'll be visiting

kinfolk arriving and tourists filling the restaurants." His father chuckled. "And there aren't many to fill."

Joseph removed his hat again and scratched his still-damp head. "*Ya*, you're right." He wanted to be alone with Beverly as opposed to being in a crowded restaurant, but the heat would be brutal even in the late afternoon.

After the post was upright and secure, his father collapsed into one of the two lawn chairs they'd brought out to the pasture. "Tell me about this *maedel*."

Joseph sat down in the other chair and smiled.

"She's the most beautiful woman I've ever met, for starters." He loved to talk about Beverly. He was sure Samuel was sick of hearing about her since that's all Joseph talked about at work. "She lives on her own and works at a bakery part-time. Her husband passed about a year ago."

His father hung his head. "*Ach*, that's tough."

"*Ya*, but she doesn't seem to dwell on it. I know she will soon, but she hasn't even talked to me about him yet. I'm sure she loved him, but she laughs and smiles a lot. And she's good with *kinner*."

His father chuckled. "Kinda like you. You laugh and smile a lot, and *kinner* always take to you."

"*Ya*, I guess so." Joseph shook his head, grinning. "But other than that, I ain't got a clue what she sees in me. Seems she could date anyone she wanted."

"Don't sell yourself short, *sohn*. You've got a lot to offer a *gut* woman."

"Like what, so I can point these things out to her?"

His father laughed. "Maybe be subtle about it, but you're a hard worker, you never miss an opportunity to help a neighbor, and you have a *gut* heart. Those are all things women like in a man."

Joseph took both their empty glasses to the pump near the barn. After he returned and handed his father a full glass, he sat down again. "Do you think there's such a thing as love at first sight? Because I'm sure I saw stars the first time I set eyes on Beverly." He chuckled. "And I'm pretty sure the earth shifts beneath *mei* feet when I'm around her." Putting a fist to his chest, he said, "She makes *mei* heart beat faster too."

"There's nothing like being in *lieb*. I felt that way the first time I saw your *mudder*. She was with a group of girls at a Sunday singing. I knew I'd marry her." His father smiled. "Sometimes you just know. Be yourself, *sohn*, and you'll be fine." He stood and stirred the cement again.

Break over. Joseph lifted himself from the chair and picked up one end of another post, then steadied it into the ground. As they worked, he silently prayed, asking God to help him not mess up his chances with Beverly. He wasn't going to change who he was, but he sure did want her to love the man he believed himself to be. This was the first woman he truly believed could shatter his heart if their relationship didn't work out.

CHAPTER 9

Beverly awoke, startled, and sat up in bed. Her battery-operated clock said it was after two a.m. It had been a long time since she'd had a dream about Enos. She reached over and touched her husband's side of the bed, remembering how long she'd refused to wash the sheets or launder his dirty clothes after he died—anything that had his scent on it. She'd been furious with her mother for taking it upon herself to wash the sheets and clothes when Beverly was out. She'd been so broken then.

But for the first time since she and Chriss had broken up, she'd let hope slip back into her life. She wasn't going to allow a dream to affect her picnic with Joseph today.

As she lay back down and closed her eyes, the dream replayed in her mind, even though she willed herself to forget it. Enos was scolding her, telling her she wasn't being fair to Joseph by keeping secrets from him, much the same thing her sister had said lately. She really liked Joseph, though, and he seemed to really like her. Maybe he could even love her, so that by the time she told him the truth, it wouldn't matter.

She'd loved her husband, but didn't she deserve happiness again? She pictured Joseph's face as she recalled his gentle kiss on her cheek. People had often told her she was a joyous person to be around. She believed that was true, with the exception of her grief when Enos died. As much as she'd loved him, though, she'd always wanted him to smile more. Joseph couldn't seem to stop smiling. Yes, words seemed to slip off his tongue without him thinking about what he was saying, sometimes to his detriment, but even when his face turned red from embarrassment, Beverly thought he was adorable. He made her insides feel warm. And safe. Something about Joseph felt safe.

As she rolled onto her side, she tried to picture another man lying where Enos had slept for two years. She couldn't. At least, not yet.

She breathed in the scent of nightfall, a dewy aroma floating in on a warm summer breeze. In not so many hours, she'd meet Joseph for another picnic. They'd have more time alone.

Her thoughts circled back to their interruption at the last picnic. She was looking forward to seeing Lydia again, along with their trip to find Margaret's house. Redemption came in many forms. Perhaps helping Margaret was God giving her an opportunity to do something good. Maybe that would make up for not being truthful with her new friends.

She rolled onto her back and stared into the darkness. No matter which way she spun it, that wasn't how God worked. And the more time she spent with Joseph, Lydia, and Samuel, the more she wanted to be honest with them.

. . .

Saturday morning, Lydia eased out of Samuel's arms when she heard Mattie cooing from her crib. Not only had falling asleep as they cuddled become the norm but waking in his arms each morning gave her hope they were moving in the right direction, even beyond the positive strides they'd made emotionally.

She was physically attracted to her husband, and she wanted to show him how much she loved him. When she tried to analyze what was holding her back, though, she realized her hesitancy was multifold.

At the beginning of their marriage, Samuel had seemed, at the very least, frustrated when she didn't want to make love. But now he seemed content just to hold her in his arms, and that was confusing. Maybe he didn't find her attractive anymore. But maybe he could sense she needed more time. Either way, if they were going to have six children, something had to change.

Although she longed to feel his touch, she was still so inexperienced. What if he was disappointed in her?

As she stepped into her slippers and tiptoed out of the bedroom, she silently asked God for help with her last concern—how to continue shedding the shame she'd worked hard to get past. Most of it was gone, but not all.

"*Wie bischt, mei* precious *boppli*." She lifted Mattie and snuggled with her, then laid her back down to change her diaper. Lydia thought again about the kind of love that came with motherhood. It was different from the love she had for her parents and sister and even for her husband. And she only had to look at Samuel to see he had that same kind of love for their daughter. It was the one emotion they shared without question, fear, or hesitation. The relationship she sought with Samuel wasn't the same as her bond with Mattie, but in her heart, a bond just as strong was what she wanted.

. . .

Samuel opened his eyes, then sat up and stretched. It was hot in the bedroom even though they'd slept with the windows open and fans were blowing full force on each nightstand. He swung his feet over the side of the bed as he recalled Lydia snuggling up to him the night before, the way she'd been doing recently. Even though they were covered with only a light sheet, her body heat made it hard for him to fall asleep. He wasn't about to tell her that, though. It felt like they were working their way to each other, however small the steps, and Samuel didn't want to jeopardize what he hoped was progress. Even if it meant a few sweaty nights. August would be behind them soon enough.

Yawning, he got dressed and found Lydia in the kitchen holding a bottle under warm water. He wondered if she had any idea how beautiful she was, even in the morning, standing in her robe, her hair matted in long tresses down her back. She was the same woman, doing the same things she'd always done, but Samuel was still seeing her in a new way. He had to wonder if he was falling in love with his wife.

"Wie bischt." On the way to the percolator, he slowed his stride to lean down and kiss Mattie, who was impatiently waving her arms in her high chair.

"Good morning." Lydia smiled at him as she lowered the bottle into Mattie's eager hands. "I'm so glad Mattie isn't having as much trouble with teething."

Samuel nodded. *"Ya,* the stuff Beverly gave you is working well." He filled his cup and sat down at the table. "I-I thought maybe we could take Mattie to the zoo since we both want to go, but it might be too hot for her, and it's Labor Day weekend."

"Ya, you're probably right. It will be too hot and crowded." Lydia opened the refrigerator and took out a carton of eggs, which reminded Samuel that he needed to work on the chicken coop. A raccoon or some other critter had been ripping away at the wire, and if he didn't secure it, they would lose some hens.

He'd rather go to the zoo, but maybe he would try to connect with his wife on another level. "Joseph is all *ab im kopp* about Beverly." He took a sip from his cup. Joseph seemed to want what he thought Samuel had. If his friend only knew how much Samuel longed to make Joseph's assumptions a reality. Maybe a conversation about another couple with Lydia would lead into a discussion about them.

"*Ya*, and she seems equally as smitten with him. When we were at the library, she told me they were going on a picnic today."

"*Ya*. He told me about the picnic too."

Samuel hadn't said much after that trip, only reiterated what he believed to be true—that Margaret might be dangerous. His wife didn't see it that way. Samuel was hoping she'd let it go since she and Beverly hadn't been able to learn anything new about the old woman. Samuel knew he could be wrong about Margaret, but he didn't want to take any chances. He didn't want to be overbearing, but his role in life had changed. He had to protect his family.

"It seems hot for a picnic." Samuel wished he could save up for an aboveground pool, but his parents' financial needs weren't going to change, so it wasn't going to happen. At least not anytime soon.

"*Ya*, I agree." Lydia started frying bacon, then cracked eggs into a bowl.

Samuel would love to give Lydia and Mattie a pool. They'd all enjoy it during the summer months. He decided to tell her his plans. Maybe it would give her something to look forward to.

"Did you see the pool the Lambrights put up at the beginning of the summer?" Samuel pictured him and Lydia in the pool with Mattie, and when Lydia smiled, he prayed he could turn that vision into a reality.

"*Ya*, I did see it." She took a paper towel and dabbed sweat from her forehead, "They're very expensive, though."

"I want to get one for us as soon as I can."

Lydia stopped flipping the bacon and turned around. "Really?" A smile filled her face as her eyes brightened. Samuel decided right then and there that he would get the pool even if he had to take on a second job. "I had no idea you'd like to have a pool too. Maybe I can get back to knitting potholders and putting together cookbooks. They seemed to sell well when I placed them on consignment at some of the shops nearby."

Samuel liked the idea of working toward a goal together. "That would be great." His wife had a full schedule, though. "But only if you have time."

She chuckled before she turned around and flipped another slice of bacon. "I'll make the time if it means we might be able to get a pool."

An excitement in her voice warmed Samuel's heart. Getting a second job wasn't realistic, but maybe he could ask for a few extra hours at work.

"As for Beverly and Joseph, I'm sure they'd rather be alone today, but we could ask if they want to come here instead." She looked over her shoulder at him, grinning. "We don't have a pool, but time inside the *haus* would be cooler than time out in the sun."

"*Nee*. Joseph said he really wants to be alone with her."

Samuel wanted to tell her he wanted to spend time alone with her too. Even though they had time by themselves after Mattie was asleep, they were usually too tired to do much talking. Maybe they needed a date—even today. He sipped on his coffee as he considered the possibilities. He couldn't ask his parents to babysit when they were down with health issues. Maybe Lydia's sister and her husband would do it. Mary and Levi loved Mattie. But they didn't keep their phones turned on because Levi was from a strict Old Order district much more conservative than the folks in Montgomery were. So even if Samuel thought of a place to take Lydia, a place he could afford, it was too far to travel to their house in Shoals not knowing if they were even home. And Lydia's parents liked to keep their Saturdays free.

Samuel also needed to check on his parents today. Lydia had been going over there most mornings, and she'd been able to do some cleaning. His mother had balked at first, but eventually she gave in. His parents were constantly on his mind. He still stopped by most evenings on his way home from work, but it gave him comfort that Lydia checked on them so often.

They'd definitely settled into a married routine, one that presented some challenges. But he appreciated that family was as important to Lydia as it was to him. Tending to those they loved was a part of their routine that worked well.

Only one thing was missing, but it was more than just a physical relationship. It was the uniting of two people into one. That was what a marriage was supposed to be. How could he and Lydia find that? Why had he let things go on like this for so long? He wanted a wife in every sense of the word. There had to be a way to connect with Lydia without pushing her away. He just didn't know what it was. They were trapped in the life they'd made for each other, and a certain loneliness had settled in. But now that they were growing in their emotional relationship, maybe other areas would improve as well.

He turned his thoughts to Joseph and Beverly. Were they

actually going to have a picnic alone in the sweltering heat, or had Joseph wised up and decided to take Beverly somewhere with more pleasant temperatures? Samuel would hear all about it at work on Monday. He'd listen with genuine interest, then detail his own weekend, which would probably include repairs to the chicken coop and possibly a fresh coat of paint on the barn door. Along with a whole lot of sweating.

. . .

As Beverly waited at Gasthof Village for Joseph to pick her up, she was nervous for several reasons. When he arrived, she repositioned Susan on her hip as he tethered his horse, then walked toward her.

"*Mei schweschder* has to work again today, and her husband is down with a bad cold. Do you mind if we take Susan with us?"

When Joseph got close enough, Susan practically jumped into his arms, which made both him and Beverly chuckle. "I do believe your niece likes me."

"*Kinner* have a way of knowing if a person is *gut*." She recalled the way both Mattie and Susan cried when they saw Margaret, but Beverly thought the babies were just feeling the tension in the air between the adults.

"I have a confession to make." Joseph handed Susan back to Beverly when the baby stretched out her arms. "I know I said I'd pick up fried chicken and supply the food for today, but I started thinking it might be too hot for a picnic. I booked us a reservation at the French Lick Winery." He grinned. "Not for wine. They have a nice restaurant there. I have a driver coming to pick us up. From there, I thought we could ride the train." He cringed a little. "I only bought two adult tickets, though, and the rest are sold out, probably because it's Labor Day weekend. I didn't ask about a child's ticket."

Beverly had heard about the restaurant inside the winery. She'd always wanted to go there, but it was expensive. And she hadn't been on the train ride since she was a kid, but she remembered the tunnel and traveling in total darkness for a stretch. Lots of girls she knew had their first kiss in the tunnel. "*Ach*, those sound like such *wunderbaar* plans." Beverly's mind was awhirl. Her parents were at an auction, so they couldn't babysit Susan.

"You know how much I love being around your niece. I just didn't think you'd have her today."

Beverly sighed. "I wasn't supposed to, but Anna got called into work unexpectedly when a coworker didn't show up."

"Samuel said he and Lydia didn't have any plans this week-end. Maybe they would watch Susan since she and Mattie play *gut* together." Joseph paused and grinned. "We could even re-turn the favor and offer to sit with Mattie some Saturday so they can go on a date. You can even bring Susan for Mattie to play with. Samuel said they never get to go out alone."

"I'll call Lydia. Hopefully she'll pick up her cell phone."

A few minutes later, Lydia and Samuel had agreed for them to drop off Susan so Beverly and Joseph could proceed with what sounded like a wonderful chance for romance. Beverly was eager to see what Joseph had in mind.

• • •

Joseph wished he'd known Beverly would have her niece to-day. He loved being around Susan, but he would have planned something different to include the baby. Maybe even going to the water park in French Lick, although it would be overly crowded on this holiday weekend. It was a blessing that Lydia and Samuel agreed to keep Susan. He was able to get a reservation at the winery only because a couple had canceled. Being there wouldn't be time with just the two of them like he'd originally planned, but his father was right. It was too hot for a picnic, and maybe a little romantic flair would win him some points.

Mr. Jenkins—the driver Joseph's family used—took them to drop off Susan at Samuel and Lydia's and then to the French Lick Winery, where they saw plenty of *Englisch* in the restaurant.

Joseph thought he might fall out of his chair when he saw the prices on the menu. He said a silent prayer, asking God to please have Beverly order the pizza, not the lobster ravioli.

"This is so fancy." Beverly leaned over the table and spoke in a whisper. "Are you sure about this?"

Joseph sat taller. "Of course. I want this to be your special day."

Beverly glowed as the fringe of her dark lashes cast shadows on her cheeks. "*Our* special day," she said.

Smiling, he could feel *Englisch* eyes on them, coming from every angle, but he didn't care if they were the only Amish people there. And when Beverly suggested they split a pizza, Joseph thanked the Lord.

"This is the best pizza I've ever had." Beverly dabbed at her mouth with her napkin.

Joseph wasn't sure half of this pizza would fill him up, but it was tasty. "*Ya*, I agree."

"*Danki* for bringing me here. I've been looking forward to

today. A picnic would have been okay with me, too, but this is so much nicer."

"I still think it would have been too hot." Joseph wouldn't have cared as much, but he wanted this to be the best date she'd ever been on. His parents might not approve of this fancy place, but Joseph had a little money saved. "Samuel told me you and Lydia met at the Bedford library to do research on that old woman."

"*Ya*, but we didn't learn anything new. It's just hard to understand how a person gets like that, especially since Samuel's parents told him and Lydia that Margaret has a *haus* and led a normal life until her parents were killed and then her *schweschder* took off." She shook her head. "It's just sad. But maybe we can help her."

"How? She doesn't seem to want any help." Joseph agreed with Samuel that it was best to leave well enough alone. The woman was surviving somehow. But he wasn't in a position to tell Beverly what to do.

"Maybe no one has tried hard enough." Beverly frowned.

Joseph wanted to keep a smile on her face, and he would throw caution to the wind to do it. "You, um . . . look really pretty today." He paused. "I mean, you always look pretty. I mean . . . you're like the prettiest woman I've ever known." He silently told himself to hush up. Telling her once would have been enough.

"*Danki.*" Her expression lit up with a smile, so Joseph assumed he was still in the game.

After they finished their pizza and declined dessert, they fell into an easy conversation about their childhoods, and Joseph quit worrying about whether Beverly was having a good time. He could tell she was—until her eyes widened and she gasped.

Her gaze was focused on an *Englisch* couple eating a few tables to their right. A small child was with them. Then Beverly's gaze fell to her lap as she scooted her chair back and grabbed her purse. "I-I need to go to the restroom. Can I just meet you at the entrance when I leave the restroom?"

"Uh, *ya*. Sure."

She rose quickly, tucked her head, and didn't look back. Not even when the man at the table called out her name. When Beverly didn't turn around, the guy went back to his meal.

Whoever the fellow was, Beverly had clearly wanted to avoid him.

Joseph paid the check and did as she asked. He waited by the entrance.

When she returned, she brushed past him and out the door. "I'm ready for the train ride," she said over her shoulder, grinning.

He forced a smile. Perhaps that was true, but Beverly was also clearly avoiding the couple in the restaurant. He wanted to ask her about it, but he decided against it. She'd tell him if she wanted to. They'd had too nice of a time so far to mess it up. And Samuel had told him about the dark tunnel the train went through—known as the kissing tunnel. Joseph was working up his nerve.

CHAPTER 10

S amuel was heating his food in the break room on Tuesday when Joseph rushed in and sat down at the table. Because the store had been closed on Labor Day, it was the first time he'd seen his friend since Saturday.

"I'm going to marry Beverly Schrock." He flashed his toothy grin and gave Samuel a quick nod.

"The date went *gut, ya*?" Samuel took his bowl of chicken and dumpling soup to the table and sat down.

Joseph nodded, still smiling. "*Ya*, it was *wunderbaar*."

"And the train ride?" Samuel raised an eyebrow before he dipped his spoon into his bowl.

Chuckling, Joseph stood and retrieved a bag from the refrigerator. "Now, *mei* friend, I can't kiss and tell." He sat down again and took a sandwich out of the bag.

"I think you just did." Samuel was happy for Joseph, but it made him long to kiss Lydia in a way that made his stomach swirl. Maybe they'd have that chance, an opportunity to squeeze some romance into their lives next weekend. "*Danki* for offering to watch Mattie this Saturday. Lydia is looking forward to a night out by ourselves." At least, he hoped so. She'd seemed excited when Beverly made the offer after she and Joseph returned to pick up Susan last Saturday.

Joseph finished chewing the bite in his mouth. "*Ya*, that was *mei* idea." His face split into a wide grin. "It's another opportunity for me to spend time with Beverly, even if it is with two *bopplis*. It'll be *gut* practice for those ten *kinner* we're going to have someday."

Samuel wanted to tell his friend to be careful, that the babies would go to sleep early, and they'd be alone in the house. But he spooned another bite of soup. He'd never told Joseph that he and Lydia had married only because she was pregnant.

Joseph lowered his sandwich. "One odd thing happened, though."

"What's that?" Samuel glanced at the clock on the wall. He had ten minutes left. He didn't want to be late getting back to work, but Joseph had an unusually sober expression on his face.

"She avoided a man eating at the restaurant who seemed to know her, a guy about our age. It was really obvious after she spotted him. She asked me to meet her at the entrance of the place right before tucking her head and almost running to the restroom." He shrugged. "I don't know. It was just weird. The man even called after her, but she didn't turn around. I know she must have heard him."

"Maybe he was an old boyfriend or someone she dated?"

Joseph shook his head. "*Nee*, he was with a woman and a small child. And Beverly told me she's dated only one other man since her husband died, a guy named Chriss. She didn't seem comfortable talking about him when the subject came up. She just said it didn't work out."

"Did you ask her why she hurried out of the restaurant?" Samuel pushed back his chair, then went to the sink and rinsed out his bowl.

"I wasn't going to, but it was bugging me, so I eventually did." He slouched into his chair, having only eaten half his sandwich. "She avoided answering the question."

Samuel looked at the clock again, then leaned against the counter. "She could have had a lot of reasons, I guess. Were they Amish?"

"*Nee. Englisch.*" Joseph picked up the other part of his sandwich and took a large bite.

"I don't know. Maybe try to bring it up again when the time seems right. I guess I better get back to work." He took a couple of steps toward the door that led to the showroom.

"Hey, what do you think about Beverly and Lydia looking for that old woman's *haus* tomorrow? I wish they'd just let it be, but they seem determined to help the old gal somehow."

Samuel stopped abruptly and slowly turned around. "I didn't know that's what they were planning to do. Lydia just said Beverly had a day off from the bakery and was coming for a visit." His nerves tensed as he took a deep breath. "I can't think of a time Lydia has lied to me. If she did, I didn't know about it. Lying is a big pet peeve of mine."

"*Ya. Ya*, I agree. I try not to lie, and I can't stand it when others do. But . . . it ain't exactly a lie, what Lydia did. She just didn't mention it." Joseph cringed. "Maybe I shouldn't have said anything."

"It's fine." He hurriedly turned around so Joseph wouldn't see the scowl on his face. Lydia knew he wasn't in favor of her growing obsession with Margaret Keim. He'd ask her about it when he got home. He wasn't sure what he was more upset about—that Lydia hadn't told him about looking for Margaret's house or that she'd breached a trust he thought they were at least working toward.

. . .

Lydia laid Mattie in her crib when she got home from Fannie and Herman's house, then stretched her arms above her head as she yawned. She'd pulled out furniture to sweep behind it, and she'd prepared several meals, dishes her in-laws could easily heat in the oven. They'd loved visiting with their granddaughter, but they still put up a mild argument about Lydia doing housework. In the end, Mattie consumed their time, and even though the extra work had worn her out, Lydia felt better when she left the house tidy.

But she'd also stayed longer than she meant to this afternoon. She was accustomed to visiting them in the mornings, but she'd taken Mattie to the doctor for her vaccinations early in the day.

Her father-in-law had more color in his face, and Fannie's bruised eye and cheek were yellowing every day as the swelling slowly went down. Lydia was hopeful they were on the mend. Not that she minded the extra work but so they could enjoy a better quality of life.

As she yawned again, she planned to turn in early. That sounded like a small thing in the big picture, but she looked forward to snuggling with Samuel at night. And she was excited about them having an actual date on Saturday.

As she put the casserole she'd made that morning into the oven, the front door opened. Samuel stormed into the kitchen without pausing to take off his shoes, and when she glanced up, Lydia could tell something was wrong by the sour expression on his face.

"Didn't you get the voice mail I left you saying I was going to your parents' *haus* this afternoon?" Lydia closed the oven door and turned to face him. "I didn't want you to think you had to stop and check on them if you didn't feel up to it, since I was going to be there."

"*Ya*, I got the message." He put his hat on the rack by the kitchen door, but he didn't sit down. Nor did the brash tone of his voice soften as he folded his arms across his chest. "Beverly is coming over tomorrow."

"*Ya*, she is. She has the day off from the bakery." She tried to sound casual before she turned around and began chopping lettuce at the counter. "Remember, I told you about it?"

"What do you have planned?"

Samuel sounded confrontational, but Lydia was too tired to argue about anything. She also didn't want to lose her spot in the nook of her husband's arm when they went to bed. Maybe a little arguing was healthy, but she wanted to avoid it tonight.

"We'll probably get something to eat. It's supposed to be a nice day, not as hot as it has been." Lydia started to chop up a tomato, hoping that would pacify Samuel. It wasn't a lie, just an exclusion of the entire truth.

"That sounds nice, a meal and a ride." Samuel sat down at the table. The harshness in his tone didn't make it sound nice.

Lydia kept chopping and cleared her throat. "*Ya*, a nice day for both."

"Do you have anything else planned?" Samuel's tone softened, so maybe Lydia had misread any irritation in his comment before.

She thought for a few seconds. "*Nee*, that's all." Now she was lying, so she quickly asked God to forgive her.

Samuel was quiet, but when Lydia turned to put the salad in the refrigerator, she looked at him sideways. By the scowl on his face and the way his arms were still across his chest, she could tell he had more on his mind.

"Is something wrong?" She leaned against the counter, faced him, and folded her arms across her chest too.

"Today Joseph and I had a conversation about something that really gets under our skin." He paused to glare at her. "Lying."

Lydia dropped her hands to her sides and sighed. "Samuel, if you have something to say, just say it." She was much too tired for this, but she'd rather break through the tension than deal with it all evening.

"You're planning to go find Margaret Keim's *haus*, even though I asked you to let that whole business go." He peered at her in a way that brought forth anger.

"*Ya*, we just might do that." She raised her chin, deciding she couldn't avoid a confrontation "As long as we were going to enjoy a ride, we thought we might drive by the *haus* where Margaret used to live, and I don't know why that bothers you so much."

"I hope you found a babysitter. I don't want *mei dochder* any-where near that place." Samuel's jaw tensed.

Lydia's thoughts about the matter bubbled to the surface. "You can't tell me where I can take Mattie. We're just going to drive by. It's just an old *haus*." She stiffened as she met his icy gaze, but she took a deep breath and forced herself to stay calm. She didn't like his tone or bossiness, but she would give him the benefit of the doubt—that he truly had concerns about Mattie's well-being. "But *mei mamm* is going to keep Mattie so I can enjoy a day out with Beverly."

"I told you. I worry that old woman might be dangerous." Samuel's expression relaxed as he unfolded his arms.

"You have no reason to think that. A lot of rumors about Margaret circle around, but maybe she just fell on hard times and needs a little help." Lydia held her stance, arms still folded.

"You heard what *mei* parents said. Folks have been trying to help her for decades. What can you possibly do that others—with more means than us—haven't been able to do?"

"If this is about money, I know we don't have any to spare. But you have no compassion where Margaret is concerned. How can you stand to see someone living in squalor the way she is? Maybe she just needs someone to take an interest in her, to show a little kindness."

"Maybe you should show a little interest in your husband instead."

Lydia's jaw dropped. Samuel was itching for a fight. She wondered how much of it was about Margaret and the house. His last comment leaned more toward the elephant in the room they'd been avoiding, the one that wandered into the bedroom each night. Maybe he was using his irritation with Margaret to mask what he was really upset about. Either way, all their issues were coming to a head in this one conversation. Lydia was only prepared to tackle one at a time.

As she stood gaping, she pondered a response. It was easier to argue about Margaret than it was to talk about their sex life—or lack of one. She had hoped she and Samuel would work toward bettering their relationship as a couple, but this sounded like bullying. Even so, she didn't want to get into their lack of intimacy, although she sensed her spot in his arms slipping away, at least for tonight. "You can't tell me what to do." She felt like a five-year-old as she lowered her arms to her sides and looked down.

"*Nee*, apparently not. Go and have fun with Beverly tomorrow." He stood, and his chair scraped across the floor so roughly that it almost tipped backward. "I'm not hungry. I'm going to go shower."

Lydia was tempted to run after him, to unleash all the emotions she'd been holding in, but Mattie began to fuss. She shuffled out of the kitchen, crossing through the living room to tend to her daughter. As she scooped Mattie into her arms, she had to ask herself if Samuel was right. Was she occupying herself with other things to avoid the issues between them? *Maybe.* But now the topic was all but out in the open, and she wasn't sure what to do. Should she try to pretend the conversation hadn't happened? Would Samuel bring it up again?

As she held Mattie close, she blinked back tears and thought about all the angry comments, knee-jerk responses, and emotions that had just boiled to the surface like hot lava. A volcano was beginning to spew. And it all led to the one emotion that kept rising to the top for Lydia—*loneliness.*

. . .

Samuel skipped both supper and devotions and went to bed. When Lydia came into their bedroom, he pretended to be asleep. As he lay there, thinking about the day, he tried to analyze what had him bothered the most and why he'd reacted the way he had.

If Lydia had any idea how much the possibility of her interacting with Margaret worried him, she would have understood his reaction. But there was more to Samuel's bad mood than he liked to admit even to himself. Yes, he wanted to be closer to Lydia in an intimate way, but he'd also been envious when Joseph told him about his date with Beverly. Would he and Lydia have fallen in love and *chosen* to be together if their relationship had progressed the way a relationship is supposed to? Would they have had that twinkle in their eyes Joseph had today? His friend was a man falling in love. Samuel was a married man who loved his wife. But it felt different, and he wanted what Joseph had. Maybe that time had passed.

He rolled onto his back just as Lydia extinguished her lantern. But he got a glimpse of her face and saw she'd been crying. He was such a jerk. He'd missed supper, he hadn't seen his daughter, and he'd made his wife cry. Not his best day.

"I'm sorry," he said softly as she laid down, far on her side of the bed and facing away from him. He rolled onto his side and stared at her back.

Samuel expected her to say it was okay or offer some other mundane response so they could go to sleep without further discussion. That's what they did. But the tension between them had never escalated to the point it had this evening.

When Lydia rolled over and faced him, he could barely make out her face in the small amount of light streaming from the propane lamp outside. But as she shifted her position, rays from a nearly full moon lit her expression, and he saw her bottom lip tremble.

"Samuel, I want to be the *fraa* you want. I want our relationship to be different as much as you do. I just don't know how to get there." She covered her face with her hands and cried.

"Come here," he said softly as he reached for her.

Sniffing, she found her place in the nook of his arm, and he kissed her on the forehead. "We'll get there. I'm sorry for the way I spoke to you. If finding out about Margaret is that important to you, then I won't give you a hard time about it—if you promise to be careful."

She lifted her head and stared into his eyes, and for a moment,

Samuel thought he saw an invitation in her gaze. "I'll be careful," she said in a whisper before she settled against him again. Maybe if they communicated more about what was important, maybe if they were more honest, their issues wouldn't intensify. Maybe they'd find a way to each other the way they wanted to.

He stared at the ceiling as Lydia fell asleep in his arms. On Saturday, they would have an actual date, just the two of them. Samuel wanted to make it the most romantic night he could— a night Lydia would never forget.

CHAPTER 11

Lydia wondered if Beverly noticed her eyes were still swollen from crying. If she had, her friend didn't say anything. Lydia wanted to spill her guts to Beverly, to tell her everything going on in her mind. But Beverly was aglow and seemingly in love, and Lydia didn't want to tamper with her happy mood. They were on a mission to learn more about Margaret Keim. Today, Lydia would let that be her distraction.

"Are you sure this is the right road?" Beverly pushed black sunglasses up on her nose as she peered ahead of them, straining to see into the sun's glare. They'd eaten fish sandwiches at Stop N Sea, and now they'd just passed the Troyers' place and the turn her father-in-law had described. Dark clouds gathered in cottony clusters overhead as the sun fought for space. As of last night, no rain had been in the forecast, but Lydia hadn't checked this morning's newspaper.

"*Ya*, I think so. When I asked him for clarification, Herman said the *haus* was on this road, just past the Troyers'." Lydia had snagged a pair of sunglasses right before she left home, but they were an old pair and hung lopsided on her face. She'd been in a hurry to get Mattie to her mother's house before Beverly arrived.

As Lydia kept the horse at a steady trot, she wondered if they should turn back. "I've never been down this road." The farther they went, the more the trees began to form a scraggly arch across the narrow street. "It's a little creepy."

"Maybe it only feels creepy because of the dark clouds hovering over us. We're on a historical mission, not living out a ghost story." Beverly giggled, but stopped suddenly and gasped. "Look!" She pointed across Lydia and to their left. "There's a house back there."

An old farmhouse loomed in the distance, a considerable way from the road. Lydia slowed the horse. "How did you even see that?"

"I must have been looking at just the right time." Beverly pushed her sunglasses on top of her head as the skies became more overcast. "Do you think that's it?"

Lydia took off her sunglasses and set them in her lap. "It certainly fits the description." She paused as they both eyed the house. "Look at the way the vines crawl up the sides, and the front windows are broken." After she took a deep breath, she said, "I don't know if we should go any closer."

To Lydia's surprise, Beverly said, "*Ya*, I agree."

Loud, rumbling thunder sounded overhead. Seconds later, a bolt of lightning caused Lydia to squeeze her eyes closed, and she covered her ears when the follow-up thunder boomed overhead. "Argh. Where did this storm come from? I should have double-checked the weather forecast."

Lydia jumped when lightning struck closer this time, causing her to pull back on the reins. Her horse's front legs came up in the air. "Chester doesn't like storms," she said as she nodded toward the nervous animal.

"There's a barn by Margaret's *haus*, but it looks like it's missing a wall." Beverly pointed to the other side of the property. "There's a lean-to. Should we at least take shelter on the front porch and put your horse under the lean-to? This is surely just a random thunderstorm passing through. It shouldn't last long."

Lydia eyed the trail to the house. It was barely wide enough to accommodate a buggy.

"Someone uses this driveway." Beverly pointed across Lydia again. "See how all that overgrowth is pressed down."

"I still don't think we should go on the property." Lydia wanted to heed Samuel's warnings, but they might not have a choice. He would want her to wait out the storm. When another bolt of lightning struck nearby, her horse grew more agitated and reared up again. "Chester has neighed and fussed when we hit a storm, but he's bucked like this only once. I'm a little afraid he might take off running. We better take shelter for now."

Beverly bit her bottom lip and then stayed quiet as Lydia backed up the horse and buggy, then coaxed Chester onto the worn path. Her heart pounded against her chest as rain poured, and still another bolt of lightning lit the trail ahead of them. Lydia had a bad feeling about this, but she kept a strong hold on the reins as her horse whinnied his way down the path. As if by instinct, Chester trotted under the lean-to and stopped, leaving the buggy exposed.

"Are we better off staying here in the buggy or running inside the *haus*?" Beverly had her eyes on the dilapidated structure. "I don't think we'll be any safer or drier on the porch. The rain is blowing sideways, so we'd get wet there."

Lydia turned that way and studied the remains of a life once lived. She wanted to know what was inside, but at what cost? "There's no telling what type of critters might have taken up residence in there."

They both stared at the once-white farmhouse, its paint chipped and peeling, leaving behind shades of gray. In addition to being engulfed in vines, the place had weeds growing through some of the slats in its porch. An old rocking chair was overturned, and several empty beer cans were strewn about.

"Maybe *Englisch* teenagers hang out here." Lydia's mind fluttered in all directions as she speculated about what they might find inside.

"Well, there isn't anyone here now. No cars or buggies." Beverly covered her ears when another clap of thunder roared. "I'm willing to take the chance and go inside. We'd be safer than sitting out here."

Lydia wasn't sure about that, but she nodded. Then they both made a dash for the house, carefully stepping around broken glass on the porch. When Lydia turned the knob on the front door, the door opened.

"I feel like we're trespassing." Beverly clung to Lydia's arm as they crossed the threshold.

"We are." Samuel's warnings rang out in Lydia's head, and as she took slow, careful steps, she blinked her eyes into focus. Without much sunlight, it took a few seconds to make out the contents of the living room. A worn gray couch looked bleached from the sun and was spotted with bird droppings. A spring protruded from one side. A coffee table sat upright but crooked in front of the couch. It looked warped, probably from rain coming through the broken windows. Two high-backed chairs in the same condition sat across the room. A horrible stench permeated the atmosphere.

"Is that mold I smell?" Beverly let go of Lydia's arm and pinched her nose closed.

"I'm not sure, but it really stinks." The rancid odor caused

Lydia to almost gag as they continued taking slow steps, their shoes crunching on even more broken window glass.

Beverly gasped and then stepped to the fireplace mantel. Only one item sat on top of a thick layer of dust and debris. Her friend picked up the framed photograph and brushed it off with her apron. "Look," she said softly as she turned to Lydia and held it out. "Margaret was beautiful."

Lydia took the frame and studied the photo as she put a hand to her heart. Margaret wore a bright-red dress belted at the waist. Long, auburn hair hung straight, and she had on makeup, a particularly bright red lipstick. Standing next to her was a handsome young man in a dark suit, and he was clean-shaven.

Beverly leaned closer. "Or is that Margaret's *schweschder* in the photo, her twin?"

Lydia shrugged. "Maybe it is. Maybe when she went away, she went with this man. *Mei* in-laws said the family was Amish, but there isn't anything Amish about this photo. Not to mention photographs aren't allowed." Lydia tipped her head to one side and studied the photo some more.

"These people are so young." Beverly eased the frame from Lydia and brought it closer to her face. "Maybe it's not Margaret or her *schweschder*."

"I don't know." The young woman in the photo stood tall and proud, her chin slightly raised, a broad smile on her face, a smile filled with perfectly white teeth. Lydia had seen Margaret just close enough to see that her teeth weren't in the best of shape. She probably hadn't cared for them in a long time.

Beverly pointed to the dress. "That's not how the *Englisch* dress these days. *Mei schweschder* and I recently went to a yard sale and saw boxes of old patterns. The dresses looked like the one here."

"Weren't photos only in black and white a long time ago?" Lydia wiped away more dust from the picture. "Since the photo is in color, it might not have been taken as long ago as we think. Maybe you're right. Maybe this isn't Margaret or her *schweschder.*"

Beverly placed the frame back on the mantel. "This doesn't feel right. We're trespassing on someone's life."

Lydia nodded, yet the urge to look through the house was strong. "We're already here, though. We might as well look around."

Beverly stepped to a window, more glass crunching beneath her black loafers. "The rain is letting up."

"We can leave if you want." Lydia longed to tour the rest of the rooms, but if Beverly wanted to go, she wasn't going to argue.

"*Nee.* Like you said, we're already here. Maybe learning more about Margaret will give us a clue about how we can help her. This *haus* is in horrible shape, but the structure looks solid. Maybe the community could come together and help her get the place livable."

"She's never wanted any help. At least, that's what everyone keeps saying." Lydia stepped into the kitchen, then held her nose. Beverly was behind her. Rusted pots sat on a wood-burning oven, and as Lydia drew closer, she eyed dried-up tea bags in one of the pots. A skillet sat crusted with something that looked like black, rotten potatoes. The counters were mostly bare except for a box of overturned quick oats and a glass canister that looked like it had sugar inside. As in the living room, bird droppings dotted everything in sight.

Beverly stepped around two lanterns on the floor, both missing their glass, and Lydia eyed a roll of paper towels on the small kitchen table that had been gnawed on. "Mice," she said softly. Four wooden chairs sat around the table, each engraved with ornate designs.

"This is a fancy dining set for an Amish home." Beverly gingerly ran a hand across the back of one of the chairs, pulling back another thick layer of dust.

"I've seen furniture like this in Amish homes before, families with money." Lydia had always wondered what the bishop thought about such luxuries. Herman and Fannie hadn't said what Margaret's father did for a living. Nor did they say the family had money. Maybe they did, though. Maybe that's why rumors about buried cash started flying.

"I can't take this odor any longer." Beverly put her hand over her mouth and nose and marched back into the living room, which didn't smell much better.

They wound their way into a mudroom that lived up to its name. Two pairs of galoshes lay toppled by the back door, both with rotted and detached soles. A bird nest in a corner hovered above an old broom propped up against the wall next to an ax. Lydia shivered when she noticed dried blood on the ax even though she'd seen her father chop off a chicken's head using the same tool.

Beverly led them into another room downstairs, a bedroom. "That's fancy furniture in here too." She pointed to the large oak bed with etchings along the back of the headboard, two end tables equally as nice, and a matching armoire. The condition of the room was the same as the others—dirty, with broken glass on the floor and bird droppings. They took a peek in the attached bathroom, where they saw muddy water in the commode, a claw-foot tub covered in lime and filth, and more remnants that told them birds and mice often occupied the space.

Lydia left the bathroom and walked to the bedroom window, then waited until she heard thunder. But it was far in the distance. "The rain stopped." She turned to Beverly, who'd followed her. "Do you think we should go?"

Beverly sighed. "*Ya*, we probably should."

When they were back in the living room, they studied the staircase to the second floor. "I can't see how going up there will provide any information about how to help Margaret." Lydia twisted her clammy hands together as she kept her eyes on the stairs. "No one has slept here or cooked in ages. It's just an abandoned old house."

"This was once a beautiful home." The sadness in Beverly's heart mirrored how Lydia felt. "It just seems like such a waste for it to deteriorate like this."

"I still wonder if Margaret would live here even if it was repaired and cleaned up." Lydia pulled her eyes from the stairs and looked at Beverly. "She's the one who let it get like this."

"Maybe she's mentally ill," Beverly said as her eyes drifted back to the stairs. "But we'll likely never come back here again, so should we see what's upstairs while we have this chance?"

Lydia looked outside again as the sun lifted above the clouds, which somehow made the venture feel less scary. Then she pointed to a stair step that was missing a board. "Just be careful. If one of us gets hurt, Samuel will be so upset. He wasn't happy we planned to drive by the *haus*. He surely wouldn't approve of us being inside."

"I don't think Joseph thought it was a *gut* idea either, but he didn't say too much." Beverly led the way, the rickety wood creaking beneath her feet. Lydia followed, and when they reached the landing, a hallway stretched before them with two closed doors on either side and a bathroom at the far end, its door swung open. They stopped in front of the first closed door on the left. All the rooms downstairs had been easily accessible, but now Beverly had to put her hand on the knob and slowly turn it until it clicked. The door opened.

Lydia scanned the room. "It looks like the rest of the *haus*." She saw a single bed, a nightstand, and a rack of hooks on the wall. Two tattered Amish dresses hung there, along with a straw hat that had seen better days. "Except with even more mouse droppings." Cringing, she eyed the small dark pellets on the bare mattress.

From there, they opened the next two doors in the hallway. One room was in similar condition as the first, except with a double bed. The other housed a treadle sewing machine, a wooden chair, and a wall of shelves filled with chewed-on fabric and various sewing accessories.

"No packed boxes, no keepsakes, just furniture and everyday items." Beverly ran a hand along the old sewing machine. "Maybe Margaret's twin took a lot of their belongings with her. It's just odd. I guess I thought we'd find some clue about why Margaret chooses to live out of a pickup truck when she has a *haus*."

Lydia moved to the shelves. "This room has more in it than the others." She picked up a shoebox filled with various sewing needles, spools of thread, and safety pins. "Someone in Margaret's family must have been a *gut* seamstress." She thought again about the photo and who was wearing the bright-red dress. The reams of fabric in this room represented colors common to the Amish—maroon, dark blues, and green, and black for men's trousers.

"We should go." Lydia acknowledged a feeling she'd learned to recognize—one she did her best to avoid. *Shame.* She should have known trespassing would trigger the emotion. "I don't feel right being in here." What had started as a goodwill mission—or possibly just morbid curiosity—had turned into a situation Lydia wished they'd resisted.

"I agree." Beverly took a final look around, as did Lydia, then they left the small room. But out in the hallway, Beverly pointed to the last closed door and the bathroom and started toward them. Lydia followed with heavy steps and a heavier heart. Everything about this place had caused a knot to start building in her throat.

She peeked over Beverly's shoulder into the bathroom with a corner shower, sink, and a commode in the same condition as the one they'd seen connected to the bedroom. Mouse droppings were everywhere. Cringing, she turned to leave, but they still hadn't opened one of the doors.

They both stared at it.

"If there's a basement, I don't feel the need to see it. But since we're already upstairs, we might as well look in this last room up here." Beverly turned the knob. "It's locked," she said when it wouldn't budge.

"Let's go." The back of Lydia's neck prickled. "We've seen enough, and it just makes me sad."

Beverly tried the door again. "But this might be the one room that sheds some light on Margaret's situation. What if it has boxes filled with trinkets that were once displayed in the *haus*? Maybe more old clothes? Or photographs like the one on the mantel?"

"Or more broken windows, mouse and bird poop, and filth." Lydia wanted to take a shower as soon as she got home. She'd felt sticky from getting wet in the rain, then even more so after being in Margaret's house.

Beverly took a few quick steps down the hallway. "These doorknobs are all original." She pointed to the hardware on the door that led into the sewing room. Then she stepped back to where Lydia was standing outside the locked door. "But this one is new and has a lock."

Lydia wasn't sure why that mattered. A locked door was a locked door.

Beverly stood on her toes, reached to the narrow ledge above the door, and then brought down a pin with a curve at its end. "I have this same kind of lock, and they all come with a thing like this." She held up the tool before she poked the straight end into a tiny hole in the middle of the lock and wiggled it. "I've had to use mine several times when I accidently locked myself out." She pushed the pin and moved it in all directions, and eventually they heard a click.

Right before Beverly eased the door open, a shot of adrenaline coursed through Lydia. She had a strong urge to pull it closed, but it was too late, and as the door swung wide, she gasped. Never in a million years could she have imagined what she saw.

CHAPTER 12

Beverly stepped into the middle of the room with her jaw dropped. Glancing at Lydia, she saw her friend had the same wide-eyed and shocked expression Beverly was sure she wore.

"I don't understand," Lydia said barely above a whisper.

Beverly's feet took her to the crib in the corner of the room. It was an older style yet looked brand-new, and as she ran her hand across the top of the rail, not even a hint of dust came up. The pink sheets and blankets were neatly folded back at an angle, and a white teddy bear sat in the corner. A pink-and-yellow mobile hung delicately above the crib.

Her eyes traveled to where Lydia was standing in front of a changing table complete with a perfectly stacked pile of folded cloth diapers, baby powder, and lotion. Lydia picked up the powder, held it for a couple of seconds, then placed it back in its spot. The packaging design wasn't anything Beverly had ever seen. It looked . . . old. Near the changing table sat a white dresser, a white rocking chair next to it. The walls were painted a light shade of pink. It was fancy for a baby nursery, by Amish standards.

Beverly lowered her eyes. "The wood floors seem freshly waxed. Someone cleans in here." She looked back at her friend, and as they locked eyes, Beverly tried to surmise why this room had been preserved to perfection. "I don't understand either," she finally said before she walked to the dresser. It held a rattle, pacifier, two folded burp rags, and a thermometer. As she continued to look around the pink-and-white room, she couldn't think of anything missing. Everything needed for a baby was here. Even a stroller leaned against one wall. It was an older style too.

Lydia pointed to the window and ran a hand across her sweaty forehead. "That explains why it's so hot in this room. This window isn't broken, and it's closed."

Beverly's mind was spinning with bewilderment "This is one time I wish cameras were allowed. I'm afraid later I'm going to think my brain deceived me and I really didn't see this." In her community, cell phones with cameras weren't allowed, let alone ones with access to the internet, and she was pretty sure Lydia's district followed the same rule. Otherwise, she thought her friend would have suggested a photo by now, rule or not.

Lydia began to pace as she tapped a finger to her chin. "Maybe Margaret always wanted a *boppli*, but she never had one and went crazy over it." Her eyes widened as she looked at Beverly. "That's why she keeps this room like this. Maybe she even has a doll she pretends is her *boppli*."

Beverly shivered at the thought. "*Nee, nee.* I don't think that's it."

"Maybe she had a *boppli*, but it died, and she keeps the room exactly as it was." Lydia's voice had dropped to a whisper.

Beverly had no idea what the intent of the room was, but a chill ran the length of her spine despite the heat. "I knew something about Margaret didn't add up. Maybe if folks had tried a little harder to help her, or even came here and found this room, she wouldn't be living out of her truck."

"We need to go." Lydia's voice trembled. "This is *ab im kopp*. I don't feel right."

"Okay, *ya*. Let's go." A part of Beverly was fascinated they'd stumbled upon something so unknown and mysterious. But warning bells rang loudly in her head. She had to consider Lydia's speculations. If her friend was even close, Margaret might indeed be crazy—or at least dangerous.

They scampered out of the room and closed the door behind them. Beverly dropped the key twice before she got it back on the ledge above the door. She stayed on Lydia's heels as they rushed down the stairs, not taking nearly the care they had on the way up. Lydia didn't even slow down as she crossed through the living room, kicking up a plume of dust and dried leaves.

Beverly's heart rate didn't begin to fall until Lydia had backed the horse out of the lean-to and they were headed down the narrow trail from the house. Neither woman said anything. Beverly was expecting Margaret to turn onto her makeshift driveway any moment. The old woman would confront them, and then what?

When Lydia made the turn onto the road, Beverly breathed a sigh of relief, but her relief was short-lived. In the distance, a blue truck came toward them, close enough that the driver would have seen Lydia turn from the path.

"*Ach*, oh dear." Beverly held her breath. Maybe it was someone else driving a blue truck. But as the truck got closer, she saw the back of the rocking chair protruding over the cab and tomatoes bobbing over one side "It's her," she whispered as her heart pounded against her chest like a jackhammer.

"Don't make eye contact. Look casual." Lydia's voice shook again as she spoke, but despite her friend's warning, Beverly did look at Margaret, and she was sure Lydia's eyes had veered in that direction too.

The woman slowed the truck almost to a stop as she passed the buggy. She held her arm out the window, almost as if she were reaching for the buggy—or Lydia. Lydia faced forward and whistled to Chester as she snapped the reins, quickly putting the horse at a faster trot. "That's the closest I've ever been to her," she said after she put some distance between the buggy and the truck.

"She knows." Beverly blinked back tears as she considered Lydia's earlier thoughts about the nursery. "She knows we were at her *haus*."

"Don't panic." Lydia spoke firmly, but Beverly heard the shakiness still in her voice. "She's not dangerous. Like everyone says, she's a fixture here. If she were dangerous, something would have already happened, or she'd be in jail. Besides, we could have just made a wrong turn and been coming out of her driveway to get back on the road. There's no way for her to know we were in her *haus*."

Beverly's nerves tensed as she swallowed with difficulty, struggling to find her voice. "Except . . ." She paused to slow her breathing. "I put the key to the nursery back, but . . ." She turned to Lydia, who was looking at her with questioning eyes. "I didn't lock the door."

. . .

Lydia just wanted to get home and forget about this day, but the expression on Margaret's face was etched into her mind. As the old woman slowed her truck and scowled, she might as well have said *I know you were in my house*. And the way she'd extended her arm as though she wanted to touch the buggy—or her—was unnerving.

"Are you going to tell Samuel about this?"

Beverly looked a mess. Her prayer covering had slipped to one side, strands of hair blew loose in the breeze, and she had a smudge of dirt on her cheek.

Lydia thought about it. "I don't want to lie to him, but if I tell him we went into Margaret's *haus*, he'll be angry." She paused, sighing, as she brushed back her own wild strands of hair from across her face. Avoiding the entire truth also wasn't going to bring her closer to Samuel, and she knew she wouldn't feel good about keeping this from him, but . . .

"I really want our date Saturday night to go well. We don't get to go out by ourselves much." *Actually, never.* She clicked her tongue and gave Chester a gentle flick of the reins to pick up the pace a little more.

"Then I won't say anything to Joseph." Beverly put her sunglasses on now that the sun's rays were back in full force. "I don't want to lie, either, so I'll just tell him we got something to eat and drove by Margaret's house." She flinched. "That much is true."

"I think I'll always wonder about Margaret, and I really did hope we could find a way to help her." She turned to Beverly. "But did you see the way she looked at us?"

"And the way she reached out toward us?" Beverly shook her head. "It was unsettling, to say the least."

The women were quiet for a while.

"We should forget about what we saw and stay away from Margaret," Lydia finally said. "We're bound to see her from afar every now and then, like we did at the school, but I don't think we can help her."

"Maybe she *is* mentally ill." Beverly rubbed her forehead. "Or maybe she never got past her bereavement. I understand about grief. But Margaret's situation is bizarre."

"*Ya*, we'll just leave her alone to live her life the way she's chosen." Lydia breathed a sigh of convicted relief. "We'll let it go."

Beverly nodded. "*Ya*, agreed."

They rode in silence until they reached Lydia's house. After they'd given Chester a sufficient amount of water, they readied Beverly's horse for travel.

"I'd ask you to come in for a while, but I need to pick up Mattie at *mei mamm*'s *haus*."

"*Nee*, I need to get home as well, but I'll see you Saturday." Beverly put a finger to her lips. "Seeing Margaret and going inside her *haus* can be our secret." She gave Lydia a long hug, the kind of embrace you give someone you haven't seen in a long time. An unspoken sisterhood had bonded them today. Lydia just wished that bond wasn't based on a secret they'd vowed to keep.

Lydia wasn't fond of secrets, especially when it meant keeping something else from Samuel. It seemed like she withheld enough from her husband, but those were feelings she didn't share. This was a tangible event he wouldn't approve of. As she recalled their blowup the night before, she was even more sure he'd be angry if he learned she and Beverly had gone into Margaret's house.

Sighing, she prepared for the shame she could feel coming. And this time, what she'd done to earn it had been premeditated, which made her feel even worse.

• • •

Samuel was anxious to hear about Lydia's day, if not a little wary. He wasn't crazy about the idea of her and Beverly searching out Margaret's house, but he refused to let anything get under his skin this evening. He had a big night planned for Lydia on Saturday, and he didn't want anything to hamper their pending date. The closer it got to Saturday, the more excited he was to have a proper date with his wife. Each day, he felt more and more like a giddy teenager.

When he walked inside the house, he breathed in the smell of oregano and garlic, savoring the fragrant aromas that signaled spaghetti for supper. Maybe even garlic bread with Parmesan cheese sprinkled on top. His mouth watered as he slipped out of his shoes and hung his hat on the rack in the living room.

"It smells *gut*," he said as he walked into the kitchen. Lydia stirred the simmering spaghetti sauce as Samuel pulled out a chair and sat down. Her hair was wet and fell past her waist.

She turned around and smiled. *"Danki."*

Mattie was already in her high chair. *"Wie bischt, mei maedel?"* Samuel leaned over and kissed the baby on the cheek, then he looked at the clock on the wall. "You showered early."

"Ya. Beverly and I got caught in the rain, and I felt sticky, so when I got home, I showered while Mattie was napping."

Samuel took a deep breath. "Did you see Margaret's *haus?*"

Lydia carried the pot of sauce to the table. *"Ya,* we did." She returned to the stove to drain some noodles in the sink. "I'm not sure how Beverly even spotted it. The *haus* sits way back from the road. It's like your *daed* said. It seems the *haus* is more or less abandoned. Vines have overtaken it, windows are broken, and it was just sad to think Margaret used to live there." She came to the table with the noodles in a large bowl.

Samuel bowed his head when she did. Then when she started

feeding Mattie tiny bites of noodles, he dug in and filled his plate. Lydia's spaghetti sauce was even better than his mother's. "Did you eat out?"

"*Ya.*" Lydia offered Mattie apple juice from a sippy cup, but when their daughter's face twisted into the expression she had right before she wailed, his wife quickly gave her the bottle she'd had sitting nearby. "We got fish sandwiches at Stop N Sea."

Samuel wanted to ask if Lydia was done trying to gather information about Margaret, but he didn't want to come across as too overbearing, the way he had last night. "They have *gut* sandwiches," he said between mouthfuls.

He'd been planning their date every chance he had. As badly as he wanted to tell Lydia what he had lined up, he'd rather she be surprised. He'd had help from Joseph, but also from his other *Englisch* coworkers. It might not be the most traditional and sanctioned date for an Amish man and woman, but if a few rules were broken along the way, Samuel hoped God would be forgiving. They hadn't had much of a *rumschpringe*.

Besides, more than once he'd heard that a woman needs romance in a relationship, and he was determined to sweep his wife off her feet, to woo her. And if their date went well, maybe they could finally work their way to a more intimate relationship. He would also be patient—not like he'd been in the beginning when Lydia was pregnant. This time would be different.

After they ate, Samuel played with Mattie in the living room while Lydia cleared the kitchen table. He looked forward to holding his wife as they drifted off to sleep tonight. These days, no one was pretending to be asleep, which eased the tension in the evenings.

After they went through their nightly devotions, he excused himself to take a shower.

. . .

Lydia shuffled into the bedroom holding Mattie, who seemed to get a burst of energy after her bottle instead of getting sleepy.

Samuel was propped up in bed, where he'd been reading a book. But now he lowered it.

"Can Mattie lie here with you while I finish cleaning the kitchen? I let her nap too late this afternoon." Lydia kissed her baby on the cheek. "But she's all smiles, and I suppose I should be thankful for that. Her first tooth finally pushed through the surface."

Samuel marked his place, closed the book, and held out his arms. "*Ya*, sure. Come here *mei* sweet *maedel*."

She handed Mattie to Samuel as the baby flapped her arms and smiled. Mattie loved her daddy, and a special kind of love was at play when father and daughter were together. A deep and fulfilling sensation warmed her heart, and she allowed herself a few more moments to watch them before she scooted off to the kitchen.

As she washed and rinsed dishes, she thought about her day, glad Samuel hadn't pushed her for more details, making it easier to avoid lying to him. It might be a while before she didn't think about the perfectly clean and decorated nursery at Margaret's house, but she was glad Beverly wanted to put the matter to rest too.

The familiar shame had tried to force itself into her heart, but she'd fought back and relied on God's grace. He wouldn't appreciate her not telling Samuel the entire truth, and for that she asked for forgiveness. She also promised she would earnestly try to avoid situations that would put her in a position to feel shame.

As her thoughts wound back to Margaret, she recalled the way the older woman had looked at them today. Lydia tried to discern why it had been so unsettling. Guilt from trespassing in the woman's house seemed to be the logical answer.

In the past, she'd gone months without seeing Margaret. Maybe the older woman would retreat to wherever she went for a while—maybe to that nursery—and stay out of sight. Meanwhile, Lydia could do only one thing for Margaret—pray for her.

As the sun began its descent, Lydia finished putting the last of the dishes in the drainboard, then wiped down the table. Yawning, she hoped it wouldn't be too long before Mattie was tired enough to sleep. Lydia was having a more restful sleep these days. Curled up in Samuel's arms gave her a sense of calm that they'd both settled into. During supper, she'd asked him what he had planned for their date on Saturday, but he'd only grinned and said it was a surprise. She loved that he was trying to make it special.

She took the kitchen towel from over her shoulder and hung it on the rack by the sink, then turned to join her husband. But something between the fading sunbeams streaming through the window caught her eye. She allowed her gaze to unwillingly trail to the end of their long driveway.

Her breath seized in her lungs when she saw a blue pickup truck parked at the side of the road. It was too far to tell if someone was in the vehicle, but there was no denying whose truck it was. Lydia could see red balls attached to green stems swaying in the gentle breeze.

She put a hand to her mouth as her heart pumped at a furious rate. What had she and Beverly stirred up? And what should she do now? Glancing toward the bedroom, she heard

Mattie giggling as Samuel spoke baby talk to her. If Lydia was forced to tell him the whole truth about today, he'd be angry. But if he knew Margaret was lurking near their house, he'd be furious.

Was Samuel right about her? Was Margaret dangerous and not just a harmless old woman? Or was she purposefully letting Lydia know she knew she'd been in her house today and warning her to stay away?

If only Margaret didn't know where she lived. Their home was tucked away, out of sight of neighbors, but since they knew almost everyone in their community, they rarely locked their doors. Lydia checked both outer doors and made sure they were locked. Then she checked the windows, ensuring they were also shut and locked despite the warm weather.

By the time she was done, the blue truck was gone. But Lydia didn't think sleep would come easily tonight—or be peaceful.

CHAPTER 13

Beverly had been looking forward to Saturday evening and spending time with Joseph. As she pulled into Lydia and Samuel's driveway with Susan late in the afternoon, she recalled the quick kiss she and Joseph shared in the darkness of the railroad tunnel. Beverly wasn't going to consider it their first kiss; it was fast and clumsy. Hopefully tonight, after the babies were asleep, Joseph would kiss her again. She wanted to see his expression, for him to cradle her face in his hands. Maybe he would see in her eyes how much she'd already come to care about him.

Joseph was a grown man who had managed to hold on to his boyish looks, and Beverly loved that about him. And he made her laugh, which was high on her list of dating qualifications. She'd spent time grieving for her husband, as was expected, but she'd spent too much time pining over the loss of her relationship with Chriss. She was ready to get on with her life, and she wanted it filled with joy and laughter.

"Are you ready for a playdate with Mattie this evening?" After she tethered her horse, she carried Susan across the yard with the diaper bag draped over her shoulder. Joseph wasn't here yet, but she'd barely made it to the top porch step when Lydia met her and grabbed her arm.

"I have to be quick. Samuel will be out of the shower any

second." Lydia was breathing so hard that Beverly worried something awful had happened.

"What's wrong?" She hoisted Susan onto her hip and adjusted the diaper bag.

"Margaret parked at the end of our driveway Wednesday night." She shook her head, cringing. "Well, not really on the driveway, but on the road right by our driveway. Why would she do that? And how did she know where I live?"

"I don't know. What did Samuel say?" Beverly had tried to forget about Margaret and her perfectly decorated baby nursery inside the crumbling house.

"I didn't tell him." Lydia straightened. "Like we agreed, I didn't tell him about going in the *haus*. And I didn't tell him about Margaret parking on the road."

"Was she there the last two nights too?"

Lydia shook her head. "*Nee*. She didn't stay long Wednesday night, almost like she just wanted me to know she knew we'd been in her *haus*. I don't know . . ." She pressed a hand to her forehead. "Maybe I'm making too much of it, but I wanted you to know, so I'm glad you got here before Joseph so I could tell you."

"*Ya*, okay." Beverly's chest tightened. She wasn't sure how much of it was from concern about Margaret or from anticipating being alone with Joseph.

Lydia blew out a long breath, and Beverly could see the relief on her friend's face. Maybe she just needed someone to know, and Beverly was the only person she could tell.

"Samuel has a special night planned." Lydia switched gears before Beverly had time to fully process what she'd told her. "And I'm so excited to see what he has in store for us." She finally acknowledged Susan by kissing the baby on her cheek.

"He hasn't told you what you'll be doing?" Grinning, Beverly sighed. "That's so romantic, that he wants to surprise you."

"I'm a little nervous." Lydia's face turned a light shade of pink.

"Why? He's your husband. I'm sure he's planned something you'll enjoy."

Lydia waved her off as she let out a nervous laugh. "*Ya*, I'm sure he has." She stepped aside. "Come in, come in. I set up Mattie's playpen in the living room. I know she's going to be happy to see Susan."

"I've been looking forward to this all week." Once inside, Beverly set Susan in the playpen with Mattie, along with a few toys from the bag she'd brought.

"Are you comfortable being alone with Joseph? I mean, I know you've been married, and I'm sure you know to be . . . um, careful?" Lydia raised her eyebrows as she offered a tentative smile. It seemed an odd thing to say, but Beverly reminded herself that Lydia was only seventeen.

"No worries, *mei* friend." She touched Lydia on the arm. "Nothing inappropriate will happen in your *haus* while you're gone. Just plan to have a *gut* time this evening."

"*Ach*, I don't even know what I'm talking about." Lydia chuckled.

Beverly's friend seemed unusually nervous for a woman going on a date with her husband. Maybe she just wanted it to be special since they rarely got to go out by themselves.

. . .

Joseph arrived at Samuel and Lydia's toting a dozen red roses, as he'd been instructed, and he placed them on the rocking chair on the porch like Samuel asked him to do. Then behind his back, he held a dozen yellow roses. He'd bought them for Beverly. He hoped the gift wasn't overkill, but he wanted her to have flowers too.

Samuel pushed open the screen door before Joseph had time to knock. He peered around the corner at the roses.

"*Danki, mei* friend." Samuel put a hand on Joseph's shoulder. "I've never given Lydia flowers, so I thought it would be a nice gesture."

Joseph eyed his friend up and down. His black slacks were pressed, along with his dark-blue shirt. "*Ach*, you clean up well." Joseph scowled. "But I can't believe you've never given your *fraa* flowers."

"I'm going to make up for it tonight." Samuel winked as he craned his neck to see what Joseph had behind his back. "Beverly is getting roses, too, I see."

"*Ya*, I can't let you one-up me." Joseph chuckled. He was eager to have some alone time with Beverly, and he hoped the flowers would help set the mood. His awkward kiss in the dark railroad tunnel could be improved upon. He wanted to kiss her properly tonight, without slamming his nose into hers.

Samuel rubbed his hands together, grinning. "Lydia and Beverly are inside feeding the *bopplis*, and then we'll be ready to go."

Joseph laughed again. "Relax, Samuel. You act like this is your first date with your *fraa*." He'd never seen a fellow so nervous about taking his wife out.

Samuel actually blushed. "*Ya*, well . . ." He shrugged before he motioned for Joseph to follow him inside.

Beverly and Lydia were lowering the babies into the playpen. When Beverly looked up, Joseph smiled and brought the roses from behind his back. "These are for you."

Beverly brought a hand to her chest and gasped a little. "*Danki.*" She batted her eyes at him, and Joseph didn't think he'd ever made a wiser investment. He'd also bought the red roses. Samuel promised to reimburse him on payday. Joseph didn't mind fronting the money for the purchase. He knew his friend helped his parents with health-care expenses.

"Are you ready?" Samuel offered Lydia his arm, and she looped hers through it and nodded.

Joseph cleared his throat. "Now, you *kinner* have a *gut* time." He spoke as deeply as he could to disguise his voice, and he stretched as tall as he could. "No coming back too soon." He turned to Beverly and winked. Then he reminded himself to not be too forward, to let her lead. Joseph still couldn't believe he was dating someone so kind and beautiful.

A car honked outside, and as everyone went to the porch, Samuel scurried to get the roses and handed them to Lydia. "A beautiful woman deserves beautiful flowers."

Joseph rolled his eyes. He wanted to tell Samuel that he was going a bit over the top, but when Lydia's eyes lit up enough to light a village, Joseph stayed quiet and just smiled.

"What have you done, Samuel?" Lydia put a hand over her mouth as she stared at the black limousine in the driveway. Their boss's brother owned a limousine service, and he'd made arrangements to have Samuel and Lydia picked up at no charge.

"Better hope Bishop Miller doesn't get wind of this." Joseph snickered before he looked at Beverly. "Don't worry. I don't need props like that to woo you. My stunning *gut* looks and delightful personality leave women swooning."

Beverly laughed, then they both waved as Samuel walked Lydia to the long black car. "Have fun *mei* friends." Joseph hoped after he married Beverly Schrock, they'd still treat every date like it was their first.

. . .

Lydia couldn't stop smiling as she climbed into the luxurious car. Inside was a long bench and a shorter one in the back, and a trail of running lights lit the floor. Samuel sat beside Lydia on the longer bench, facing a bar with glasses, bottles of alcohol and soda, napkins, and a tiny refrigerator. An unopened bottle of nonalcoholic champagne sat in a bucket of ice. "Samuel, can-can we afford—"

"*Ya*, we can." Smiling, her husband reached for two long-stemmed glasses, then opened the champagne and poured it. "We didn't get to toast at our wedding." He handed her a glass before gently clicking his against hers. "To us."

Although their people rarely drank alcohol, it was often available at weddings. But their wedding had been thrown together so quickly that there wasn't much fanfare. Lydia was glad Samuel had chosen something bubbly for them, but she was glad it was nonalcoholic. She wasn't even of age to drink. But if this was any indication of how the evening would go, it might possibly be the best night of her life. Samuel was going out of his way to be romantic, and his effort touched her even more than what he'd arranged so far.

It was a short ride, and Lydia was surprised when they stopped in front of the furniture store where Samuel worked. She couldn't imagine how this could be part of the surprise— unless he'd been working on a special piece of furniture for their house. She wasn't sure they had room for anything else.

Dressed in a dark suit with a white bow tie, their driver

extended his hand to help Lydia out of the car. Samuel stepped out behind her and took her hand, and then they followed the man to the store's entrance. He pushed open the door with ease and led them inside.

They wound down a dimly lit aisle, maneuvering around pieces of furniture, until they turned into a narrow hallway that led to the small break room. Lydia had been back there before, where the employees often ate their midday meal. She was tempted to ask Samuel why they were there, probably having something to eat in this rather mundane place, but she didn't want to hurt his feelings. The roses and the car—all his effort— had already overwhelmed her. Just being on a date with him was enough for her.

When the driver opened the door to the room and motioned Lydia inside, she couldn't move at first. It didn't even look like the same place. She took two careful steps across the threshold and eyed the transformation. The table was covered with a white cloth, and the extra chairs had been removed, leaving two covered in a white draping, a red ribbon encircling each one. A single, tall red candle was lit, fancy blue-and-white dinnerware had been set, and silver holders held cloth napkins. She forced her mouth closed when the driver excused himself after putting her roses in a vase already filled with water on the counter.

A man dressed similarly to the driver stood with a white napkin folded over his arm. "Good evening." He pulled out a chair for her to sit down. Then he did the same for Samuel. Soft music played in the background, violins and piano. Two rules already broken—the fancy car and the music—but Lydia was floating too high off the ground to give it more than a brief thought.

The older man, presumably a waiter, cleared his throat, then held up a bottle of the same type of champagne they'd had in the car. "May I?"

Lydia nodded, but her eyes were fused with Samuel's as the man filled two flutes with the bubbly drink. Her husband had never looked more handsome. Not only was he dressed in clothes he must have ironed himself when she wasn't around, but his eyes shone with a kindness that made Lydia swell with happiness.

An unfamiliar but wonderful aroma hung in the air, yet she wouldn't care if the man served them hot dogs or pizza. The evening was already perfect.

The waiter left the room but returned in less than a minute with two small bowls, which he placed on top of the plates in front of them.

"Morel mushroom soup to get you started, Madam." He left and returned with a basket of bread. "Enjoy," he said before he exited the room again.

They bowed their heads, and when she lifted hers, Samuel was smiling ear to ear.

"*Danki* for this," she said softly.

The look in his eyes made Lydia almost want to get up and leave, to go and be with her husband in the intimate way she thought they both wanted. But then she tasted the soup, and not even her love or desire for Samuel would be able to drag her from this meal.

"This is the best soup I've ever had in *mei* life." She dipped the spoon for more.

"*Ach*, I don't know." Samuel grinned. "Your chicken soup could compete with this."

Lydia swallowed, then laughed. "*Nee*, I think not." She reached for one of the rolls in the basket, which were warm and smelled of herbs. One bite, and she was sure she never wanted to leave this room. She'd always thought her mother made the best bread ever, but apparently someone else could bake a roll better than Lydia could have imagined.

"How did you do all this?" Lydia tipped her head slightly to one side, knowing she couldn't stop smiling if she tried.

"I had a little help from the fellows at work." He smiled. "And from Mr. Bargas."

Mr. Bargas owned the furniture store, and he'd always been good to Samuel. Lydia was sure it was because her husband was a hard worker and nice to everyone he met.

Samuel had finished his soup, and Lydia was nearly done. She wondered if they could ask for seconds just as the waiter returned with two small plates. Lydia's eyes widened. She'd never seen anything quite like the offering in front of her. A large tomato had been sliced into thick wedges with mozzarella cheese in between them. Lydia could smell basil, and something else was drizzled on top.

"Caprese salad, Madam." The man nodded before he put the other plate in front of Samuel and left. Lydia breathed in the basil as a hint of garlic wafted up her nose.

"I might want to stay here forever." She quietly giggled. "*Danki*," she said again to her husband.

"I should have done this a long time ago, taken you on a proper date." Samuel's eyes twinkled as the flame from the candle danced in the middle of the table.

As they cut into their salads, Lydia thanked God for Samuel and for this wonderful meal, uninterrupted and heavenly.

"This exceeds a proper date." She gazed into Samuel's eyes. "I didn't know they made food like this." She laughed. "I wonder if that man would share these recipes. I like how the mozzarella cheese is stuffed into the tomato, and I can taste basil and garlic, but something else makes this so *gut*, and I can't figure it out."

"We still have the main course coming." Samuel raised and lowered his eyebrows several times as he grinned. "And dessert."

Lydia felt like a princess. As she stared into her husband's eyes, she tried to identify the emotion she was experiencing right at this moment. After only a couple of seconds, she knew what it was. She felt loved. It overwhelmed her that Samuel would do this, and even if his intentions might hold hopes of something more intimate between them when they returned home, that was okay. Lydia smiled on the inside. His efforts were working.

When they finished, the man took their salad plates as well as the large plates that were already on the table when they arrived.

"Where do you think he's getting all this food?" Lydia leaned forward a little and spoke in a whisper.

"He must have prepared it ahead of time and kept it in a warmer in another room." Samuel reached for another roll. "I'm glad you're enjoying this."

She leaned her head back and closed her eyes, and when she opened them, she gazed at him. "This is a perfect surprise. I've never had a meal like this." She glanced at the red roses on the counter before looking back at Samuel. "*Danki.*"

Samuel laughed. "You can stop thanking me."

Lydia lowered her head as her cheeks warmed.

"You look beautiful, Lydia, today and every day." Samuel stared into her eyes. "I know I don't tell you that enough." He paused. "I also don't tell you what a *gut mudder* you are often enough." Stopping again, he took a deep breath. "I know our life together didn't start out the way we might have planned, but I love you, Lydia."

Certain this night couldn't get any better, she brought a hand to her chest. "I love you too." She'd wondered if Samuel heard her when she'd whispered that she loved him in his ear, but it felt good to tell him now. So many times, she'd wanted him to know how she felt, and just now the words had slid off her tongue as naturally as breathing.

The waiter returned with two more plates. "Pork chops with fig and grape agrodolce, Madam."

"With what?" Lydia cringed. She hadn't meant to blurt what she was thinking.

The man smiled. "Agrodolce is Italian, Madam. It's a sweet and sour sauce. The figs and grapes are cooked in honey and a balsamic vinegar reduction sauce."

Lydia had no idea what that meant, but the moment the first bite met with her palate, she was in love. "I would do anything to cook like this."

"Our cook insists it's not hard." The waiter folded his hands in front of him as he nodded. "Enjoy, and I'll return with dessert when you're ready."

"This is the best night I've ever had." Lydia took another bite of the pork chop, then looked at her husband. "I really would love to know how to make this."

Samuel just smiled. Lydia couldn't wait to see what was for dessert. She hoped Beverly and Joseph were having a good night, but she doubted it could compare to hers.

. . .

Beverly sat next to Joseph on the couch. The babies had fallen asleep, and Joseph had just placed two lit lanterns on the fireplace mantel next to a lavender candle Lydia put on the mantel before she left. It was lit, too, and the mood was set.

"You're so *gut* with the *bopplis*."

Beverly turned to face him and laughed softly. "Even when Mattie spit up all over your shirt?" Joseph glanced down at the wet spot where Beverly had helped him clean up. "Sorry I laughed, but the look on your face was so funny." She giggled again just thinking about his expression.

"I've got younger siblings, but none of them ever puked on me." He grinned as he scratched his head. "But I'm not sure I ever gave any of them a bottle."

"She probably didn't burp *gut*." Beverly's leg brushed against Joseph's. "I hope Samuel and Lydia are having fun. What you told me he planned sounds so romantic."

Joseph rolled his eyes, still grinning. "*Ach*, I'm sure they are. I ain't never seen a man go to so much trouble for a date, especially with his *fraa*." He shrugged before he leaned back into the couch. "I mean, he's already won her over, so why go overboard?"

Beverly rolled her lip under. "I hope whoever I marry will still want to do romantic things like that after the wedding."

Joseph rolled his eyes again and sighed. "I thought we'd already established the fact that I'm going to marry you and bless you with ten *kinner*."

Beverly gave him what she hoped was a teasing look. "Do you always say exactly what's on your mind?"

"*Ya*, way more than I should." He straightened and twisted to face her. "And I've been wanting to kiss you since the moment I arrived." He scratched his cheek. "I botched it up pretty *gut* in that dark tunnel. I promise I can do better."

She tapped a finger to her chin. "Hmm. Is that so?"

"*Ya*, I'm a *gut* kisser. I'm sure of it." He didn't even crack a smile when he said it, but Beverly laughed.

"Guess there's only one way to find out, Joseph." Beverly batted her eyes at him. She was being way too flirty, but she'd fallen hard for this man. A life with him would be filled with laughter.

But he wasn't laughing when he gently cupped her cheeks in his hands and eased her face closer to him. He kissed her with his eyes before his lips ever met hers, and by the time they did, she was already floating on a wispy cloud of euphoria.

"Now, did I lie? Was that not the best kiss you've ever had?" he whispered as he slowly pulled away.

Beverly thought she might fall down if she tried to stand up. "*Ya*, it was," she managed to say as she breathlessly wondered if he would kiss her again.

"I guess it's no secret that I like you very much." Joseph still wasn't smiling. His expression was so serious, and Beverly liked seeing this more somber side of him too. He balanced his qualities well.

"I like you too." She smiled. "Do you want to come over to *mei haus* next weekend for supper? Or am I being too forward?"

"I would love to go to your *haus* next weekend for supper." Grinning, he added, "Are you a *gut* cook?"

She playfully slapped him on the arm, but before she could say anything, he kissed her again with the same passion.

She'd made up her mind. Next weekend, she'd tell Joseph the truth. It was time.

CHAPTER 14

Samuel helped Lydia into the fancy car, knowing this would be the last time they would travel in such luxury. He hoped God would forgive this overindulgence.

The waiter had emptied most of the water from the vase so Lydia could take her flowers home in the limousine, and Samuel found a spot where they wouldn't get jostled. He pointed to the bar and raised an eyebrow, but Lydia shook her head.

"I can't put one more thing in *mei* mouth." She looked down at the folded papers in her lap. "It was so nice of that man to share these recipes with me." As she gazed into Samuel's eyes, she'd never looked more beautiful. "Every time I make one of these dishes, I'll be reminded of this perfect evening." She paused but kept her eyes on him. "This was the best night of *mei* life," she told him for the second time.

A noise clicked from the front of the car, and Samuel looked that way just in time to see the driver closing the small window between him and his passengers.

When Samuel gently trailed a finger down his wife's cheek, she didn't jump or move away as she'd done in the past. She stared at him with a longing Samuel understood. When she parted her lips and initiated a kiss, her touch was like a whisper of what was to come, and it sent Samuel's insides swirling.

They stayed in each other's arms during the short drive

home, but not more than a few seconds went by before their lips found each other again. Samuel could feel his wife's desire building the way he'd longed for it to since the early days of their marriage. Love was erasing those memories and making room for better ones they could carry in their hearts forever.

They were almost home when Samuel saw something out of the corner of his eye, and he eased Lydia away to have a better look. Peering out the dark window, he could see what it was once they got closer.

"That's the old lady's truck." He turned to Lydia. "Why would Margaret be parked at the end of our driveway?"

His wife looked past him, then said, "She's really more on the side of the road." She began to twirl one string of her prayer covering and avoided his eyes.

As they drove past the truck, the woman waved. Samuel's stomach twisted into a knot. "I don't like that, her parked there." He looked at Lydia again. "Doesn't that make you feel unsettled?"

His wife shrugged as she chewed on her bottom lip.

Something is up.

The driver stopped in the driveway and then opened their door. Samuel followed Lydia out of the car, then pulled a ten-dollar bill from his pocket to give to the man. But the fellow shook his head as he waved him off.

"It's already been taken care of, Mr. Bontrager." He nodded. "Enjoy the rest of your evening."

Lydia started toward the house, but Samuel caught up to her and grabbed her arm. "Wait." He gently coaxed her farther into the yard, away from the open windows. "Why are you acting like this?"

She shrugged, then finally looked at him. Samuel thought

he saw fear in her eyes, which made him press her even more. "Do you have any idea why Margaret is parked out there?"

Lydia raised her shoulders again, dropping them slowly as she kicked at the grass and kept her eyes cast downward.

"Lydia." He gently lifted her chin until her eyes met his. "What aren't you telling me?"

Huffing, she walked away from him. Then she turned around, her arms folded across her chest, and sighed. Samuel stepped closer to her.

"What's going on?" He looped his fingers beneath his suspenders and took a deep breath. He didn't want to mess up this evening. "Whatever it is, you can tell me," he said softly so maybe Lydia would talk to him.

"She was parked there Wednesday night too." She pointed to Margaret's truck, then quickly resumed her stance.

"Why didn't you tell me?" Samuel squinted as he shifted his weight.

"I didn't want you to worry."

"Is there a reason I should be worried? I mean, more worried than I am when she's parked at the end of our driveway, which seems odd?" He looked in the direction of the truck. Its lights weren't even on. "This doesn't feel right."

Lydia huffed again and lowered her arms to her sides. "Promise you won't get mad."

Samuel took another deep breath and blew it out slowly as he held up his palms. "I won't get mad." He hoped it was a promise he could keep.

"Everything I told you about driving by Margaret's *haus* is true, but . . ." She bit her lip.

"But there's more?" Samuel glanced at the house to see if Beverly and Joseph were watching from the window. They must have heard the car pull up, but all he could see was the flicker of lanterns.

"Remember, you promised you wouldn't get mad." As she peered up at him, her lip rolled under in a pout. She looked like a child about to be scolded.

"*Ya*, okay, okay. I've promised. Just tell me." He heard the irritation creeping into his tone.

"We had a bad storm on Wednesday. I showered early that night because I was sticky and wet. Remember?"

Samuel thought back. "*Ya*, I remember."

"We didn't just get wet. We got caught in the storm, right as we were passing Margaret's *haus*. Chester got spooked and reared up, and I was afraid he would take off, so we turned onto the path that led to the *haus*. There was nowhere to take shelter, but we could see a lean-to in the distance. Chester instinctively went right to it, but the buggy was still exposed. So . . ." Lydia cringed. "We went into the *haus* to wait out the storm."

Samuel stiffened. "You broke into her *haus*?"

"*Nee*. The front door was unlocked. The place is an absolute mess. Mostly, it doesn't look like anyone has been there in ages other than maybe teenagers hanging out. We saw beer cans on the porch. But there were leaves and bird droppings and . . ."

Samuel stood quietly as Lydia described the interior of the house, but he was seething. She'd kept this from him. He thought they'd reached a new level of emotional intimacy, but he must have been wrong. Not only had Lydia put herself in a dangerous situation but she'd made a conscious choice not to tell him about it.

"But there was one room upstairs, a *boppli*'s room, that was clean and lovely."

His hands curled into fists at his side. "So she caught you in her *haus*?"

"*Nee*." Lydia let her arms fall to her sides as she slouched, her eyes cast down again. "She didn't catch us in her *haus*, but she might have caught us turning out of her driveway." Before Samuel could respond, she threw her hands into the air and paced the yard. "But the nursery door had been locked, and Beverly forgot to lock it again, so Margaret probably figured out we were in her *haus*." She stopped pacing as her hands landed on her hips. "You promised you wouldn't get mad."

It was too late. Promise broken. He stretched out his arm and left it there, pointing at the truck. "So now she's stalking us?"

"I'm sorry." Lydia's voice was shaking, and Samuel wasn't interested in comforting her.

"Have you put our family in danger? Didn't I tell you to stay away from that woman?" He took off his hat, ran a hand through his hair, and put the hat back on. Shaking his head, he stepped closer, now pointing a finger at her. "It's *mei* responsibility to take care of this family." He shifted his finger toward the house. "We have a *boppli*. What about Mattie?"

"Just because Margaret is parked at the end of our driveway doesn't mean she's dangerous." Lydia's voice shook even more than before. "And you said you wouldn't get mad."

"Well I lied." His blood pounded against his temples. "Kind of like you did." He marched toward the house.

"I didn't lie!" She screamed it loud enough that Joseph and Beverly were at the door by the time Samuel reached the porch.

"How was the date?" Joseph looked over Samuel's shoulder. "Uh, why is Lydia crying?"

Beverly rushed past the two of them and into the yard.

Samuel stormed inside the house, and Joseph followed. After

Samuel paced the room for a few moments, he repeated everything Lydia had just told him.

Joseph scratched his head. "Is Margaret's truck still out there? It might not be safe for Beverly to drive home alone."

"Doesn't it bother you that they both lied to us?" Samuel was upset on several levels. A perfect night had turned sour.

"Uh . . . it wasn't exactly a lie. They just didn't tell us everything."

Samuel grunted. "You sound like Lydia."

"I mean, I ain't happy they did that, but I'm not really in a position to tell Beverly what to do or get mad because she chose not to tell me something."

"Well, I'm in that position with Lydia. She's *mei fraa*, and she should have told me." Samuel tossed his hat on the couch and sighed.

Joseph walked to the window. "Lydia's still crying." He looked over his shoulder at Samuel. "Maybe just forgive her, and don't let it mess up your night."

"It's already ruined. Margaret might be dangerous, and now she probably knows Lydia and Beverly were in her *haus*. And she knows where we live. I have to protect *mei* family."

Samuel wanted to trust God's will and put his faith in the Lord to keep them safe, but an instinctive protectiveness was overpowering the way he'd been taught to passively deal with conflict. He wasn't sure what to do, but now it might not be enough to just stay away from a woman who might want to harm his wife, maybe even his daughter.

"The truck is gone. I just saw the headlights turn on, and she drove away." Joseph returned to where Samuel was standing. "Maybe don't be so hard on Lydia."

"You and I recently had a conversation about how much we dislike lying."

Joseph held up a palm. "*Ya, ya.* I know. But I'll say it again. Lydia didn't exactly lie."

Samuel scowled. "It was a big omission of the truth."

. . .

Lydia dabbed at her eyes. "I should have known something would go wrong. Nothing ever seems to go as planned with Samuel and me." She blinked back more tears.

Beverly rubbed her arm. "Just try to focus on how great things were tonight up to this point. Samuel will get over this."

Lydia had spent so much time closing herself off, hiding her feelings, and pretending she and Samuel had the perfect marriage. Carrying the load alone was exhausting. But Beverly was growing into her closest friend, and she needed to unload some of her emotions before she exploded.

"Our marriage has been challenging for Samuel and me." She wasn't ready to divulge everything, but she longed for nurturing, and she wasn't going to get any from Samuel right now. She'd pray about it later, but Beverly's sympathetic eyes drew her in. "This was an important night for us, and I wanted everything to be perfect. Why did Margaret have to choose tonight to park down by the road?"

Beverly shook her head. "I don't know. But no marriage is perfect. It takes a lot of work." She turned around when she heard the screen door close. Joseph had Susan over one shoulder and the diaper bag over the other, and he was carrying Beverly's roses.

If things weren't bad enough, Lydia realized she'd left her flowers in the limousine.

"I'm real sorry about this, Lydia," Joseph said in a whisper before he turned to Beverly. "I'm going to follow you to your *haus* just to be safe."

Beverly nodded before she hugged Lydia. "You'll be all right. Samuel will realize he's overreacting."

"*Ya*, he might be overreacting a little." Joseph passed Susan to Beverly and turned back to Lydia. "But he's fiercely protective of his family. You're all he talks about at work, you and Mattie."

Lydia swiped at her eyes again. "I'm sure Beverly's right. Everything will be fine." She forced a smile. "Did the *bopplis* do okay?"

"*Ya*." Beverly rubbed Lydia's arm again, offering a comforting smile.

Beverly and Joseph said their goodbyes and headed to their buggies. When Joseph reached for Beverly's hand, Lydia fought another round of tears building. She was happy for the couple, but she couldn't understand why God kept giving her and Samuel a glimpse of the life they longed for only to present them with more challenges.

She shuffled across the grass, the recipes still in her hand but with no plans to prepare them. They would only remind her how this night ended.

Samuel wasn't in the living room when she went inside the house. She locked the front door behind her, and then as she checked all the windows, she considered why Margaret had been there again. Horrible thoughts crossed her mind. Maybe Margaret wanted to steal Mattie, so she'd have a baby for the only livable room in her house. Or would she try to harm

Mattie? Or her. Even Samuel. Or was Margaret's presence merely a warning to stay away from her house? Maybe she just wanted someone to pay attention to her.

She had no way to know if any of those scenarios were true. All she could do was try to salvage this night. Maybe if she apologized to Samuel, told him he'd been right to worry and that she'd never keep anything from him again—maybe then they could resume where they left off.

When she eased open their bedroom door, Samuel was already in bed, on his side, even lightly snoring. *But is he really asleep?*

Lydia checked on Mattie before she changed into her gown and brushed her teeth. Then when she returned to the bedroom, she gave the bed a little bounce as she climbed in. But Samuel didn't budge. Until tonight, he'd been rolling onto his back, stretching out his arm, welcoming her as she settled into her nook.

It didn't look like that would happen tonight.

· · ·

Beverly hoped Joseph wouldn't want to come inside or need to use the bathroom when they got to her house. She was glad he followed her home, but she wasn't ready for him to see the inside of her home. It needed a good cleaning, and she wanted it to smell of beef stew slow-cooking on the stove when he arrived next Saturday. She wanted lanterns lit and placed where they'd shed just enough light but not too much. She wanted everything to be perfect.

When she parked her buggy near the barn, she left Susan asleep on the seat beside her so she could tell Joseph goodbye properly. She'd already told him she was keeping the baby overnight.

"*Danki* for a *wunderbaar* evening." She stood close enough for him to kiss her.

"I didn't do anything. Lydia left us a pizza, and the *bopplis* entertained themselves." Joseph nodded to her buggy. "Do you want me to carry Susan in for you?"

"*Nee*, I'm used to it. I've told you. I've always kept her a lot. She's the only *boppli* in our family." She hadn't thought about him offering to carry Susan in.

"At least let me put your horse in the barn for you. It's late."

"All right. *Danki*."

She lifted Susan and the diaper bag from the buggy, then quickly went inside to lay the baby down before returning to wait for Joseph. She didn't have to wait long for him to come back to the front of the house.

"I know this is a bit early, but is four next Saturday okay?" She was eager to say good night, sure it would be followed with a kiss.

Joseph grinned. "I'll bring *mei* appetite."

Beverly closed her eyes when Joseph kissed her, hoping her neighbor wasn't peeking out her window. She also thought about how important next Saturday would be. Joseph was everything she wanted in a husband. Even though he joked about getting married and having ten children, she could envision such a life.

Saturday, Joseph will know the truth.

CHAPTER 15

L ydia sat on Herman and Fannie's couch Monday morning, happy to see her mother-in-law's face looked much better. Mattie was in her grandmother's lap and didn't seem as bothered by the discolored eye and cheek.

Samuel hadn't attended worship service with Lydia and Mattie yesterday, saying he needed to check on his parents. He could have done that in the afternoon, so it seemed more likely he was avoiding her. Lydia wondered how much he'd told his folks about what happened with Margaret. Her father-in-law wasn't his cheerful self, and Lydia couldn't recall a visit when he didn't have a joke or funny story to share.

After a few minutes of small talk, Herman cleared his throat from where he was sitting across the room. "Don't look so nervous, *mei maedel*. We're not planning to scold you about Margaret." He crossed one leg over the other and grinned a little. "We figure Samuel has done enough of that," he said, confirming that her husband had confided in them.

Lydia sighed. "It was a dumb thing to do, but once we were in the *haus*, our curiosity got the best of us. We just wanted to see if we could find any clues about why Margaret lives the way she does."

"And did you discover anything?" Fannie bounced Mattie on her lap, smiling at her granddaughter as the baby quietly sucked on her pacifier and held a teething ring in her hand.

"Did Samuel tell you about the *boppli*'s room?" She wondered if they knew more about Margaret than they'd shared during their last conversation about her.

"*Ya*, he did." Fannie shivered. "I find that very strange. I mean, we all know Margaret is odd, but that's unsettling."

"Did she ever miscarry a *boppli*?" Lydia still wanted to know about the old woman, especially since she'd taken up residence at the end of their driveway on at least two evenings.

"Herman." Fannie turned to her husband. "I don't recall Margaret ever losing a child, do you? She never married."

An uncomfortable silence loomed, all of them surely thinking about Lydia's pregnancy out of wedlock.

Lydia's father-in-law broke the silence. "Even if she had miscarried, we wouldn't have known about it. When Margaret was young—when we were *all* young—such things weren't discussed."

Lydia recalled what they'd found on Margaret's mantel. "She looked so pretty in the photograph, even though she was wearing *Englisch* clothes, which seemed odd."

"What photograph?" Herman raised an eyebrow.

Lydia tried to remember if she'd told her husband about it. "I might have forgotten to mention that to Samuel." She cringed. "He was already so mad at me."

"We spoke with him about the power of forgiveness when he was here yesterday. Give him a little time." Fannie maneuvered her wheelchair, now facing Lydia and Herman. "Tell us about the photo."

"Margaret was wearing a fancy red dress and standing next to a young man. Or maybe it was her twin *schweschder* or even someone else. The photograph was framed and sitting on the mantel among the dust and leaves and . . . bird droppings."

Herman stood and walked to the window, where he lowered the shade. The sun had been shining right in his face. He seemed to be doing much better too. He sat back down, but he did flinch a little as he did.

"Margaret's *schweschder* had been baptized when she left—both girls had been—so she was shunned by members of our community," Fannie said. "I do remember that much, even though I can't recall the girl's name. I know Margaret was terribly upset, but over time, I think everyone just forgot about her twin—especially since no one was really allowed to talk about her. Back then, shunnings were enforced more than they are now." She snapped her fingers. "Delila. That was her name." She looked at Herman. "Right, Herman?"

He nodded. "*Ya*, I believe so."

Delila.

"I was surprised when you told me she had a *schweschder*. I'd always heard Margaret didn't have any family." Lydia stood and picked up the pacifier Mattie dropped. She gave it a quick wipe with her apron and handed it back to her daughter before she sat back down.

Herman stroked his beard. "Folks would have to be our age or older to remember that far back."

The wheels in Lydia's mind were spinning. "Maybe someone should find Delila and let the woman know how Margaret is living."

Herman cleared his throat again. "I'm going to speak in Samuel's absence and say you'd be best to leave it all alone, *mei maedel*. I admit, this information is interesting, and it's challenging not to be lured into a mystery of sorts. But some things should be left in *Gott*'s hands." He paused. "Especially since Margaret has rejected help in the past."

Lydia knew he was right, but she could already feel another temptation brewing, and she wasn't quite ready to dissolve the conversation. Fannie and Herman's interest in Margaret had provided some new details. "I've always heard twins have a special bond. It must have torn up Margaret when her *schweschder* left."

"*Ya*, I'm sure it did," Fannie said. "Especially since I believe Margaret didn't understand why Delila left." She frowned. "Neither do I. Delila was protective of Margaret. I remember that too. As a child, and even when she got older, Margaret seemed a little odd."

"Like maybe her mind wasn't right?"

Herman scratched his cheek. "*Ya*, maybe. And if so, I suspect the family would have tried to hide it as much as they could. People weren't as open about these things back then."

Margaret's sister had likely married, changing her last name, and she could be anywhere now. Not to mention Samuel would be furious if he thought Lydia was further involving herself with Margaret. Maybe if she were up-front with him about it, he would be more understanding and tolerant. Samuel was fearful of the woman, but he'd seemed to be equally mad that Lydia hadn't been completely truthful with him.

She wanted to tell Beverly what she'd learned, but she was hesitant. If Margaret was troublesome, did she want to put her friend in harm's way? Also, Beverly had taken on more hours at the bakery since a coworker went on maternity leave. She said that meant she couldn't babysit Susan for her sister as often, but fortunately their mother was available.

She wondered if Samuel would work late. He'd worked hard outside all afternoon yesterday, even though it was Sunday, no doubt to keep avoiding her. She'd tried twice to apologize again for not telling him the entire truth, but he said he didn't want to talk about it. Just like Saturday, last night he'd showered and gone to bed before Lydia had even bathed Mattie. By the time she went to bed, he was curled up and snoring. No outstretched arm. No nook for Lydia to snuggle into. He was mad, and Lydia didn't blame him. He'd gone to a lot of trouble to plan a perfect date, but they'd slipped back into the relationship they both wanted to abandon. Emotional intimacy seemed to go along with physical intimacy, and at the moment, both were floundering.

Lydia's stomach growled. "I'm going to heat up the casserole I brought." She stood.

Fannie groaned. "This is not necessary, you or Samuel coming daily. I'm feeling fine, and Herman is getting his energy back."

Lydia smiled. "I enjoy our visits." It was true, and especially since Samuel's parents were much older than hers, Lydia wanted to make sure they saw Mattie as often as possible. "But I also know privacy is important to you. I'll talk to Samuel about us not coming by so often, although he worries about both of you."

Herman smiled. "It's the boy's nature, to worry."

Lydia nodded. "I know."

As she made her way to the kitchen, she thought about Samuel. Lydia didn't want him to worry so much. But she wasn't sure she could abandon her curiosity about Margaret's sister, who must be out there somewhere—if she was alive. And seeking information about Delila didn't mean she had to have any contact with Margaret.

. . .

Samuel stared at his food, leftovers from last night's supper that he'd barely touched. Lydia had made some of his favorites—pork tenderloin, twice-baked potatoes, and roasted green beans.

Joseph walked in with a bag from Taco Bell and held it up. "We had to drive right past it in Bedford. That's where our last delivery was. And since I walked out and forgot the sandwich *mei mamm* made for me, I didn't want to starve." Chuckling, he pulled out a chair across from Samuel. "I might have forgotten that sandwich on purpose." He pulled out half a dozen tacos, then eyed Samuel's plate. "Although that sure looks *gut*."

Samuel's stomach growled, but his appetite seemed to have taken leave. "*Ya*," he said softly as he took a bite of the pork.

Joseph unwrapped one of the tacos. "I'm going to guess things did not go well after Beverly and I left Saturday night? Not as you'd hoped?"

"You know how much effort I made to give Lydia the perfect date night she deserves." Samuel had told his friend only that he was hoping for a romantic night, not that he wanted to make love to his wife for the first time since they'd been married. That felt too personal. "And, *ya*, I was hoping for . . ." He shrugged, assuming Joseph knew what he meant.

"*Ya, ya.* I get it. But you've got to forgive her, Samuel. You were too hard on her." Joseph spoke with a mouthful of taco.

"I forgave her." Samuel hadn't said the words, but he kept repeating them in his mind, so he'd be able to tell her soon.

"Ha. You're as sulky as I've ever seen you, so I doubt that's true." Joseph finished off his first taco and then unwrapped a second one and took a bite.

Samuel took a deep breath and considered letting the

comment go, but Joseph was already under his skin. "It upsets me, what she did. And she hid it from me."

Joseph swallowed. "*Ya*, I know you were mad at her, but you could have talked it out, forgiven her, and not let it ruin the night. But I'm real soft when it comes to women crying." He downed the rest of the taco.

"I'm the head of the household." Samuel heard the way he sounded—childish. But he couldn't seem to help it. "That's the way it's supposed to be."

Joseph chuckled. "You sound like *mei daed* when *mei mamm* is winning an argument. Times have changed. Us men don't get to rule the roost all the time. *Mei mamm* lets *mei daed* have the final say, but she puts up a pretty *gut* fight when she feels strongly about something. *Daed* once told me he had to choose his battles with *Mamm*. I reckon that's how marriage works."

Samuel wanted to think about Joseph's comments, which surprisingly made some sense. He didn't like seeing Lydia cry, and he'd missed her curling up with him in bed. He'd been sure their date would lead to a perfect night together. As Joseph started rambling about his upcoming supper at Beverly's, Samuel's mind wandered—back to the drive home from the restaurant, how good it felt to kiss his wife.

By the time he'd finished eating, he'd decided he would apologize to Lydia for being so harsh with her. He would tell her he'd forgiven her and mean it.

. . .

Lydia pulled into Sarah Mae Yoder's shop around one o'clock and found the old woman knitting behind the counter.

"*Wie bischt*, Lydia." Sarah Mae set her knitting needles aside. "What can I help you with?"

Lydia looked around. "Um, I haven't been here in a while, so I just stopped to browse."

She couldn't ask Samuel's parents more questions without drawing suspicion that her quest to learn more about Margaret and Delia wasn't over. But Sarah Mae would be about Margaret's age—like Herman and Fannie were—so Lydia thought she might have more information about the Keim sisters. Besides, if the town had a gossip, Sarah Mae was it. She was a kindhearted woman, but she seemed to know a little bit about everything and everyone, and she didn't mind sharing what she knew.

"Where's that precious *boppli*?" Sarah Mae struggled to stand from the stool she'd been sitting on.

"*Mamm* is watching her for a little while." Lydia smiled before she started up and down the narrow aisles and tried to think of something she might need. Sarah Mae carried all kinds of odds and ends—kitchen tools, sewing supplies, handmade blankets, knitted scarves, toys, and even some books. Lydia didn't think she had more than five dollars in her purse, but she wanted to buy a little something. She chose a set of measuring spoons. Hers were hand-me-downs from her mother, and they were so old she could barely read the faded markings.

After a few more minutes perusing the store's wares, she made her way back to the counter. "You know, I've recently seen the old woman in the blue truck around town." She paused. "I think her name is Margaret?"

Sarah Mae frowned. "*Ya*, that's what I've heard, that she's roaming the streets in that old truck of hers again." She shook her head. "Something's wrong with that woman. I wish she could get right."

"Do you think she's dangerous?" Lydia found her five-dollar bill and handed it to Sarah Mae.

"*Nee*, she's not dangerous. Just crazy."

Lydia had been wrong. Now that she was standing in front of Sarah Mae, she realized the woman probably had ten years on Herman, Fannie, and Margaret. The lines of time stretched across her face like a road map of a life lived in the sun.

"Hmm . . ." Lydia said as she waited for her change and tried to think of a way to get more information.

Sarah Mae handed Lydia her twenty-eight cents in change. "I heard a fella say he thinks Margaret's got something called dementia. I don't know what that is, but I suspect it's a case of crazy she's had for a long time."

Lydia had never heard of dementia either. Was that a form of mental illness? "I-I heard she has a twin *schweschder*. Someone said her name is Delila." Lydia glanced up at Sarah Mae as she dropped the change into her purse.

"*Ya*, she did. But she just up and vanished one day. Those *maeds* pretty much raised themselves after their parents were killed." She paused, a faraway look in her eyes. "Car accident. Tourist from somewhere down south plowed right into their buggy and killed them both. The townspeople wanted to take in the girls, but they were sixteen and stayed in their farm-house. I guess I can understand that." She shook her head. "It's a terrible shame Margaret let that *haus* go the way she did. I reckon she can't help it, though." She tapped a finger to her head, scowling. "You know, with her mind and all."

"Her *schweschder* never came back?" Lydia pulled her purse up on her shoulder even though she was in no hurry to go.

Sarah Mae confirmed what Herman and Fannie had said, that Margaret's sister had been baptized and shunned when she left.

"But she could have come back and redeemed herself, right?"

"*Ya*, she could have come back. Margaret kept telling people Delila would be back, and I remember her being real angry if anyone suggested otherwise. But months went by, then years. Margaret never heard from her again, as far as anyone knows."

Lydia thought about the photo on the mantel and wondered again if either Margaret or Delila was the woman in it. "I guess seeing her again made me feel sorry for her." Lydia shrugged, still trying to appear only mildly interested.

"She's had plenty of people try to help her over the years, but"—she tapped a finger to her head again—"Like I said, she's *ab im kopp*."

Lydia thought about the reasons Margaret might have parked at the end of her driveway. Her in-laws and Sarah Mae didn't seem to think she was dangerous, but couldn't crazy be dangerous? A voice in her head said to leave it alone, but she was pretty sure it was Samuel's voice. Another voice boomed louder and said *Help her*. Lydia recognized that voice, but she didn't have a clue what she could do to help Margaret. Apparently, lots of people had tried.

Gott, *I don't know what to do. I don't want to put* mei *family in danger. If I'm being called to help Margaret somehow, then I need Your guidance.*

"*Ach*, Delila left such a long time ago." Sarah Mae smiled. "I know we're taught not to be prideful, but oh my, Margaret and Delila Keim were beautiful girls, inside and out. Everything just seemed to go downhill for them after their parents died. Everyone knew Margaret was a little odd, but she had a sweet nature." She paused for a long while. "I guess if any of us had known she'd end up like this, we would have tried harder to help her back then." Lydia heard the regret in Sarah Mae's voice, but the woman groaned as she waved away her own comment. "But what's done is done. Margaret won't let anyone help her, so—I hate to say it—she remains a human eyesore in our community. And she needs a bath."

Lydia wanted to ask Sarah Mae if she thought Margaret was an eyesore because she reminded everyone how they'd failed her, but that wouldn't do any good. Sarah Mae hadn't provided much new information, but Lydia couldn't seem to shed the feeling that she was supposed to help Margaret. Was this really a calling from God? Or just her relentless curiosity? Either way, she was going to find Delila Keim.

But was it worth the price she'd pay when she told Samuel her plan? Or did she care?

CHAPTER 16

Samuel had flowers for his wife again, promising to pay Joseph back for this batch on payday as well. He hadn't realized they'd forgotten the roses in the limousine until later, but that wasn't the only reason he was bringing Lydia flowers now. He needed them as part of his apology.

When he pulled his horse and buggy to the barn, he was surprised to see her buggy and horse were missing. She was always here when he got home from work, usually with supper ready. Inside the house, he set the flowers on the kitchen table and searched every room. In his heart, he knew she wasn't there, but visions of Margaret having her tied up somewhere raced through his mind. He flipped open his phone and called her, but no answer.

Pacing the kitchen, he tried to recall a single time he'd come home to an empty house. Once, when Chester had stepped on a piece of glass and Lydia had to call a vet from wherever she was. She'd been late getting home that day. He couldn't recall any other time.

Maybe she left me. Had he treated her so badly that she decided to stay with her parents? Just the thought caused his eyes to moisten. He vowed right then and there to never make his wife cry again.

He bolted to the front door when he heard a buggy, then

breathed a huge sigh of relief when he saw her coming up the driveway. Samuel waited on the porch until she got closer, then he met her at her buggy.

"You scared me. You're always home when I get here." He slipped to the other side of the buggy and got Mattie out of her carrier, pressing the baby to his chest. "Where were you?"

"*Mamm* kept Mattie for a while so I could run some errands." She raised her chin. "I'm sorry. I'll get supper started now."

She was still mad. No doubt about it. But maybe the flowers would help. He followed her into the kitchen, then swooped by her and lifted the flowers from the table. As he pushed them toward her, he said, "I'm sorry about Saturday night. I'm sorry I made you cry. I'm not going to tell you what to do. We're a partnership." He forced himself to be quiet since he was beginning to ramble.

Lydia took the flowers. "*Danki.*" She found a vase, then filled it with water before she shoved the flowers in. *Shoved.* He was sure that was an accurate description. He'd thought he'd at least get a hug. Something.

She turned around and leaned against the counter. "I'm glad you're not going to tell me what to do, because today I learned Margaret's *schweschder*'s name—Delila. Margaret is sick. She needs help whether she wants it or not. I could be wrong, but I feel like I'm being called by *Gott* to help her. I can't get her off *mei* mind, and I believe the community let her down when she was young. They should have made her accept help." Her chin got even higher. "I'm going to find Delila." She folded her arms over her chest and crossed her ankles. Her nostrils flared. She was ready for battle, and that only fueled Samuel's temper.

"*Nee*, you're not," he said calmly, even though he was shaking with fury on the inside.

She grunted. "You just said you weren't going to tell me what to do."

Samuel didn't like this side of Lydia, but he was sure she didn't like plenty about him too. "You're willing to go against *mei* wishes and put our *dochder* in danger just to try to help an old woman who doesn't want help from anyone? I don't think this is a calling from *Gott*. The woman has been stalking us."

Lydia rolled her eyes. "She hasn't been stalking us."

He came closer to her, still holding Mattie. "You're doing this just to spite me. But if you want to punish me for making you cry, which I just apologized for, then please do it in some other way. Margaret is dangerous."

"No, she's not. And I'm not planning to interact with Margaret. I would just like to find her *schweschder* to let her know that Margaret is sick in the head." She put her hands on her hips. "You're just trying to forbid me from doing this because I haven't slept with you. It's your way of trying to control me, and I don't like it."

"I-I'm head of the household. What I say goes." Samuel recalled what Joseph had said, about times changing, but Lydia was pushing every button he had. "And you're denying me *mei* husbandly rights!" He regretted it the moment he said it.

Lydia was in his face within seconds, and Samuel felt like they'd just jumped back a year, all that resentment and bitterness worming their way back into their lives. He was trembling, he was so angry.

"Samuel, would you have married me if I hadn't gotten pregnant? Or even dated me?" Maybe it was because she was yelling, or the fact that Mattie started to cry, but he blurted an answer without thinking.

"*Nee!*" His eyes widened as his chest tightened. "I didn't mean that, Lydia."

She eased Mattie out of his arms and marched from the room with their screaming child. Samuel had never heard his parents bicker in front of him. He'd wanted to carry that over into his own marriage, and he'd already failed before his daughter even had her first birthday.

Samuel hung his head. He felt sick about everything. Mostly, he was worried about Lydia's involvement with Margaret. His wife might think she was being called by God, but temptations didn't come from God. Either way, Samuel wasn't going to let anything happen to Lydia and Mattie. Maybe he was better off jumping onboard the ship with her instead of letting her capsize on her own—or endanger their daughter.

. . .

Lydia leaned over Mattie and changed her diaper. Then she wiped a tear from her daughter's face, a tear that had fallen from one of Lydia's eyes. Mattie had stopped crying and just stared up at her. Lydia tried not to cry in front of Mattie, but she'd failed plenty of times.

"I'm sorry, Mattie," she said in a whisper before she picked her up and held her close. She pressed her cheek to her baby's and repeated herself. "I'm sorry."

She blinked the last of her tears away. Samuel's answer hurt her more than she'd expected, even though deep down she'd always known it was the truth. They'd had sex in the barn, not dated or fallen in love. They'd been friends who grew up together, were attracted to each other, and succumbed to temptation. They loved each other, but was it the way a husband and wife should?

Lydia also had to consider if there was any truth to Samuel's saying she'd been withholding sex from him. That might have been true in the beginning. Only sixteen and pregnant, she'd felt cheated out of her running-around period, and she hated that their parents had forced them into marriage. Even though she knew she had to take personal responsibility, she'd resented Samuel's role in all of that. Yet she thought she'd moved on.

She fed Mattie, bathed her, and eventually got her settled in her crib. Samuel sat out on the front porch the entire time with his head in his hands. Lydia finally went out there and sat down in the other rocking chair.

Samuel didn't lift his head. "I didn't mean what I said, about not dating you."

She heard the shakiness in his voice. She wanted to believe he had just lashed out in anger, that he loved her the way she loved him. Theirs wasn't the relationship either of them wanted, but they'd been taking baby steps forward. This felt like a giant step backward.

"Don't you think I want to feel close to you, Samuel . . . in every way?"

He finally looked up, his eyes watery. "I don't know what you want, Lydia. I really don't."

She placed a hand over her trembling lips, trying not to cry. For once, they needed to communicate. "What I want is for us to talk, really talk, about how we feel. We've never done that. We grew up together, but we were close only when we were kids. You hit your *rumschpringe* way before me, and by the time we started to get close again, we'd grown into different people. Once we were married, you were like a stranger to me.

I think I've been getting to know you ever since." She shook her head. "That probably doesn't even make sense."

They were quiet. Samuel's elbows were still propped on his knees, and his head found its way back in his hands again.

"I was bitter," she said. "But that's only part of why I avoided intimacy, why I . . . rejected you. I had morning sickness that managed to turn into all-day-long sickness, and I also felt fat and unattractive. I still do. I-I'm still carrying baby weight."

Samuel turned to face her. "You are the most beautiful woman in the world."

Lydia thought she'd never seen such sincerity in her husband's expression. It took everything she had not to burst into tears and run into his arms. But they needed to talk this out. It had taken her a long time to realize that.

Samuel held the expression. "Lydia, I know I pushed you in the beginning. I was angry too. Mostly at myself. I'm older, and I should have known better than to let my attraction to you run away with me. Every time I looked at you, I felt guilty. But I was still angry that you didn't want any part of me in the bedroom."

"Samuel, it's not that I didn't want any part of you. And now . . . sometimes I want all of you, in every way. But we didn't start out the way couples are supposed to."

Samuel pulled his eyes from her and stared straight ahead as he leaned against the back of the chair. "What do we do from here?"

Lydia reached over and touched his arm. "We talk instead of shutting down. If you don't like something I'm doing, or vice versa, we talk it through instead of getting angry or staying silent."

. . .

Samuel thought about his earlier resolve, then turned to face her. "I'm not going to go against you trying to find out about Margaret's *schweschder*. I'll even help you. I'd rather be involved and know what's going on. If this is something you feel called to do . . ." He still wasn't convinced this was a true calling, but he would be there for her either way. "Then I'll be by your side."

"Do you mean that?" She twisted in the chair to face him, dabbing at her eyes.

"*Ya*, I do. And please don't cry. I never want to make you cry again."

She smiled. "You will make me cry again. And we'll get mad at each other again. But that's just part of marriage, *ya*?"

He nodded, still hoping he'd never make her cry again. "How are you planning to find Margaret's *schweschder*, and what if she doesn't want anything to do with her? She knows where she is, I'm sure. And what if she isn't even alive anymore?"

"I wish I knew why I feel called to do something about Margaret, but I don't. It's our *haus* she's been parking in front of. Somehow, she found out who I am and where I live. I'm sure she could have found out who Beverly is, too, but apparently, she didn't. All I'm going to do is try to locate Delila. She might be the only one who can get help for Margaret. No one should live the way she's living."

"What about the creepy *boppli* room?" Samuel cringed when he thought about it.

"It's a beautiful room. It's chilling only because it's the only livable room in the *haus*. Maybe Margaret always wanted a *boppli* and tended to that room in hopes of having one someday."

"Um, that time has long passed for Margaret." Samuel rubbed his temples.

"I saw Sarah Mae Yoder today, and she said Margaret might have something called dementia. I think that's a form of craziness. So maybe her *schweschder* can help her."

"What's your plan?" Samuel's stomach growled.

Lydia stood. "I don't know yet. But I hear your tummy rumbling, and I'm starving too. Maybe we can talk about it over supper." She reached out her hand to him, and he took it and stood.

They walked hand in hand to the door, but before they stepped over the threshold, Samuel stopped and waited until she turned to face him. "Lydia, I do love you. It might not be the kind of love we thought it would be, but I'd throw myself in front of a train for you or Mattie."

She smiled again, which warmed his heart. "Let's hope you never have to do that. And I love you, too, Samuel. I believe we have the kind of love we wanted to grow into, but we missed the growing phase, the romance part." She looked down, then back up at him, her lip trembling. "I know your patience must be wearing thin, but when we truly are together the way we both want, I want it to be just right." A tear rolled down her cheek, and Samuel could feel his heart cracking. "I'm afraid I won't be very *gut* at . . . it. And that scares me."

Samuel had often thought about the three-year age difference between them. It didn't sound like much, but Lydia had basically been a child having a child. Women had children young in their community, but rarely as young as sixteen. Still, it had never occurred to him that she might be afraid or worried about how they would be together as an intimate couple.

"I'll tell you what." He heard the shakiness in his voice, so he cleared his throat. "You find your way back to the nook in my arm tonight, and I'll give you all the patience in the world.

I miss you being next to me when we sleep. We'll take things slow, and I'll try not to be so overbearing, especially about Margaret. I'll see if I can take an afternoon off from work, and we can go to the library or do whatever else you have in mind. We can even drive by her *haus* if you want."

"That sounds *gut*." She smiled, and they started back inside. Once there, Samuel grinned. "But if you ever want to repeat those kisses, the ones we had in the limo last Saturday, I'd be all for that."

"Baby steps, Samuel."

He wasn't sure exactly what that meant, but he took her smile as a good thing.

CHAPTER 17

Enos used to tell Beverly her stew was the best meal she prepared, and as she breathed in the beefy aroma, she hoped Joseph would think so too. Joseph loved to eat, and he ate a lot, so Beverly doubled the recipe. If she had any leftovers, she'd offer to send them home with him.

She'd cleaned house since early this morning, even the windows. Her table was set for two, and she'd plucked a few roses from her yard and put them in a vase in the middle. Four lanterns were placed throughout the living room and kitchen. It was almost four o'clock on a cloudless day, but she hoped Joseph would enjoy himself enough to stay until dark.

Lydia had called earlier and filled her in about Margaret's sister, as well as about how she was going to try to find her. As exciting as keeping a quest secret had been, Samuel was onboard now, and that was probably best since no one knew about Margaret's mental state for sure. Meanwhile, Beverly wanted to focus all her efforts on her budding relationship with Joseph, but she would pray often, asking God to keep both Lydia and Samuel safe.

As she gave the stew a final stir, she heard a buggy pulling in. After brushing wrinkles from her apron, she strode across the living room and waited for Joseph at the front door. He had flowers again. Yellow roses. She smiled as she pushed the screen door open.

"I love a man on time." Beverly accepted the flowers, then hugged him. "Welcome to *mei* home, and *danki* for the flowers." She motioned for him to come in.

Joseph hung his hat on the rack by the door, then sniffed the air. "*Ach*, something sure smells *gut*."

"*Danki*. I hope you like it. It's beef stew." Beverly hadn't decided when she would share the secret she'd been keeping from Joseph. She presumed the right opportunity would present itself, and she'd prayed about it several times.

Joseph's eyes drifted to the playpen filled with toys. "You *do* keep your niece a lot."

"*Ya*, I do." She waved an arm. "Follow me. Supper is ready, and if I've learned anything about you, it's that you enjoy a *gut* meal. I hope you'll be pleased."

A sober expression settled into his features as they entered the kitchen, which didn't happen often. "*Danki* for having me, Beverly. I'm happy you're comfortable enough to have me in your home."

She kissed him on the cheek. "I'm very happy you're here."

His eyes traveled around the room and landed on the pot simmering on the stove. He closed his eyes and took in a long deep breath. "If this meal is half as *gut* as it smells, I might drop to one knee and propose right here and now."

Beverly laughed at his teasing, but his words caused her heart to swell.

"Have a seat," she said before moving to the stove. She turned off the burner and then carried the pot to the table before placing a warm loaf of bread near the stew. "I just need to get the salad, and we should be ready."

After Beverly sat down, they bowed their heads in prayer. When she looked up, Joseph was staring at her.

"You look very pretty." His hair was flattened on top of his head, and her supper date had a late afternoon prickly shadow on his face. She'd felt it when she kissed him. But when he smiled . . . that cheeky grin won her over every time. She hoped he retained his boyish features as he aged, but if he didn't, it didn't matter. He'd already stolen her heart.

"*Danki.*" They locked eyes, then Beverly said, "Eat while it's hot."

After she'd served him some of her stew, Joseph took one bite, closed his eyes, and swallowed. "This is the best stew ever." He chuckled. "But don't tell *mei mamm* I said that."

Beverly's insides swirled. She was thrilled to learn he might want to introduce her to his family soon.

He ate all of his stew before Beverly had even finished a third of hers. She ladled more for him. "Save room for dessert. I made a rhubarb pie."

Beverly stood when she heard cooing coming from the back of the house. "*Ach*, well, we almost made it all the way through supper before she woke up from her nap."

"I didn't even know you had Susan tonight."

She smiled and left the room.

. . .

Joseph's vision of sitting on the couch, kissing Beverly, slipped from his mind, but that was okay. Beverly was good with her niece, and Joseph loved being around them both. She'd be a good mother someday. *To our ten kids.* He smiled and looked around her kitchen. He saw empty bottles in a drainboard by the sink, a high chair folded against one wall, and a porta-ble stroller in the corner by the back door. Beverly was really involved in her niece's life. *Maybe we'll have more than ten kids.*

When she came back into the room with Susan on her hip, the baby yawned.

"She played hard today. Normally she doesn't take a nap so late in the afternoon, but it worked out okay since we got to eat most of our meal without being interrupted."

Joseph waved at the baby. "*Wie bischt*, Susan." He nodded to the high chair. "Do you want me to pull it up to the table."

"*Ya, danki.*"

He popped it open and carried it to the table. Beverly slid the baby into the seat, then placed a plastic bowl with dry cereal on the tray. "I'll feed her a real meal shortly. It takes her a few minutes to wake up."

Joseph gazed at the woman across the table from him. "You're a *wunderbaar aenti*. Your *schweschder* is blessed to have you. I'm sure she enjoys having breaks since motherhood is hard work." He paused to roll his eyes. "Or so *mei mudder* tells me."

Beverly looked at the baby as if seeing her for the first time, her expression filled with love. Joseph pictured her looking at their children like that someday, then reminded himself—again—that it was too soon for those kinds of thoughts.

"Joseph . . ." She gazed into his eyes. "I'm not Susan's *aenti*. I'm her *mamm*."

As an unfamiliar pain squeezed his heart, Joseph's jaw dropped. "What?" Had he misheard her?

"Susan is *mei dochder*, my and Enos's child."

Joseph was rarely speechless, but no words came together to form a sentence. Finally, he found his voice. "Why . . . why would you tell me she's your niece?"

"I wanted you to have a chance to get to know me first." Her bottom lip trembled. "Some men are open to raising another man's child, and some aren't. I thought if you liked me, then you would accept Susan too." Pausing, she took a deep breath. "I didn't want you to decide not to date me just because I had a *boppli*."

Joseph was too stunned to say anything as he slouched into his chair and put a hand over his full stomach. The playpen, the stroller, the high chair, the bottles in the drainboard—how had he not caught on? His thoughts traveled back to meeting Beverly at Gasthof Village, specifically when she said she had to babysit because her sister had to work. The truth must have been that her sister had to work and couldn't babysit Susan. Then there were all the references to her being Susan's aunt. How many lies had she told since the day he met her? Was that why she'd avoided that *Englisch* couple in the restaurant in French Lick? Would they have mentioned Susan was her daughter? Their child appeared to be about Susan's age, and she knew them somehow.

"Maybe it was too soon to tell you." Beverly pressed her trembling lips together.

How could she say that? "Too soon?" He scratched his forehead. "Um, you should have told me a long time ago, like the first time we met at Lydia and Samuel's *haus*." His eyes opened wide. "Were they in on this? Do they know Susan is your *boppli*?"

"There's nothing to be in on. It wasn't really a deception, more a testing of the waters." She blinked her eyes a few times. "But, *nee*, they don't know Susan is *mei dochder*."

Joseph was drowning in those deceptive waters, struggling to wrap his mind around this. "Lydia is your friend. It seems you would have told her." *And me.*

"I didn't really know Lydia the day we went into the furniture store. We'd bumped into each other on the street, and then I went inside with her to use the restroom. We had seen each other once or twice, but just in passing. I was going to tell her, but then so much time went by, I decided I wanted to tell you first." She smiled.

Joseph gave his head a little shake. "I don't believe this." He was pretty sure the tone of his voice revealed his thoughts, and he reminded himself there was a child at the table. He wasn't going to lose it in front of Susan. He took a deep breath. "Don't you think Lydia and Samuel—especially Lydia—are going to be upset when they find out you've lied this entire time?"

Her eyes filled with tears. "I didn't think they would be. I thought they'd understand. The man I told you I dated, Chriss, didn't want to raise another man's child. I-I wanted to see what kind of person you were, if you would break *mei* heart the way he did."

"Beverly." He gazed into her eyes. "I never would have broken your heart, and I would have loved Susan like she was *mei* own."

She smiled. "I knew I was right about you. I just needed to be sure."

Joseph slowly stood and looked back and forth between Beverly and Susan. "The only broken heart is mine."

She stood as her smile faded. "What do you mean?"

Joseph walked over to Susan, leaned down, and kissed her forehead. Then he straightened and looked at Beverly. "*Danki* for supper. I enjoyed the meal very much"—fearful his voice would crack, he paused—"But I don't want to see you anymore."

Then he took long strides out of the kitchen, hurried through the living room, and tried to block out Beverly's cries for him to please wait as he took his hat from the rack. By the time he got to his buggy, a tear spilled down his cheek.

He allowed himself to feel the pain all the way to Samuel and Lydia's house, then dried his eyes and climbed the steps to the porch. September had brought cooler temperatures, and their windows were closed, but through one of them he could see Samuel and Lydia sitting on the couch. Samuel was bouncing Mattie on his lap. Joseph stood there watching them for a while, envisioning how it might have been with Beverly. He finally knocked on the door.

"I thought you were going to Beverly's *haus* for supper," Lydia said when she found him there. Samuel walked up behind her, still holding Mattie.

"Can I come in?" Joseph looked down and hoped he wouldn't cry again. He didn't remember the last time he'd wept.

"*Ya, ya.*" Lydia put a hand on his arm. "Did something happen?"

Joseph shuffled to the couch and fell into its cushions. He leaned his head back and closed his eyes. "Susan isn't Beverly's niece. She's her *dochder.*"

When no one said anything, Joseph opened his eyes and lifted his head. Samuel's eyes were wide, and Lydia's jaw had dropped. "She's been lying to us the entire time," he said.

Samuel paced with Mattie over his shoulder, rubbing the baby's back, and Lydia sat down in one of the rocking chairs. "I don't understand," she said. "Why wouldn't she just tell us Susan is her *dochder*?"

Joseph did his best to explain Beverly's reasons for lying to them.

Lydia was quiet for a few seconds. "I guess I can understand her thinking, at least a little."

"I don't understand her thinking *at all*." Joseph looked up at Samuel. "You don't either, do you?"

Samuel shrugged. "I don't understand women in general." He winked at Lydia, smiling a little.

Joseph was glad to see his friends had apparently worked through Lydia's omission of the truth lately, but this was different. "I told her I didn't want to see her anymore."

He looked back and forth between them, and their expressions mirrored the looks on their faces when he'd told them Susan was Beverly's daughter. "Why are you looking at me like that?"

"I know how you and Samuel feel about lying. I don't condone it either." Lydia cringed. "But I know how much you like Beverly, and it just seems extreme to cut all ties like that."

He raised his eyes to Samuel's. "And your thoughts?"

Samuel glanced at Lydia, then turned back to Joseph. "Someone recently lectured me about forgiveness." He cleared his throat in an exaggerated way. "I agree she should have been up-front, but obviously Beverly was afraid if you knew she had a *dochder* before you even got to know her, you might reject pursuing a relationship." He ran a hand through his beard, still pacing with Mattie. "And I know how much you like her too."

Joseph fell against the back of the couch again, took off his hat, and put it in his lap. "I'm in love with her." He shook his head. "But when I look back, I realize one lie just rolled into another lie, and now I feel like I've been riding a roller coaster of deception." He threw his hands into the air. "I think she thought I'd be thrilled because she knows how much I like Susan. But now it seems like everything I feel was built on lies."

"I'll bet Beverly is heartbroken." Lydia hung her head before she looked back at him. "Was she crying when you left?"

Joseph nodded. "It broke *mei* heart even more. I would have loved Susan just like *mei* own. A child wouldn't have affected *mei* feelings for Beverly at all."

"But apparently her existence made a difference to that Chriss fellow. She might not have made a *gut* choice by deceiving you, but like I said, I can understand her reasoning, at least a little bit." Lydia sighed and shook her head. "Poor Beverly."

"Poor *Beverly*?" Joseph tossed his hands up again, then slapped them to his knees. "What about poor Joseph? I just lost the only woman I've ever loved."

"By your own doing," Lydia said in a whisper as she avoided his eyes.

"Let this soak in overnight." Samuel handed Mattie to Lydia, along with the cloth he'd had over his shoulder. "She burped *gut*." Then he turned back to Joseph. "You might feel differently in the morning. Is the relationship worth fighting for?" He glanced at his wife, who smiled.

"I would have fought with everything I had for this relationship. I thought I was. But that's a big lie to tell a fellow, and then to let it go on for so long . . ." He shook his head, but then he donned his hat and stood. "I best be getting home. I'm not getting nearly enough sympathy from you people."

Samuel followed him to the door. "*Mei* friend, you had your whole life planned out with Beverly. You need to at least talk to her."

Joseph turned around and said goodbye to Lydia, then looked at Samuel. "*Nee*. I probably wasn't *gut* enough for her anyway."

CHAPTER 18

Beverly was glad it wasn't a church Sunday. She didn't want to face anyone. Joseph, Samuel, and Lydia were in a different district, but Beverly didn't want to face her sister today either. Anna had warned her repeatedly that the lying would blow up in her face.

Still in her nightgown at ten in the morning, she sipped on coffee as Susan played with a set of blocks on the floor. She'd been careful not to cry in front of her daughter so far today, but it had been a constant battle. The night before she'd sat in bed, wept for hours, and eaten half the rhubarb pie she'd baked.

If she'd only known Joseph would be so accepting of Susan, she never would have lied to him. But Chriss had insisted he wasn't bothered by the fact that Beverly had a baby, and then, three months into the relationship, he told her he didn't love her enough to raise another man's child. She never could have predicted that. And when she met Joseph, she'd just wanted a man to love her so much that Susan would be an extension of that love.

Beverly stared at her phone, sitting next to her on the couch. She was sure Joseph had already told the Bontragers what she'd done. Wouldn't Lydia have at least called to check on her? But maybe she planned to end their friendship just as Joseph had ended their relationship.

Despite her best efforts, tears slid down her cheeks. She quickly wiped them away. Then she went to the kitchen and returned with the rest of the rhubarb pie and a fork.

. . .

Lydia changed Mattie's diaper before reminding Samuel to rub some of Beverly's ointment on their daughter's gums if she became fussy. Mattie was cutting another tooth, and until it pushed through the surface, it seemed to be painful for her.

"*Danki* for keeping Mattie while I go see Beverly." She picked up her small black purse and stepped to where her husband was now holding the baby on the couch.

"I readied Chester and the buggy for you." Samuel bounced Mattie on his knee. "I hope Beverly is okay, but"—he shook his head—"That's a whole lot of lies she told, and about her own *dochder*."

"It's not our place to judge. Only *Gott* can do that. And I don't think Beverly would have lied if she hadn't had such a bad experience with the man she dated before Joseph."

"*Ya*, I know." Samuel frowned but nodded.

"I won't be gone too long."

After kissing Mattie's forehead, she cupped her husband's cheek and parted her lips, her mouth feather-touching his, until he reached around and put his hand on the back of her neck, pulling her closer. She lingered, savoring the intimacy they were building. Samuel moaned a little as she stood, a hungry look in his gaze, a teasing smile on his face.

"Hurry back," he whispered.

Lydia grinned before she turned to leave, looking back over her shoulder at her family. She winked at Samuel, wondering if he had any idea how attractive he made her feel when he looked at her the way he just had. Desire was brewing inside them both, and with that, they were growing closer emotionally— although Lydia thought the emotional growth was probably fueling the physical part of their relationship, not the other way around. Either way, she looked forward to kissing her husband when he left for work, when he returned home, and when she settled into the nook of his arm at night. Their physical relationship was moving forward, but at a pace Lydia was comfortable with, and she appreciated her husband's patience.

After she had Chester settled into a steady trot, she thought about what she'd say to Beverly. She had mixed feelings about what her friend had done, but she cared for her a great deal, and she was worried about her. She'd also meant what she said to Samuel, that they weren't in a position to judge.

At the end of her driveway, she turned right. They lived off a road rarely traveled, but in the distance, a vehicle was stopped on the side of the road. A blue truck. And she could tell by the mess in the back of the pickup that it was Margaret's. Her stomach clenched as she drew closer, and she was tempted to turn around. The truck was even on her side of the road.

Lydia gently pulled back on the reins, slowing her horse so she'd have more time to decide what to do. She recalled Sarah Mae telling her Margaret wasn't dangerous, just crazy. Lydia still wasn't sure dangerous and crazy weren't one and the same. But she couldn't live her life fearful of the old woman, so she kept going.

She picked up the horse's pace when she passed the truck, hoping Margaret wouldn't follow her. But as she glanced to her right, she saw that the old woman's head was resting on the steering wheel.

Lydia wondered if she was dead. It was an extreme thought, but whether Margaret was dead or just injured or sleeping, Lydia knew she had to stop. But she had nowhere to tether Chester, so she went a little farther up the road until she had room to pull over the buggy and tie the reins around a tree.

She fumbled with the process a few times, then jogged back to the truck. Her insides churned with each hurried step as she speculated about what she might find. Lydia had never seen a dead person, but she wondered if that might be better than the old woman grabbing her around the neck and choking her to death. Margaret was a large woman who looked like she could take down a big man. She could easily snatch Lydia by her neck and dangle her off the ground until she couldn't breathe. Such horrible thoughts to have, but when she reached the truck, she stayed back about ten feet.

"Margaret, are you all right?" Lydia spoke as loudly as she could without yelling. She started to tremble when the old woman slowly lifted her head and looked at her. Her dark eyes met Lydia's, then she smiled, showing the teeth she still had. Up close, Margaret didn't look as scary, but maybe that was because a tear trailed down her cheek.

"I've been watching you, waiting for you." Margaret reached an arm out the window of the truck.

Lydia took a slow step toward her as saliva ran down Margaret's chin.

"Where's *mei boppli*?" She cried harder, and Lydia considered bolting back to the buggy. Her previous outlandish thoughts were real. Margaret did want Mattie, and Lydia began to tremble all over.

Now Margaret sobbed, and when she opened the truck door, Lydia backed up as fast as she could, but not fast enough.

Margaret stepped out of the truck, ran to her, then grabbed her and yanked her so hard that they both fell to the ground.

Lydia turned to see a red sports car whizzing down the road—a car that would have hit her if Margaret hadn't pulled her out of the way. Lydia scurried to stand, stumbling as she got to her feet. Backing up again, she waited for Margaret to get up, but the woman stayed facedown in the grass that lined the narrow road.

"Margaret!" Lydia yelled this time. "Margaret, get up!"

After a few seconds, the woman still wasn't moving, so Lydia edged closer and squatted beside her. She wasn't sure if the horrible stench she smelled was coming from Margaret or the contents of her truck. As she jostled Margaret's arm, the woman didn't rise, but she turned her face toward Lydia.

"Where have you been?" Margaret whimpered as she spoke, red lipstick smeared around the lines of her lips. She also wore a pair of dangling blue earrings, almost the same color as the Amish type of dress she was wearing, and black galoshes. Every other time Lydia had seen Margaret, she'd been barefoot.

Lydia's phone was down the road with her buggy. But since Margaret wasn't getting up, not even lifting her head, Lydia knew she needed to call someone.

"I was on *mei* way to your *haus*, you know." Margaret spoke through tears. Lydia got a whiff of the woman's breath and began to hold her own. "But you been avoidin' me, so I changed *mei* mind and turned around. But I want *mei boppli*." She moaned as if she was in pain. "Bring her to me. Bring me the *boppli*!"

Lydia hurried to her feet and backed up, careful not to get too close to the road again.

"Bring me the *boppli*!" Margaret yelled again as saliva continued to run down her chin.

Lydia was shaking so badly that she didn't move at first. But when Margaret closed her eyes and opened her mouth, Lydia feared she'd just witnessed the old woman's death. On shaky legs, she bolted back to her buggy and fumbled for her phone, only to find it was dead. She had planned to charge it at a store on the way to Beverly's house, but now here she was with no phone and possibly a dead homeless woman on her hands. Samuel would be angry with her for letting her phone die.

She looked over her shoulder, and it didn't look like Margaret had moved. Tears gathered in Lydia's eyes as she tried to control her shaking legs and pounding pulse. Gott, *what do I do?* She put a hand to her forehead as Chester whinnied and kicked at the grass. She grabbed her purse, threw her phone inside it, and ran back to where Margaret was lying lifeless on the ground.

Crying, she said, "Margaret, wake up. Please wake up."

The old woman opened her eyes. "I love you," she said in a whisper as she reached for Lydia's hand. Margaret's hand was rough and filled with calluses, but when it went limp and Margaret closed her eyes again, Lydia grew so dizzy she hoped she wouldn't faint.

"*Gott* help me!" she yelled. She touched Margaret's arm. "Wake up!"

Margaret didn't move. Lydia tried to control her crying so she could see if the old woman was breathing, but she couldn't tell.

When Lydia heard a car coming, she stood and waved her hands in the air, careful to stay far enough off the road.

A tan car pulled over and screeched to a halt in front of Margaret's truck. A small woman about Lydia's mother's age ran toward them.

"I don't know if she's dead. I can't tell!" Lydia cried out. "Her head was on the steering wheel and—"

The woman ran past Lydia and knelt beside Margaret, quickly putting a finger to her neck. "She's alive." The lady pointed to her car. "Go get my purse and find my phone, then call nine-one-one."

Lydia did as the woman asked, and after she'd made the tearful call, she ran back to where the woman was. She had her hand on Margaret's face and was clearing matted, gray hair from her cheek. Was that dried blood on the old woman's hair?

"I'm surprised she's lived this long," the *Englisch* woman said as she stroked Margaret's face. "But she has a pulse." She looked up at Lydia, who was still crying and had a hand over her mouth. "Hon, I think she's dehydrated." She nodded to Margaret. "See how her lips are so incredibly chapped. She looks like she's been out in a desert. And although the bleeding has stopped, she has a deep cut on her scalp."

So it was blood. "I-I called nine-one-one. They're sending an ambulance." She paused, squeezing her eyes closed, and prayed Margaret wouldn't die. That felt a little strange since the woman wanted to steal Lydia's baby. But she didn't want to witness her death, especially since Margaret had pulled Lydia out of harm's way. Maybe she'd get the help she needed now.

It took almost twenty minutes for the ambulance to arrive, and Lydia was still crying so hard that the *Englisch* lady— who had introduced herself as Sharon—led the conversation with the men, relaying what Lydia had told her, including Margaret's name.

After they'd loaded Margaret into the ambulance and hooked her up to a lot of wires and machines, Lydia asked one of the men if Margaret was going to die.

"I don't think so, but her blood pressure is really high, and she's dehydrated and lethargic. Plus, it looks like she was hit on the head, maybe hours ago."

Margaret had opened her eyes a few times, and each time she'd looked from person to person, locking eyes with Lydia when she saw her.

They informed Lydia and Sharon what hospital they were taking Margaret to and then left. Sharon put a hand on Lydia's arm. "Sweetie, can I take you somewhere?"

Lydia shook her head. "No, thank you." She pointed to a distraught Chester. "I can't leave my horse, and I live right around the corner."

"It's a good thing you noticed Margaret was slumped over the steering wheel. A lot of people would have just driven by without a look. You might have saved her life. I doubt that woman has ever been to a doctor. There's no telling what all could be wrong with her." She shook her head. "Hers is a sad situation."

Lydia wiped her eyes with her hands as she thought about Margaret saving her life.

"If she doesn't make it for some reason," Sharon added, "I can't think of a single person who will miss her." She sighed. "And that's a shame, but it's her own doing."

"Someone said she might have dementia," Lydia said, still sniffling. "Or some kind of mental illness."

Sharon tucked short blond hair behind her ears. Lydia hadn't known the woman before today, but she obviously lived nearby and knew about Margaret. "Well, that's an entirely different situation. If that's the case, she can't help that. The doctors will find out. And at least the woman will get cleaned up and be given something to eat."

"You're a nice lady, to stop." Lydia took a deep breath.

"So are you," the woman said. "Be safe on your way home. I'll phone the police and tell them about her truck. They'll want to get it off the road."

Lydia nodded, and then Sharon returned to her car and drove away.

Chester calmed down when Lydia rubbed his nose and talked to him in a whisper. "It's okay, boy." She waited until she'd gathered herself a little more, then she checked for traffic and guided Chester to turn around. She wasn't in any condition to continue her trip to Beverly's, and all she wanted to do was hold Mattie.

By the time she pulled into her driveway, she was crying again. She ran across the yard, then up the porch steps, and flung the screen door wide. "Samuel!" she called when she didn't see him or Mattie.

Samuel came out of Mattie's bedroom, his eyes wide. "What's wrong?"

Lydia rushed to her daughter's crib and put a hand on Mattie's tummy. Then she closed her eyes and thanked God that her family was okay.

Samuel came up behind her. "What's wrong?" he asked again, this time in a whisper.

They returned to the living room and sat down on the couch. Lydia tearfully told him what happened. "I thought she died in front of me." She twisted her hands in her lap. "But she was alive, and she made no sense. She kept telling me to give her the *boppli*, which made me think she wanted to steal Mattie. Especially when she said she'd been watching me." She shivered at the recollection. "But she also told me she loves me. And, Samuel . . ." Covering her face with her hands, she sobbed, then looked back at him. "I was so scared and nervous, but if Margaret hadn't lunged at me and pulled me out of the road, that car would have hit me. She saved *mei* life."

Samuel pulled her into his arms. "Thank *Gott* you're okay, and I'm so sorry you had to go through all that."

She eased away from him and stared into his eyes. "Please, please don't argue with me about this. I want to go to the hospital. I have to know she's all right."

Samuel nodded as he pushed loose tendrils of hair away from her face, then kissed her tenderly. "I'll call for a driver. And I'll come with you."

Lydia wasn't sure she'd ever loved him more than at that very moment, and she told him so.

. . .

By the time they arrived at the hospital, Lydia's tears had dried, but her heart was still pounding. She couldn't shake the image of Margaret telling her she loved her but also demanding Lydia give her a baby. None of it made sense.

They learned Margaret had been admitted, and by the time they'd found the right nurses' station, Lydia was sure Margaret must at least have the form of craziness Sarah Mae mentioned—dementia.

"What a precious baby," the nurse behind the counter said as she smiled at Mattie, who was wiggling in Samuel's arms.

"*Danki*," he said.

Lydia needed her pulse to slow down. "We're here to find out about Margaret Keim." The smell of the hospital wafted up her nose, and she fought the urge to vomit. She'd been to a hospital only a few times, and one of those times was when her grandmother died. The odor had reminded her of death ever since.

"Are you family?" the nurse asked.

"*Nee.* I mean no," Lydia said. "But I'm the one who found her on the side of the road, and I'd just like to know how she is."

The young woman put down the pen she'd been twirling between her fingers. "Okay. Let me go see what I can find out."

She returned with an older woman who had short, gray hair. "I'm Dr. Finley. You're the one who found Miss Keim?"

"Yes, in Montgomery. I was on *mei* way to Odon." Lydia bit her bottom lip.

"She's going to be okay physically, we think. We're going to run some tests. She was dehydrated, malnourished, and very dirty, which I'm sure you noticed. I'm guessing she's homeless."

Lydia nodded. They were at the hospital in Bedford, so it would be unlikely any of the staff knew Margaret.

"She also has a deep cut on the right side of her head, like perhaps she was struck by something heavy." She locked eyes with Lydia. "I know your people don't cut their hair, but we had to shave a fairly large section of her head to stitch up her wound. It's unfortunate, but we see a lot of homeless people victimized."

"She doesn't have anything to steal, unless you count her dilapidated truck," Samuel said, frowning.

The doctor sighed. "Most of the homeless we see don't have much of value. The world just has a lot of bullies."

Lydia cringed. No matter Margaret's looks or situation, how could someone hit an old woman? "Does she have something called dementia?"

"We'll know more after the tests, but based on some of the things she said, we suspect she might have some mental issues. Or it could just be confusion from the blow she took to the head. Do you know of any family we should call?"

"*Nee*," Lydia said, electing not to say her community thought Margaret had mental issues too. "I recently learned she has a sister somewhere, but I don't think they've been in contact for many years. Her name is Delila Keim. But that would be her maiden name. I don't know if she's married." She thought again about the photograph of the woman in the red dress with the man standing next to her.

"Okay, great. We have someone who's pretty good at tracking down long-lost relatives. We'll see what we can do."

Relief washed over Lydia. Surely the hospital staff would have more resources at their disposal than she and Samuel had.

"She's resting, but you can go in and see her if you'd like." The doctor pointed to a door down the hall. "She's in room 426. I have to run, but if you'll leave a contact number, we can call you with any updates." She looked back and forth between Samuel and Lydia. "Do you have a cell phone?"

"*Ya.*" Lydia reminded herself to charge hers in the lobby, even if just for a few minutes. But a big part of her wanted to leave and never think about Margaret again. The hospital had the best chance of finding any relatives she might have, and now she would get the care she needed. Lydia had every reason to just walk away.

But the woman had said she loved Lydia and saved her life. *And is she really a threat to Mattie?*

Lydia owed the woman at least one visit, but she wouldn't leave a phone number for follow-ups.

"Go ahead," Samuel said softly. "I know you want to see her. Mattie and I will wait in the hallway."

Lydia appreciated the way her husband was starting to understand the way she thought without her having to tell him. "*Danki.* I won't be staying long."

With a heavy and grateful heart, she took the few steps to room 426, then gently pushed open the door. Her eyes widened when she saw Margaret. She had a big bandage above one ear, but her face was clean, and her hair wasn't the matted mess it usually was. Despite the tube attached to her arm, this was a small glimpse at who Margaret Keim must have been at one time. She'd never seen the woman smile the way she did now, and even though her teeth were discolored, somehow Margaret looked softer, less scary. She stretched out one of her large arms and motioned for Lydia to come closer.

She took two slow, careful steps toward the bed.

Margaret was still smiling. "Delila, I knew you'd come. I knew you'd come home one day. And here you are, as beautiful as ever."

Lydia folded her hands in front of her. "Um, Miss Keim . . ." She'd decided to follow the doctor's lead and address her more formally. "I'm not Delila, but the hospital staff is trying to find her. I'm the woman who found you in your truck on the side of the road."

"Truck?" Margaret's face shriveled. "I don't have a truck. I don't even know how to drive."

Lydia chose not to argue with her. It seemed pointless. "I just wanted to make sure you were okay."

"*Ya,* I am." Smiling, she said, "I forgive you, Delila. I love you just as much now as I ever did."

Lydia was too curious to let it go, so she decided to play along. "Forgive me for what?"

Margaret blinked back tears. "For stealing *mei dochder.*"

Lydia didn't move as she tried to decide whether Margaret would believe her if she said she hadn't stolen her baby. Then she excused herself—she said she had to go to the bathroom—

and never returned. But she left her phone number at the nurses' station, after all, asking that the doctor call her with any updates. Mostly, she wanted to know when Margaret was back on the streets again. If the woman thought Lydia had stolen her baby, she might come looking for Mattie.

CHAPTER 19

Joseph listened as Samuel detailed the events of the previous day.

"That's a wild story, *mei* friend. Are you and Lydia worried she might try to kidnap Mattie when she's released from the hospital?" Joseph needed a distraction so he wouldn't think about Beverly, but he wished Samuel had better news.

Samuel's spoon clinked against his empty bowl as he leaned back in his chair. As usual, they were the only ones in the break room. Their *Englisch* coworkers usually went out to eat.

"We're hoping she just needs some medication to get her head straight," Samuel said. "I guess we'll know whether to worry when Lydia hears from the doctor."

Joseph finished a bite of meat loaf. His mother had gone overboard on his dinner, knowing her son was having a rough time. Even thoughts of Beverly couldn't keep him from devouring it along with potatoes, green beans, and bread. But his heart still ached.

"You haven't talked to Beverly, have you?" Samuel frowned.

Joseph put the lid on his food container, hoping he could talk about her without feeling like he might cry. "*Nee.*"

"Are you going to?"

Joseph looked across the table at his friend. "What's the point?"

"Uh, the point is that you *lieb* her." Samuel stood and pushed in his chair.

"I don't know if I can get past the lies." But Joseph also wondered if he could live without Beverly in his life. He'd fallen for her hard.

"Forgiveness. It's a win-win. You free her, and you free yourself."

Joseph packed up his plastic containers. "That's easier said than done."

Samuel waited until Joseph looked at him, then said, "It doesn't have to be. Forgive her. And love her. You'll argue and fight, make up, and do things that require forgiveness again. It's a relationship, and that's how it works." He paused. "And if you let true love slip away, you have no one to blame but yourself."

"I'm not the one who lied." Joseph heard the angry tone in his voice.

"You're also not the One who hung from a cross, the One who forgives us daily, and the only One who has the right to judge. Lydia is going to see Beverly this morning. She lied to us, too, and I know it hurt Lydia a lot. But we want her and Susan in our lives, so we'll forgive her and not speak of it again."

Joseph didn't say anything—for fear of crying.

. . .

Lydia sat on the couch with Beverly once Mattie and Susan were playing on the floor.

Beverly hung her head. "I don't know how many times I've asked *Gott* to forgive me for lying, and I feel like I need to tell you and Samuel I'm sorry at least a hundred times. And Joseph."

"*Gott* forgave you the very first time you asked Him to forgive you." She moved her purse from the couch to the coffee table and twisted to face Beverly. "Samuel and I forgive you too. And hopefully, over time, Joseph will forgive you as well, although I have no way to know for sure."

"I just want what you and Samuel have. I know you said you've had challenges, but"—she looked at the babies—"I really wanted those ten *kinner* with Joseph."

When it came to deception, Lydia had slipped well into a gray area—although more with omissions of truth than actual fibs. There was no easy way to tell her friend the truth, but she wanted to be honest with her. She hung her head.

"Our marriage had a rough start because Samuel and I were intimate before we were married in a way only married people should be. It was just one time, but once we knew I was pregnant, our families practically forced us to get married. We weren't in love. We were just physically attracted to each other, and we succumbed to our desires." Lydia looked up.

Beverly's jaw had dropped. "But you seem to love each other so much. I see it in your eyes."

"We do love each other. But we never dated and fell in love the way most married couples do. I was only sixteen when I got pregnant, and we were both bitter about the way our families rushed us to marry, to save face. Especially me."

Lydia paused as she recalled their wedding day. "Neither one of us meant our vows when we recited them. Mattie drew us together more than anything because of our shared love for her, but we've been trying to work our way into a more romantic relationship only recently. For a long time, we lived like roommates, and our married relationship is still far from typical, but like I said, we're working on it."

"I'm so sorry." Beverly briefly touched Lydia's arm as she shook her head.

"Don't be. In a lot of ways, we're getting to know each other's hearts. Instead of walking around in a bitter haze and staying detached emotionally, we talk things out, even when we're angry."

Beverly was quiet. "I guess that's how marriage is supposed to work. Enos and I always talked things over."

"I think it is. I know forgiveness has to be part of it too. Samuel told me he was planning to talk to Joseph about forgiveness today at work. We talked to him about it the night he came to our *haus*, right after he left your place. But he was so upset. In the end, he said you were probably too *gut* for him anyway."

Beverly shook her head. "How could he even think that? I felt like the luckiest woman in the world when Joseph took an interest in me. I made such a bad choice."

"Give him time."

Then Lydia told Beverly about Margaret, and her friend gasped more than once. "I bet you were so scared," Beverly said as she brought a hand to her chest.

"I was so scared Margaret would die in front of me."

Then Lydia told Beverly what she'd found out about Margaret and Delila from Sarah Mae. "I left you out of it only because I wasn't sure where the whole process was headed or if she really was dangerous, and then Samuel offered to help, including going to the hospital with me."

"*Ach*, wow. I hope the hospital can find her *schweschder* and get her the help she needs."

"*Ya*, me too. But hopefully she's in *gut* hands even if they don't locate Delila."

Lydia reached for her purse when her phone buzzed. "I better see who that is. We try not to use our phones, but . . ."

"Same here," Beverly said. "But once you start using them, it's hard to stop."

Lydia didn't recognize the number, but she answered. When she was done with the call, she told Beverly she needed to leave. "That was the doctor who cares for Margaret at the hospital. She asked me to come talk to her." She looked at Mattie and bit her bottom lip.

"I can keep Mattie for you," Beverly said. "She can take a nap when Susan does."

"I really don't want to be involved, but if they're releasing Margaret, I need to know if we should be worried. All her talk about a stolen *boppli* makes me nervous." Lydia shook her head. "It's all very confusing." Lydia glanced at Mattie before she looked back at Beverly. "Margaret is in the Bedford hospital, so I'll need to hire a driver." She paused, wondering if she should tell Samuel. She didn't want to make him mad by not telling him, but she hated to bother him at work. Besides, she wouldn't be in any danger at the hospital. "It would be *gut* if you can keep Mattie."

. . .

Lydia made it to the hospital an hour and a half later. She stopped at the same nurses' station and asked to speak to Dr. Finley, and in another fifteen minutes, the doctor opened the door to a hallway and motioned for Lydia to follow her.

She looked so serious that Lydia's knees began to shake. "Did she die?"

Dr. Finley opened a closed door and motioned for Lydia to step inside. "No, she didn't die."

Lydia sat down in front of a large desk with files stacked everywhere. Dr. Finley ran her hands along the desk and over the files until she found a pair of glasses and slipped them on. As she searched for something else, Lydia read the framed documents on the wall. She wondered how long the older woman had to go to school to get all those certificates.

"Miss Keim has a lot going on, both physically and mentally." Dr. Finley studied a file in front of her. "We haven't been able to locate any relatives, including the sister you mentioned, and you're the only one we have a phone number for. I understand you're just the person who found Miss Keim, but I promised you updates, so here goes."

She lowered her head and read for a few seconds before she set the glasses on her desk. "She appears to be in her late sixties or early seventies, but she can't remember her birthday. She told us she grew up Amish, but that God kicked her out of the organization." She paused. "Do you know if she did something to be shunned?"

With so many Amish in the area, Lydia wasn't surprised Dr. Finley knew about shunning. Lydia shook her head. "I don't really know anything about Margaret. I just remember her always being around and driving a blue truck from the time I was little. We were told to stay away from her."

"I'm afraid we had to restrain her last night. She was crying and trying to leave her room. She pulled out her IV twice."

Lydia's eyes widened as she pictured Margaret strapped to a hospital bed. "Will she get better?"

"No, I'm afraid not. She has an inoperable brain tumor. We

believe it was aggravated further by the blow to her head. Right now, it's hard to know how much of her confusion is because of the tumor or because of mental illness." Dr. Finley sighed. "She also believes she has a baby that's been stolen from her. Have you heard anything about that?"

"She told me that, but I don't know anything about her having a baby." Lydia wondered why she was even involved in this. The initial plan to find Margaret's sister had turned into a larger ordeal than Lydia could have predicted. If the hospital staff couldn't find Delila Keim, it was highly unlikely that she or Samuel could have found her. Lydia had misread what she'd believed to be signs from God. She couldn't do anything for Margaret.

"When will she be released from the hospital?" Lydia's thoughts circled back to Mattie and whether Margaret would come looking for them. She'd told Lydia she'd been watching her.

"We don't believe Miss Keim has long to live." She scratched her head. "We're a little surprised she's lived this long. The tumor on her brain is one of the largest we've seen. And when you take into account the way she's lived, it's even a bigger surprise that she's still here."

"Will she be sent home to die?" Lydia's daughter was first and foremost on her mind, but picturing Margaret alone in that rundown house caused her stomach to clench.

"No. But we don't have the proper facilities to care for her here. We also believe she might be a danger to herself or others. Since she doesn't have any relatives, she'll become a ward of the state and be sent to a facility that's equipped to care for her. There's also the fact that she's indigent."

Lydia raised her eyebrows. "She's what?"

"Indigent, meaning she has no money or way to pay for her own care."

"She has a house and property," Lydia said. Even though she didn't want to be involved in this, it seemed like someone should be advocating for Margaret. "Can't it be sold so she can get good medical care?"

"I assure you Miss Keim will be taken care of. We assign a social worker to cases like this. And we know about her house, but she owes thousands of dollars in back taxes. Plus, we aren't in the business of liquidating assets. I know that might sound cold, but you'd be surprised how many indigent people we get with mental disabilities."

"All right. I'll pray that her final days are peaceful and pain free." Lydia was ready to pick up Mattie and go home.

"She keeps crying and asking for Delila." Dr. Finley shook her head. "I wish we could have found her sister."

Lydia pressed her lips together, deciding how much she should tell the doctor. "She called me Delila yesterday, and she also told me she loves me and that she forgives me for stealing her *boppli*—baby."

"Maybe you look like her sister, the way she remembers her." The doctor shrugged. "But, of course, we don't know anything about a baby either."

Lydia thought about the woman in the red dress again. Maybe she wasn't either twin. Maybe Delila had a daughter, although how would Margaret have a photo of a niece unless Delila sent it to her? That seemed unlikely. Either way, she didn't know enough about *Englisch* clothing styles to even guess how long ago the photo was taken. Beverly hadn't been sure either.

Dr. Finley stood and held her arm across the desk. "You did

a good thing by stopping to help this woman. At least she'll receive proper care during her final days. You're welcome to stop by her room and see her. I don't know what day she'll be relocated. So much paperwork for these things." After they'd shaken hands, Dr. Finley handed Lydia a brochure. "This is where she'll be."

Lydia thanked her, put the pamphlet in her purse, and left. She was almost to the hospital exit when she went back to the elevator. Even though she was relieved that Margaret wouldn't be roaming the streets, it seemed wrong not to have some sort of closure with the woman who had saved her life.

When she walked into room 426, Margaret was lying on her back and staring at the ceiling. Her arms were secured to the bedrails, and Lydia wished she hadn't come. Then Margaret looked at her, and the woman's bottom lip began to quiver.

"Delila, they have me tied up. I must have done something bad again."

Lydia edged forward, cautiously. "I think they're just worried you'll get hurt. Are you in any pain?"

"It doesn't matter. You're here now." Her lip still trembling, she managed a smile. "Will you sit with me for a spell? I've missed you so much."

Lydia wanted to be home before Samuel arrived, and she still had to call a driver and pick up Mattie. "I can't stay long. I have to get . . ." She didn't want to mention Mattie—although Margaret couldn't hurt her daughter from an institution. "I have to get home soon."

"*Ya*, we'll go home soon." Margaret scrunched up her face. "Why were you gone two weeks? I was worried."

Lydia didn't want to lie, but Margaret clearly didn't realize that when Delila left, it was for good—and for a lot longer than two weeks ago. "Well, I'm here now," Lydia said as she tried to smile.

"Why haven't you brought Rebecca to see me?" Tears formed in her eyes. "It's been too long. I've seen you with her. You've been keeping her away from me, but I don't know why."

Lydia's temples throbbed. She didn't know what to say.

"I was in an accident. A blue truck hit me. But I'm all right now. Can you please bring Rebecca to see me?" Now the tears trailed down Margaret's face. "Please. I have an odd feeling I'm going to die. I know I'll go to hell, but my dying wish is to see Rebecca."

Lydia didn't believe God would send anyone with Margaret's disabilities to hell. "Do you want me to ask a member of the clergy to come and speak to you about that, Margaret? I don't think you'll go to the devil." Lydia recalled briefly wondering that about herself, whether God would deny her a place in heaven. But she realized He wouldn't. Lydia and Samuel had sinned, but Jesus had died for their sins.

"*Ya*, I will. I made a *boppli*, and I wasn't married." She cried harder. "And *Gott* stopped loving me."

Lydia recalled the shame she'd worked so hard to overcome. "*Gott* doesn't stop loving us, not even when we make bad choices. A *boppli* is a gift, and it's His grace that frees us from shame." The moment she said the words, she realized she hadn't worked to shed her shame. She'd leaned on God, and He carried it for her, allowing her the freedom to work through her situation in a way that might make sense. Despite all her back and forth about whether God had called her to help Margaret, she felt sure He had.

"Ben loved me. We were going to get married at *mei haus*." Margaret sniffled. "But he moved to another town after you left with *mei boppli*."

Lydia fought the knot building in her throat and wondered if Margaret really did have a daughter out in the world somewhere. And could this be true about the man named Ben? If so, Lydia's heart hurt even more for Margaret. Maybe that's why she no longer wanted to live in her house. It was supposed to be the place she got married and raised a family.

Squeezing her eyes closed, Margaret sobbed. "I can't even wipe *mei* own eyes."

Lydia pulled a tissue from the box nearby and dabbed at Margaret's eyes.

"*Danki*, Delila." Sniffling, she said, "Can you take me home?"

"I can't do that. It's best you stay here." Lydia needed to tell Margaret goodbye and leave before her own waterworks started.

"Then I'm begging you to please bring Rebecca to see me!" Margaret's cries were so loud that two nurses rushed into the room.

One of the women checked the restraints while the other one said, "I'll give her a sedative."

"*Nee!* Please, Delila. Please don't let them give me more drugs that confuse me. Just promise to bring Rebecca to see me!"

Lydia swallowed hard. It was all just too heartbreaking. "Okay."

CHAPTER 20

Samuel stopped to see his parents on the way home from work, and then he promised them he and Lydia would stop visiting so often. His mother said they loved them but insisted they were doing fine. Samuel was relieved their health had improved. He was also glad he could go straight home more often.

Lydia had called to say she and Mattie were fine, but they'd be home late. Then she asked if he could please bring home a pizza. She'd never asked him to do that, and it sounded like a nice, affordable treat.

When she got home, they decided to feed Mattie, get her bathed and down for the night, and then enjoy supper alone. Lydia said she had a lot to tell him. By the time they sat down with the pizza, Samuel was starving. As Lydia told him about her day, he realized his love for her was growing daily as he learned more about her. His wife was compassionate. He'd known that, but the quality seemed to shine brighter than in the past. Maybe he hadn't been paying close enough attention.

But when she got to the part about taking Mattie to see Margaret tomorrow . . . He didn't want to be demanding or tell her what to do, but he was sure that was a terrible idea. Yet he'd learned that forbidding Lydia to do something only made her want to do it more. Samuel just needed to help her think it through.

"Are you sure that's a *gut* idea?" He spoke softly before he took a bite of pizza.

"Her arms are strapped to the bedrails." His wife's voice cracked as she shook her head. "It's just awful. I wanted to run out of there and never see Margaret again, but when someone tells you something is their dying wish, it's hard to say no."

Samuel didn't have an argument for that except about Mattie's safety.

"Mattie will be safe," Lydia said before he could say anything. "There's an entire hospital staff, and she can't hold Mattie. She believes Mattie is her *dochder*, Rebecca." Her voice shook even more as she locked eyes with him. "Can you even imagine someone denying us time with Mattie, keeping her away from us?"

Samuel shook his head. "*Nee*, I can't. So, then, Margaret got pregnant, and her *schweschder* ran off with her *boppli*?"

"I don't know. Maybe her *schweschder* had a *boppli* and Margaret just thought it was hers. Today, she didn't even remember that she knows how to drive." Lydia had only taken one bite of pizza. "It was just so hard. She called me Delila too."

"Maybe there is no Delila or *boppli*." Samuel eyed the last slice of pizza, but he wiped his mouth and put down his napkin. Lydia should have it.

"*Nee*, both your parents and Sarah Mae said Margaret had a twin *schweschder* who left a year or two after their parents were killed, and they all remembered her name was Delila. And the existence of a baby named Rebecca must be why Margaret's always kept the nursery so clean." She blinked her eyes a few times. "*Ach*, Samuel, Margaret's been waiting all this time for Delila and Rebecca to return home." She covered her face with her hands before looking back at him. "Margaret also told me she'd been in love with a man named Ben, who I assume is the father of her child. She said they were supposed to get married in her *haus*." She shook her head, sniffling. "It's just all so heartbreaking."

Samuel had to agree. "Do you think anyone will try to find Ben?"

Lydia shrugged. "I don't know. I doubt it. He left her all those years ago. Maybe he had similar problems, like Margaret. Who knows? I guess if anyone finds Rebecca, who might not know the truth, it will be up to her whether or not to seek out her father."

Samuel wasn't going to try to talk Lydia out of visiting Margaret. He didn't think he could, even if he wanted to. After she'd eaten another bite of her pizza, Samuel asked, "How was Beverly?"

"Heartbroken. What about Joseph?"

"The same."

"Do you think he'll be able to forgive her?" Lydia nodded to the last slice of pizza. "I'm not going to eat that, so go ahead."

Samuel reached for it and put it on his plate. "I hope so. I thought they were cute together. I liked watching them be so playful and falling in love."

A dreamy expression filled Lydia's face. "*Ya*, me too." She set down her slice of pizza and leaned over and kissed him, something he'd never tire of. "I know we started out living vicariously through our friends, but now we're finding our own way. She smiled. "Even if Joseph and Beverly don't reconcile and get back together, let's not let our progress slow." Grinning, she added, "I'm enjoying getting to know *mei* husband."

Samuel thought he heard a *but* coming.

"But I wish we weren't married yet so that when we said our vows, we truly meant them."

Samuel was thankful that her *but* hadn't led to anything worse, but this was a regret he also had. "During devotions later, we should pray for Beverly and Joseph, for *Gott*'s will to be done but also to help them see that love really does conquer all."

Lydia smiled again. "That's a *wunderbaar* idea." He knew they'd be praying for their own relationship too. "We'll pray for Margaret and her situation as well."

His wife kissed him again. "I *lieb* you."

"I *lieb* you too."

. . .

It was dark by the time Joseph got to Beverly's house. Susan would be asleep, which would be good in case anyone cried. Joseph realized he was just as apt to cry as Beverly might be. He wasn't ready to resume a courtship with her; maybe he never would be. But he would forgive her. She needed that, and he needed it too. Carrying his hurt and anger was like having a weight around his neck.

Beverly opened the door before he knocked. "Joseph, what are you doing here?" She wore a long white robe and had a scarf draped over her head.

"I'm sorry I came so late. Can I come in? I won't stay long."

Her face lit up, and Joseph felt like a heel. She probably thought he wanted them to see each other again. "*Ya*, of course. I can make some coffee if you'd—"

"*Nee*." He took off his hat and held it at his side. "I just want to tell you that I forgive you for lying about Susan."

She threw her arms around him. "*Danki, danki*. I'm so sorry. I handled that so badly."

Joseph wished he hadn't come. This was harder than he'd thought it would be. He gently eased her away. "I do forgive you"—he paused, hoping he would put this in a way that wouldn't make her cry—"But I still don't want to date you." Shaking his head, he said, "It was just too many lies. I don't know how to get past that."

She lowered her head, and when she looked back at him, she had tears in her eyes. "I understand."

Joseph didn't think she did. His heart was breaking, and he wanted nothing more than to take her in his arms and hold her for the rest of his life. But if he didn't leave soon, he would cry too. He was a grown man, but he'd never cried as much as he had over detaching himself from Beverly. Adding to his pain was the fact that he'd grown to love Susan almost as much as he loved her mother. The thought of not seeing the baby again was also proving to be harder than he'd thought.

Joseph put his hat back on. "I need to go. But I did want you to know I forgive you."

She nodded before he turned to leave.

"Joseph."

He slowly turned around.

"*Danki* for coming to offer me forgiveness. I'm trying hard to forgive myself." She dabbed at the corners of her eyes.

Joseph took a deep breath. "*Gott* forgave you, and I forgive you. It's time you forgive yourself." *Turn around. Leave. Go home.* He couldn't take his eyes off her, and he feared he would miss her for the rest of his life.

She took a step closer to him, sniffling. "I understand and respect your feelings, but you should know something else."

He waited, hoping it was something bad, something that would make him stop loving her.

Her lip trembled. "I *lieb* you. That won't change. But I know you'll find someone else, and she'll be a blessed woman."

Joseph opened his mouth to say something, but then he turned around and left. He didn't even make it to his buggy before he started to cry. Again.

. . .

Sobbing, Beverly watched Joseph from the window. She'd been foolish to think he was coming back to her, willing to resume where they'd left off. Like Chriss, Joseph just didn't love her enough. Their reasons were different, and Beverly took most of the blame for this relationship falling apart, but the hurt would be with her for a long time.

She'd been surprised to hear about the way Samuel and Lydia had begun their relationship, but she was happy her friends were working toward a more romantic marriage. Why couldn't God grace her with a lifelong love? She thought it had been Enos, but he'd been taken from her at a young age. Then she'd thought it was Chriss, but any man who couldn't love Susan like his own wasn't the right person either. Joseph was everything she wanted in a man. And she'd blown it by lying. How silly she'd been to think he would be happy to hear that Susan was her daughter.

She vowed right then and there to never tell another lie. She knew in her heart she'd never fall in love with another man the way she had with Joseph. It was her penance that he chose not to be with her. Joseph had all the qualities she'd loved about her husband. He was honest, a hard worker, good with children, handsome . . . and there was a kindness about him she'd picked up on right away. But it was Joseph's humor, the way he was constantly smiling, and his zest for life that made Beverly realize he was the one for her. She'd loved Enos with all her heart, but if the man had one fault, it was his lack of laughter, and he seldom smiled.

But now I've lost Joseph too.

. . .

Lydia snuggled next to her husband that night, and as they grew emotionally closer, they were also becoming more physical with each other. It was slow, and Samuel had more patience than she deserved. But as she grew less nervous about what was surely going to happen soon, something else bothered her.

Even though she and Samuel were married, it didn't feel like they'd earned the right to be together intimately. Marriage was a union blessed by God, and on the day of her wedding, she hadn't meant one single thing she said. The vows she barely remembered saying had been meaningless, and she didn't love Samuel then. In a way, she and Samuel had lied to each other, in God's name.

Her unresolved feelings about their marriage vows—and what they should have meant—stayed in her thoughts, more so lately. She wasn't even sure she realized it until she and Samuel began to form more of an emotional connection. She wanted to tell him how she felt now and not stay trapped in the emotions that still plagued her sometimes. But even though they'd come a long way, she wasn't sure he'd understand.

When he began snoring, a sound she now found comforting, she shifted her thinking. Tomorrow she would take Mattie to the hospital to see Margaret. It was the woman's dying wish to see her baby, and Mattie would play the part. Then Lydia

wouldn't have to see her again. She'd been glad Samuel hadn't
put up a fight about her plan.

. . .

When Lydia arrived at the hospital the next morning, she wished
she'd waited until Mattie was in a better mood. Her latest tooth
still hadn't pushed through the surface, and even the herbal
balm didn't seem to be giving her much relief. Her daughter
wiggled and fussed as they walked the halls of the hospital to
Margaret's room.

Lydia's chest tightened as she pushed open the door to room
426, then it clenched even more when she saw that Margaret's
arms were no longer restrained. She would want to hold Mattie,
and Lydia wasn't comfortable with that. She briefly considered
leaving, but Margaret had already seen them.

Mattie continued to wiggle and fuss, but Lydia held her
extra tight and prayed for God to place a protective canopy over
them.

"You came." Margaret stretched out her long arms as she began to weep. "Bring her to me. Come here, Rebecca. I've waited
so long."

Before, Margaret said Rebecca had been gone for two weeks.
Now she thought they'd been gone much longer.

Lydia didn't move for a couple of seconds as she considered
getting a nurse to come supervise the visit just in case Margaret
went crazy. What if she did something to Mattie? Then Lydia
realized Mattie had stopped wiggling and fussing, and when
Lydia slowly moved toward Margaret's bed, Mattie nearly
jumped from her arms and into Margaret's.

"*Ach, mei* little *boppli*." She held Mattie up a little, which caused Lydia's heart to pound. The instinct to snatch her child and run out of the room was strong, but when Mattie giggled, her nerves settled a little. Margaret brought the baby to her chest and cuddled her, and Lydia sat down in the chair beside the bed, pulling it as close to Margaret and Mattie as she could get it.

"We can't stay very long," Lydia said. "But I promised you a visit."

"You are the most beautiful little person in the world." Margaret's eyes glistened as she spoke tenderly to Mattie. "I've missed you so much."

Lydia's stomach continued to settle even more. Babies had a keen sense about people, and Mattie was clearly happy with Margaret. And since this would be the last time she'd see the woman, she wanted to talk to her about heaven.

"Margaret, do you remember when I asked if you wanted to talk to a member of the clergy? Would you like for me to see if I can arrange that?"

"*Nee. Gott* has forsaken me." She rubbed noses with Mattie, much the same way Samuel's mother had always done. Mattie giggled and cooed.

"*Gott* doesn't forsake us. He's always with us." Lydia wasn't sure if this was worth the effort, but she thought she heard a voice in her head. *Bring her to Me.*

Lydia wasn't qualified to lead Margaret to God. Her people weren't known to minister to the *Englisch*—although Margaret seemed to be a mixture of *Englisch* and Amish. Besides, Lydia had misread signs from God before, so she might be misreading them now.

"Margaret, you were baptized into the Amish faith, right?"

The old woman kissed Mattie on the cheek. Her expression

shone with happiness, so much so that she almost didn't look like the same person. Lydia thought about the nursery at Margaret's house and how bittersweet this day was.

"*Ya*, I was baptized." Margaret chuckled. "You know that. We were baptized together."

Lydia reminded herself that Margaret thought she was Delila, so she needed to be careful with her questions. She also tried to sort out what was fact and what was only in Margaret's imagination.

Neither Samuel's parents nor Sarah Mae had mentioned anything about a baby, so if Margaret did have a child, no one in the community knew about it. Lydia sighed. Was there a child? Yesterday, she'd been sure Rebecca was real, but now she wondered again if Margaret had just always longed for a child. Maybe she'd never had a baby except in her mind. She also recalled Dr. Finley saying that Margaret told her she'd been thrown out of the Amish "organization," but she knew that wasn't true. Their community wouldn't oust a woman with Margaret's mental issues.

She'd just have to accept the fact that she might never know the whole truth.

"If you were baptized, then you were free to stay in the community as a practicing member." Lydia honestly wasn't sure if that last part was true, so she silently asked God to forgive her if she'd lied unintentionally. "Did someone tell you otherwise?"

Lydia couldn't believe how much Mattie was cooing and giggling, which kept Margaret focused on the baby.

"*Nee*. Only *Gott* told me I wasn't welcome anymore."

Lydia knew medical professionals would help Margaret with her mental issues, but would they lead her back to God?

"*Gott* never pushes us away. He wants all His *kinner* to know and love Him."

For the first time since they'd arrived, Margaret's expression turned sour, and she stilled Mattie in her lap. A shot of adrenaline shot through Lydia's veins as she became fearful Margaret might toss Mattie onto the hard floor—or do something worse.

"I love *Gott* very much." She paused as she locked eyes with Lydia. "But He doesn't love me anymore. I was bad, and I'll never get to heaven."

This was becoming much too complicated for Lydia. "I don't think that's true. But I do know *Gott* loves you and wants to be in your life."

Margaret smiled as she began bouncing Mattie in her lap again. "That would be very nice." She turned to Lydia. "Delila, when you come back again, will you please read to me from the Bible, the way you did when we were young? When I had trouble understanding the words."

"Uh . . ." Lydia sighed, not sure how to tell Margaret she wouldn't be coming back.

"Maybe if you read to me, I can learn to know *Gott* even better. I want Him to love me. I want to go to heaven, Delila." Margaret's voice had an edge to it, but she was still holding and playing with Mattie. "You can show me how to get there, *ya*?"

If Lydia denied this request, she wondered how she'd ever live with herself.

"Okay," she said softly, now sure this wouldn't be her last time with Margaret.

CHAPTER 21

When Samuel walked into the break room, Joseph was already there, slumped in his chair with a full meal in front of him. Samuel was losing patience with his friend. Ever since he'd gone to forgive Beverly for lying to him, his attitude and mood had worsened.

"Looks *gut*." Samuel nodded to Joseph's bowl as he took a seat at the table, then unpacked his own food—a turkey sandwich, chips, and an apple. Lydia had also included a generous helping of peach cobbler. Samuel would gladly give the dessert to Joseph if it would cheer him up.

"*Ya, Mamm* is still making all *mei* favorites." Joseph slowly dipped his spoon into a simmering beef stew. "Too bad she didn't know this is what Beverly made for me when I was at her *haus* for supper."

Samuel popped open his bag of chips. "Lydia has been with Beverly the past two days. Wednesday, they went to a Sister's Day, and yesterday, they ate dinner together and then did some shopping in the afternoon. I think she likes having a friend with a *boppli* close to Mattie's age."

"I miss us all hanging out together." Joseph swirled his spoon in the stew.

"Then do something about it." Samuel tossed a chip at him.

"Hey." Joseph scowled. "I can't be with someone who lies."

Samuel missed a lot of things. He missed spending time with Joseph and Beverly as a couple, and he missed Joseph's sense of humor, which had perished the day he broke it off with Beverly.

"Well, it's a *gut* thing you're perfect, someone who never makes a mistake, a non-sinner." Samuel took a bite of his sandwich as he raised an eyebrow.

Joseph grunted. "*Ya*, it's hard being me." If his voice hadn't been laced with a heavy dose of annoyance, the man might have resembled his old self.

Samuel decided to change the subject. "Lydia is taking Mattie to see Margaret where she'll stay until she passes." He bit into the apple, then said, "I'm not sure if she should be taking a baby to a place like that, but Lydia says she can't not go. She said *Gott* must want her to guide Margaret home." He paused, unable to deny he was starting to believe his wife had a calling when it came to Margaret. "Although, I'm not sure how Lydia is going to read the Bible to the old woman and tend to Mattie at the same time. She's crawling everywhere now, so she's not so content to stay in someone's lap."

"I loved the way little Susan always looked at me. She had this cute little grin . . ." Joseph groaned even louder this time. "I can't even get her *dochder* off *mei* mind."

They sat in silence as Samuel finished his meal. Then he decided to try a new tactic. "Joseph, the two of you weren't even seeing each other very long. You'll get over Beverly."

"I'll never get over her."

Samuel placed both his palms on the table and leaned forward. "Then get past this and get back together with her." He pushed back his chair, packed up everything but the cobbler, and stood. "She loves you. You love her." Samuel rolled his eyes and grinned. "Although, I don't know *why* she chose you." He slid the container of cobbler across the table.

"Ha, ha." Joseph grinned a little. Maybe that was the push he needed. Samuel hoped so—or he would have to find somewhere else to eat.

. . .

Lydia lifted Mattie out of the car seat and then grabbed the diaper bag. She thanked the driver and asked him to return in thirty minutes, then made her way inside the facility, where she inquired about Margaret. The receptionist led her down a narrow hallway to a nurses' station, and then an *Englisch* nurse, who introduced herself as Daisy and looked almost as old as Margaret, led her to a room with a handwritten sign on the door. *Margaret Keim.*

"You're the only person listed as approved to visit Margaret. You must be her only relative, but all she's talked about since she arrived yesterday is how much she's looking forward to her twin sister and daughter visiting her. But I have to say"— frowning, she looked at Mattie, then back at Lydia—"You sure don't look like her twin, and this can't possibly be her daughter."

"*Nee*, but she thinks we are. We're here because she said seeing her baby daughter is her dying wish, and I wanted to somehow give her that. She also wants me to read the Bible to her. She thinks *Gott* doesn't love her, so she won't get to heaven."

Daisy made the sign of the cross. "Well, God bless you." She pushed the door open and stepped aside so Lydia and Mattie could enter the small room. "Margaret, you have visitors." She looked at Lydia. "There's a button on the wall if you have any problems," she said in a whisper. Lydia wanted to ask what kind of problems, but she nodded.

Margaret was lying in the bed, but her eyes widened when she saw Lydia and Mattie. "I was afraid you wouldn't know where to find me." She smiled. "But here you are."

"And I brought *mei* Bible so I can read to you." Lydia sat down in the chair by the bed. The room seemed like a large closet with only the hospital bed, a bedside table, a small dresser, and a door that presumably led to a bathroom. A window overlooked a courtyard, but black metal bars crisscrossed the panes and obstructed the view. It also smelled like a hospital.

The bedrails on both sides of the bed were raised, but she was still hesitant about letting Margaret hold Mattie. Mattie could crawl over one of them if Margaret didn't have a good hold on her. Still, they seemed to have taken to each other, and Lydia didn't know how else she could read to Margaret.

"Do you, um, want to hold Mattie? I mean, Rebecca?" Lydia cringed at her fumble.

"I want to snuggle with her more than anything in the world, but I'm feeling rather weak today. I'm afraid she might tumble over one of these rails and onto the floor. I'd never forgive myself." Margaret's arms stayed folded across her abdomen.

It was the sanest thing Lydia had heard Margaret say, and even though she was relieved, she still didn't know how she'd hold Mattie and read at the same time.

"Do you remember when we crossed the river in that canoe?" Margaret chuckled. "It was way above Williams Dam, but *Mamm* whipped us both so hard *mei* bottom almost bled." She laughed again, which was quickly followed by a deep, grumbling cough. "I could hear you crying in the next room, knowing you were next."

Lydia stared at her, unsure what to say, so she just nodded and tried to smile. Then she fished around in the diaper bag for a bottle for Mattie before taking out her Bible. She tried to get Mattie comfortable tucked into her left arm with the bottle and hold the Bible with her right hand. She didn't know how she'd turn the pages, but she had only thirty minutes, and she wanted to keep her promise.

"Delila, I'm so glad you're here. And *danki* for bringing Rebecca to see me." She pressed her lips together as her eyebrows drew inward. "I don't think I'm going to be alive much longer, but it gives me comfort to know you'll take care of *mei dochder.*"

Lydia readjusted Mattie in her lap and set the Bible on the small table. "Why don't you think you'll be here much longer?" It was true, but Lydia wondered how she knew that. Does a person feel their body shutting down? Lydia suddenly felt a strong sense of urgency. If she was going to help Margaret know God, she needed to get busy. She didn't want to let Margaret down—or God.

Margaret sighed. "I just know. I don't know how I know."

Lydia reached for the Bible. "You asked me to read to you from the Bible. I want you to feel like you know God and know He loves you. He'll welcome you into heaven, and I don't want you to have any doubts about that."

Margaret's eyes widened. "Delila, I know I'll go to heaven. *Mamm* and *Daed* are waiting for me. But I don't know if your *daed* will be there, Rebecca."

"I'm confused. I thought you were concerned about not going to heaven." Lydia wondered if her work here was done. She was also curious about the man Margaret referred to as Rebecca's father. "Why won't Rebecca's father go to heaven?"

"Because he's dead. Ben is dead."

Lydia awkwardly cleared her throat. "Oh," she said as she began to nervously tap her foot against the tile floor. She stopped herself and sighed. Her purpose here wasn't clear anymore. "How did he die?" Lydia wasn't sure she wanted to know, but the last time Margaret mentioned Ben, she said he left her after Delila took the baby.

"How did *who* die?" A shadow of alarm touched Margaret's face.

Lydia shifted her weight. Mattie was almost out of formula, and Lydia would be out of time soon. "Ben. You said Ben died."

Margaret sighed. "He's only dead in *mei* heart."

Lydia was still processing Margaret's comments when she spoke again.

"Delila, do you remember that time we crossed the river in that canoe?" Margaret smiled. "We were above Williams Dam, but . . ."

Lydia smiled and nodded as she listened to the story again. Mattie sat up and let out a healthy burp just as Margaret stopped talking. The older woman burst out laughing. "That's *mei* Rebecca," she said as her face glowed with a familiar warmth Lydia understood. *Motherhood.*

. . .

Samuel listened in awe—and confusion—as his wife told him about her visit with Margaret. They'd eaten supper early with Mattie, deciding to catch up on their day after they'd showered and retreated to their bedroom for the night.

"I don't know what *Gott* is calling me to do." Lydia fluffed her pillows behind her. "I thought it was to minister to Margaret, but now I really don't know."

"Maybe it's just to make her happy during this last part of her life." Samuel had never wanted to make love to Lydia more than he did right now. Her compassion, combined with the way she was with Mattie and how beautiful she was, made him wish for more than the good-night kisses they'd been sharing.

"Maybe so. I remember Mary telling me that she, Levi, and Natalie felt called to be with Adeline up until she died. But they had a relationship with her. They were all friends. I barely know Margaret." Sighing, she turned on her side to face him. "How does a person end up like that, with no one? Not one single person in the world will miss her when she's gone." She paused for a while. "Although I'll be sad when she dies. She glowed when she told stories about her and her *schweschder*. And I was thinking today, if Delila is deceased, the hospital staff would have found an obituary in the newspaper, *ya*?"

"Probably, if she died in this area. I think death records can be found other ways too." Samuel yawned, but he wanted to listen for as long as Lydia wanted to talk. He could tell the whole situation with Margaret was weighing on her heart.

"Everyone has always been afraid of Margaret." She found Samuel's eyes and held his gaze. "We were too."

"People are scared of what they don't know and understand. But the community tried to help her, and she wouldn't let them. I don't know how you can help someone who doesn't want to be helped. Are you going back to visit her?" Samuel stifled another yawn. He wasn't uninterested, just tired.

"*Ya*. If I don't show up, I'm afraid it will break her heart. And next time I go, she might think she isn't going to heaven again. Either way, it seems cruel not to go back." There was another long pause, and Lydia hadn't made any attempt to extinguish the lantern on her side of the bed. "What happens to a person like her when she dies? I mean, the doctor called her indigent, which means she has no money. Will she be buried here in our community cemetery even though she hasn't been to a worship service in decades and she doesn't seem to be Amish anymore? She still speaks the *Deutsch*, but she doesn't wear a prayer covering or anything. I'm just wondering. Will there be a funeral of any type? What if no one besides me goes?"

"I'll go with you." Samuel reached out his arm, and she extinguished the lantern and curled into what had become her space. He kissed her on the forehead.

"Would she be buried in an Amish coffin? Or would they send her body somewhere?" Lydia's voice cracked a little.

"I don't know the answers, but you could ask someone who works at the place she's living. Or the bishop." Making sure someone had a proper burial seemed important, but Samuel didn't have money for that.

He yawned even more, and when Lydia closed her eyes, he did too. But before he slept, he prayed for his family, and he prayed for Margaret Keim.

. . .

Lydia and Mattie visited Margaret on Monday, then skipped Tuesday and Wednesday. She'd explained to Margaret that she couldn't come every day, although she wasn't sure the woman understood. Not only was hiring a driver expensive, but Lydia had other responsibilities. Samuel's parents insisted they were fine, but she still stopped for a brief visit on Tuesday. And because she'd missed wash day on Monday, she'd had to spend time playing catch-up on the laundry as well as on other household chores.

When she walked into Margaret's room Thursday morning, a momentary look of discomfort crossed the older woman's face. Black circles sagged from beneath her dark eyes, even more than usual, enhanced by her pale face. As Margaret stared at her from beneath craggy eyebrows, Lydia wondered if she knew who she and Mattie were.

Today she had Mattie in a baby carrier she could place on the floor. Margaret hadn't wanted Lydia to read to her on Monday, and she'd said she was too weak to hold Mattie. She'd only wanted to tell more stories about when she and Delila were growing up. Lydia had just smiled and nodded again. Her attempts to talk to Margaret about God had failed. Margaret told her she had a wonderful relationship with God, but she didn't want to talk about Him. Maybe Samuel had been right when he said God just wanted Margaret to have someone who cared for her up until the end.

"Wie bischt?" Margaret said barely above a whisper.

Lydia's chest tightened. She couldn't believe how much Margaret had gone downhill in three days. She recalled Dr. Finley saying she didn't have long, but Lydia hadn't expected a decline this rapid—even though on Monday one of the nurses said Margaret was receiving hospice care now.

"Wie bischt?" Lydia set the carrier on the floor. Mattie sucked on the corner of her blanket, something she'd just started doing. "Are you in pain?"

A hazy expression settled over Margaret's somber face. *"Ya,* I guess so. Are you the person coming to give me the medication?"

Lydia hadn't realized how vested she'd become in Margaret's

well-being, and not being recognized stung more than Lydia would have expected.

"Um, *nee*. It's me, Delila." She lifted the carrier by the handle. "And I brought Rebecca." *I'm sorry for the lie, Gott.* Lydia didn't know what else to do. She longed for a time when lies and avoidance of truth would no longer be a part of her life.

"Nice of you to come." Margaret flinched, and Lydia wondered if she should find a nurse.

"Do you want me to read to you?" Lydia reached for the Bible she'd left on the table by the bed.

"*Nee*, but *danki* for offering." Her eyes were glassy, and she slurred her words a little. Maybe they were giving Margaret too much medication. "*Mei dochder*, Rebecca, was here earlier." She spoke in a whimper. "Somehow, she's all grown up now, and I don't remember how that happened. I could have sworn she was still a *boppli*." A look of despair spread across her face. "But I told her where the money is buried. I figure she'll need it to bury me."

Lydia's mouth fell open, and she suddenly felt very protective of Margaret. If the rumor about buried money was true, then someone was taking advantage of Margaret. Or did she really have a grown daughter taking advantage of her mother after not bothering to see her all these years? A more likely scenario was that Margaret just thought someone else was Rebecca.

"I'm going to go see about your pain medication." Lydia lifted the carrier and was almost out the door when she turned back around, her heart heavy. "Do you need anything else?"

"*Nee*," Margaret said softly as the hint of a smile came across her face. "That's a lovely *boppli* you have."

"*Danki*." Lydia tried to smile but quickly left the room. She knew she and Mattie had become endeared to Margaret, but she hadn't realized how mutual the sentiment was until now. At least she hoped it was mutual. Maybe Margaret would know them if they came back tomorrow.

She stopped at the nurses' station, which had been vacant when she'd first arrived. Now Daisy was seated behind the counter.

"Did Margaret have a visitor today?" There was a little hostility in her voice, and the woman must have heard it since she frowned.

"Yes. Her daughter was here."

Lydia waved her arm around the area. "No one was here when I arrived this morning. Did the woman just walk into Margaret's room? She could have been anyone."

Daisy stiffened as she glared at Lydia, her early friendliness gone. "If no one was here when you came by, I assure you, this station was left unattended for only a few seconds."

"I'm sorry. It just worries me that someone might be trying to take advantage of Margaret. At the hospital where she was before she was moved here, no one could find her daughter."

"Well, the woman here earlier *was* her daughter, and when I mentioned you, she was worried about the same thing. But we do *not* let people visit patients unless they've been cleared by a doctor. Or they're a relative, which you, by the way, are not. I would think you'd be happy Margaret has a family member."

Lydia lowered her head. Then sighing, she looked back at Daisy. "Did she tell you her name?"

"Yes, she did. And she had all the paperwork to prove she's Margaret's daughter."

"Can you tell me her name?" Lydia's heart pounded.

"I suppose I can." She fumbled around on her desk until she found a tablet lined with names. "Rebecca Henderson."

Lydia was speechless.

"Oh, and we made a copy of her birth certificate." She scrounged through all the unorganized papers on the desk. "Here it is. She was born Rebecca Marie Keim. Her mother is Margaret Catherine Keim, and the father is listed as unknown."

"I know this will sound odd, but I really need to find this woman. Did she say where she was going?"

Daisy huffed. "Well, since Margaret seemed to think you were her sister, and your little one her daughter, I can see why you'd want to talk to her real daughter. She said someone had deeded her a house, and she was going to see about it. I only know that because she asked me if I knew where it is, which I don't."

Lydia set down the carrier, then found her phone and called Samuel. All the while, she willed her heart to stop beating so fast.

CHAPTER 22

L ydia and Samuel dropped Mattie off with his parents, and when they arrived at Margaret's house, they saw a car with an Indiana license plate in the dirt driveway. Lydia didn't know much about cars, but this one was shiny and black. It looked fancy and like a smaller version of the limousine that had taken her and Samuel on their date.

Samuel quickly tethered the horse.

Recollections of how this all started swirled in Lydia's head like a tornado as she and Samuel held hands walking across the yard and up to the porch. Mostly he helped her step through the overgrown weeds and debris, but recently they'd started holding hands during devotions in the evenings—one more way they were growing closer.

"It's as bad as you described," Samuel said as he guided her around a loose board.

"Wait until you see the inside." Lydia paused at the partially open front door. "Should we knock?"

Samuel shrugged. "You would think whoever is here would have heard the buggy pull up."

When Samuel's light knock brought no response, Lydia followed her husband inside, staying close behind him. They stopped in the middle of the living room, and she noticed the framed photograph of the woman in the red dress wasn't on the mantel.

"Hello?" Lydia spoke louder than she normally would, but she didn't yell. They stood quietly but heard no answer.

"I hear someone crying," Samuel said as he moved toward the stairs. He pointed upward, then began the ascent to the second floor with Lydia on his heels.

At the top of the stairs, they made their way to the nursery, where the sobbing was coming from. The door was open.

"Hello?" Lydia spoke softly from behind Samuel, her head peeking around him.

The woman sitting in the rocking chair jumped, clinging to the frame she held tightly against her chest. "I'm not robbing the place. Apparently, I own it."

"Are you Rebecca?" Lydia came from around Samuel.

"Yes. Do you know my . . . mother?" Rebecca stood with the photograph still pressed against her. Lydia thought she looked to be in her fifties, maybe. She wasn't good at guessing people's ages. Her wavy brown hair was parted to one side and tucked behind her ears. Like Margaret, she was tall and big-boned but not overweight. Her eyes were dark like her mother's too.

"We know her, but not well." Lydia glanced at Samuel, who was looking around the perfectly decorated, well-supplied nursery.

"Is this where she lived? Before she was institutionalized?" The woman took a tissue from a pocket and wiped her nose.

Lydia had questions of her own, like how Rebecca learned Margaret was in that facility. Had someone finally tracked down Delila? She supposed it didn't matter now. But before she could answer, the woman pierced her with a glare, causing her to shiver.

"Are you the Amish girl visiting my mother with a baby you were pretending to be me?"

Samuel cleared his throat. "Margaret was parking her truck close to our house, the truck she seemed to live in, and at first we felt threatened by her. Then we realized she thought my wife was her sister and that our daughter was you. Lydia went along with it because the doctor said Margaret was dying. She thought it would give her joy until she journeyed home."

Lydia held her breath. Surely Rebecca had been told Margaret was dying.

Rebecca sniffled. "This house should be condemned." She sat back down, then lifted the framed picture. "This is me at my senior prom. It seems cruel that my mother . . . that Delila would send this to her."

"Mother? Or aunt?" Lydia found Samuel's hand and squeezed it.

Rebecca shook her head as more tears flowed. "Well, until a few days ago, I thought the woman who raised me was my mother. She waited until she was dying before she revealed that her sister is my biological mother." Slamming her hand to the glass in the frame, so hard that it broke, she cut her hand in the process. Samuel was quick to offer her his handkerchief.

"Thank you." She wrapped her hand, which looked like it had already stopped bleeding. "I mean, I guess I should try to understand that my mother was trying to protect me." She tossed her head back. "My aunt. My mother is my aunt. I'll just keep saying that until it sinks in."

"Maybe your aunt was trying to protect you too. Maybe because Margaret isn't right in her mind." Lydia squatted beside the rocking chair. "But there might have been a better way to do it. And I suspect Margaret tended to this room all these years because she was waiting for Delila and you to come home. That's just my speculation based on what Margaret has said. But, please know, I wasn't intentionally trying to deceive Margaret."

Lydia told Rebecca about the hospital trying to find Delila and how no one really knew if there was a baby. Then she filled her in on other details, like when Margaret pulled her out of the road and saved her from getting hit by a car.

"I guess you felt you owed her after that." Rebecca had stopped crying and was listening intently.

"Maybe a little," Lydia said. "But I felt sorry for her, that she had no one. I was afraid she would die alone, never knowing anyone cared for her. I also thought she'd lost her way with *Gott*, but she goes back and forth on that."

"I'm sure you know my grandparents were killed in a car accident, and that my mom—Delila—and Margaret were alone from the time they were sixteen." Lydia nodded. "I didn't know anything about that, nor that Delila, as I'll be calling her from now on, even had a sister, much less an identical twin. When I went to see Margaret—my mother—it seemed like I was looking at a ghost. Margaret . . ." She sighed. "I don't even know what to call her. But although their features are identical, Margaret has obviously led a much harder life than Delila did."

Did. So Delila had already died.

"This must all be such a shock for you." Lydia remained squatted beside the chair. Samuel had a hand on her shoulder.

"Did Delila tell you why she took you and left?" She nodded to the photo. "Clearly she didn't continue to practice her Amish ways, and you didn't grow up Amish."

"My mother . . . Ugh." She grunted. "Delila was my mother for over fifty years, so it's hard to just drop the title." Putting a hand to her forehead, she blew out a long breath. "*Delila* was lucid up until the time she died, so I have no reason not to believe everything she told me. She said Margaret had mental health issues starting early in life, but she did have a boyfriend, someone named Ben. She got pregnant, and he left. Delila said that was the beginning of a total meltdown for her. Margaret talked constantly about having a wedding in the house and raising her baby with her husband, but it was like a five-year-old playing house. With baggy dresses, it was easy for them to hide the pregnancy, and she had the baby at home. Can you imagine? With only her sister there? These days, young unwed girls would tell someone what was going on. Well, maybe. But they were scared, so they kept me a secret.

"Then when I was two months old, Margaret—my mother—closed me up in a dresser drawer when I wouldn't stop crying." Her eyes traveled to the white dresser against the wall. "By the time Delila found me, I was turning blue. And there were other things." She shook her head. "So Delila packed me up and ran away, sure I'd never be safe with Margaret."

"I'm so sorry." Lydia spoke in a whisper even though it wasn't intentional. Saying sorry didn't seem to be enough.

"I loved the woman who raised me very much. She loved me, too, as did my father, who died last year. Well, apparently, he wasn't my father, but I just found that out as well. And he knew the truth all along." She shook her head again. "They'll always be my parents, but this lie they carried . . . They should have told me long ago. Margaret seemed so confused when I visited her. She didn't believe I was truly Rebecca at first. But after I recalled some things my mother told me about her childhood, like the tire swing that hung from a tree in the yard, she did believe me. Before I left, she said, 'Goodbye, Rebecca.'"

Lydia stood, and out the window, she could see the old tire barely attached to a rotting rope.

"I guess what's so upsetting is that she lived like this for most of her life, mentally ill and waiting for her sister and baby to return." Rebecca unwrapped her hand, which barely had a nick on it. She locked eyes with Lydia. "Why didn't any of your people try to help her?"

Samuel cleared his throat again. "People have been trying to help her for decades, but she wouldn't allow it. As children, we were told to stay away from her. And to be honest with you, at first, I wasn't happy that my wife was having anything to do with her. We were concerned for our *boppli*—baby."

"But I had planned to continue visiting her." Lydia took a deep breath. "They did tell you that she doesn't have long to live, right?"

Rebecca nodded. "Margaret told me money is buried on the property—even where—so I'd have enough to bury *her*. Honestly, I have all the money I need, so I have no plans to dig up the yard. Delila didn't say anything about buried money, so I doubt it's even true. Even if it exists, it's probably not much anyway. My mother said once she got settled, she sent Margaret cash every month. But it must have been just enough for her to get by."

She paused. "Once I let the shock of this situation sink in, I have to decide what to do with this house and property. But for now, I'm going to spend as much time with my mother as I can, whether she knows who I am or not."

Lydia's heart ached for the woman. "Do you have a place to stay?" She glanced up at Samuel, who nodded in agreement. She'd known he'd be fine moving Mattie's crib into their bedroom so Rebecca could use the twin bed in their daughter's room. Lydia had been glad for that bed when their newborn had her up much of the night.

"It's so crazy. We live in Indianapolis. All this time, we've been only two hours away from here. But I'm staying in a hotel in Bedford, which is less than a mile from Margaret's facility." She stood and walked to the crib, gingerly running a hand along its railing. Then she moved to the dresser and pulled open the top drawer. She lowered her head and stared into the empty space. Delila must have taken all the baby clothes.

Lydia moved to put a hand on her arm. "Please be our guest. I know our house isn't as close to Margaret as the hotel in Bedford is, but we'd really like for you to stay with us."

Rebecca lifted her head but kept her eyes on the drawer. The woman was older than Lydia's mother, but at the moment, Lydia didn't think she should be alone. "You don't even know me," Rebecca said as she shook her head.

Lydia smiled. "In some ways, I feel like I do. Besides, you have a car, and all this hiring drivers back and forth is bothersome." She was only halfway joking, but Rebecca turned her way and smiled.

"You still plan to visit her?"

"Unless you don't want me to. It might confuse her. When I was there earlier, she didn't seem to think I was Delila. But her thoughts and ideas seem to shift from day to day. Either way, I'd still like to visit her—if you don't mind."

"That would be lovely. You obviously know her better than I do, and I'll just follow your lead." Rebecca's shoulders slumped in defeat.

"My wife is a very good cook," Samuel said. "And you'd be welcome in our home."

"It's a kind offer, but I feel like I'd be intruding."

Something about the way Rebecca said that led Lydia to believe she really would prefer to stay with them. "It will be no intrusion, and we would enjoy having you there. If you like babies, of course. Our Mattie is eight months old."

Rebecca's expression came alive. "I'm going to be a grandma for the first time in about a month, maybe sooner."

"How many children do you have?"

"Just one, a daughter. Her name is Dawn." Rebecca's face was still glowing. "At first I just assumed I would sell this place. My husband, Peter, wouldn't do well out in the country. But I might hire contractors to clean it up and then give it to Dawn and her husband. They wouldn't be able to live here because of their jobs, but a piece of history would stay in the family. And they've always said they would love a place in the country. It's close enough to Indianapolis that they'd be able to come here often."

She paused. "Peter knows I'm here and why. I'll tell Dawn about this, too, but not until I can do it without crying. It took her and Liam a long time to conceive, and it's been a rough pregnancy. I don't want to upset her. I was a bit vague when I told her I was taking a short trip here, saying it had to do with a piece of property I'm interested in." She shrugged. "Partial version of the truth, but I just needed to process all this on my own first. I even asked Peter not to come."

After she closed the dresser drawer, she laid the photograph on top of the white piece of furniture, then looked first at Lydia, then Samuel. "Wow. I've had a total breakdown, telling you my life story when I'm sure you both have places to be."

"We're just happy that you exist." Lydia folded her hands together in front of her. "Although I'm sorry about the circumstances."

Rebecca wrapped her arms around Lydia and held her tightly. "Thank you for listening to me, but mostly for being good to my mother, which couldn't have been easy."

Then she hugged Samuel. "Thank you, too, for listening."

They left the room, and Rebecca closed the door, locked it, and put the key back where she'd obviously found it. Then she placed a palm on the door and lowered her head. Lydia believed she was praying, so she also said a prayer—for Rebecca and her family, asking God to give them peace.

. . .

Samuel didn't think he'd ever been prouder of Lydia. He'd married a girl who was not only growing into a strong independent woman but was also compassionate, almost to a fault. Maybe he would be her voice of reason if necessary, but he could also learn to be more compassionate from her example. *Balance.* They had much to learn from each other.

Lydia and Rebecca sat on the couch with Mattie between them.

"You're a natural *grossmudder.* That's what we call grandmothers."

Mattie giggled every time Rebecca tickled the bottom of her feet. "Do you think so? I'm beside myself excited about being a grandma. You would like my daughter. Actually, you remind me of her, even though she's probably older than you. She's levelheaded and calm, and I'm quite sure she would have reacted much better to this situation than I did today."

"I think you handled it well under the circumstances," Samuel interjected before he went to the kitchen to get something to drink. As he poured a glass of tea, he thought about their day. No wonder he felt emotionally exhausted. He chugged the tea, then poured two more glasses and went back to the living room, handing one to each of the ladies. They'd already eaten supper, and Rebecca had raved about Lydia's pork tenderloin. Samuel thought Rebecca was a likeable person. It had been hard to watch her suffering so much, and it was nice to see her laughing and playing with Mattie.

"If you still think you want to restore your mother's house, I can refer you to several contractors who will do a good job for a fair price." Samuel didn't want to dampen her mood, but he wanted her to know he could help. She didn't know anyone else here.

"The more I think about it, the more I would like to restore it, so I appreciate that, Samuel."

Someone began beating on the door. Now that the September air was cooler, they kept the doors and windows closed, and amid the laughter and Mattie's giggles, Samuel hadn't heard a buggy pull in.

When he opened the inside door, Joseph already had his hand on their storm door, and he pulled it open and burst into the room. "I'm doing it. I love her. I'm doing it." He paced back and forth, not even noticing Lydia and Rebecca on the couch with Mattie, shaking his head. "I love that woman, and I'm going to marry her. I'm doing it! I'm going to her *haus* and—"

Joseph finally saw Lydia and Rebecca with the baby. "Uh, hello," he said as his eyes widened. Then he took off his hat and bowed at the waist, which couldn't have looked any goofier. "My apologies, ladies."

"Well, hello there," Rebecca said, smiling. "You sound like a man in love."

"Most definitely." He straightened and held out his hand. "I'm Joseph."

"Nice to meet you, Joseph. I'm Rebecca."

Samuel chuckled. "I'm glad you enjoyed Lydia's delicious meal, but Joseph is our entertainment."

"Ha-ha." Joseph rolled his eyes at Samuel before he looked back at Rebecca. "When a man makes up his mind about something as important as spending the rest of his life with the woman he loves, it seems worthy of spreading the news."

"I agree." Rebecca gave him a quick nod.

Samuel smiled. Rebecca's world had been rocked, and earlier she seemed to be drowning in pain and tears. Now, as she laughed, played with Mattie, and tolerated Joseph, she looked like a different woman.

Samuel laughed when Joseph asked Rebecca if she wanted to hear a joke.

Gott *always has a plan*. Samuel had a plan, too—even though the timing for it wasn't right just yet.

CHAPTER 23

Beverly's heart skipped a beat when she saw Joseph tethering his horse in front of her house. Then she cringed. This would be the second time he caught her in her robe. She grabbed a scarf and covered her head.

"What are you doing here?" she said when she opened the door. She didn't think her heart could take another blow. Was the man here to chastise her for lying even more? But why would he do that when he'd said he'd forgiven her?

"May I come in?" He sounded unusually formal. Maybe he was nervous. Or had something happened? Maybe to Samuel or Lydia? Or to Mattie?

She stepped aside. "Is everything okay? Are the Bontragers all right?"

"Every*one* is fine." Joseph took off his hat. "But every*thing* is definitely not okay."

Beverly swallowed with difficulty and found her voice. "What's wrong?"

Joseph took a step closer to her. "It angered and upset me that you lied to me."

Beverly hung her head. "Joseph, I . . ." They'd been through all this. Didn't he think she'd been punished enough?

He gently cupped her chin and brought her gaze in line with his. "Even though I forgave you, I still thought I could be without you. But I was wrong." He lowered his hand back to his side and moved closer as his lips slowly descended to meet hers. It was a gentle kiss but packed with emotion. "I don't want to be without you," he whispered before he kissed her again.

Beverly savored the moment and thanked God for bringing Joseph back to her.

"Can you stay a while? Let me get dressed, and I'll make coffee."

"I'd like that very much." He smiled. "We can talk about our future and those ten *kinner*."

Beverly smiled, knowing it was much too soon for Joseph to propose, but she felt warm all over, ecstatic he was talking about a future together again.

"And there's lots to tell you about Margaret." Joseph sat down on the couch.

She hadn't heard from Lydia in a while. Her friend knew she'd been working extra hours lately and wanted to spend all her free time with Susan. "I can't wait to hear. I'll go get dressed." But she didn't move. She wasn't ready to take her eyes off him.

"Do you need something?" He raised an eyebrow.

She smiled. "*Nee.* I'm just very happy you're here."

"I know. I have that effect on people." He flashed his boyish grin but quickly sobered. "I'm glad I'm here too."

• • •

Lydia and Rebecca stood outside Margaret's door the following morning. Rebecca wanted to carry Mattie, saying it was good practice for her.

"How do we explain who we are?" A muscle in Rebecca's jaw quivered, and Lydia could sense her nervousness.

"We could tell her the truth, but if she becomes aggravated, then maybe just go along with her. What do you think?"

"I guess so."

Lydia pushed open the door and let Rebecca and Mattie go in first, then she stepped into the room. Margaret was propped up in bed, looking much better than she had the day before. She had a little color in her face, and someone had braided her gray hair to one side. The large bandage covering the wound on her head had also been replaced with a smaller Band-Aid.

Margaret's gaze ping-ponged between them as her bottom lip quivered. Lydia was waiting for her to identify who she believed everyone to be, but as Margaret blinked back tears, Lydia was pretty sure they'd made a mistake. She eased Mattie from Rebecca's arms. "Do you want to hold Rebecca?"

Lydia would have to stand right by the bed to make sure Mattie didn't fall, but she held Mattie under her shoulders and began to lift her over the railing. Margaret shook her head.

"*Nee, nee.*" Her eyes stayed on Rebecca, so Lydia took a step back with Mattie. "I want a mirror," Margaret said as annoyance hovered in her gaze.

Lydia didn't have one, but Rebecca dug in her purse and took out a small compact. "Here you go." She opened it and gave it to Margaret, who held it close to her face. She stared at her reflection, then at Rebecca, then back into the mirror. She did that several times before tears broke loose.

"You're Rebecca, *mei* grown *dochder.*"

Rebecca put a hand over her mouth as her own eyes filled with tears. She nodded, and stepping closer, she lowered her hand. "Yes, I am."

Lydia smiled, but her stomach churned. Margaret's state of mind could change on a whim, and Lydia didn't want to see Rebecca more emotionally scarred than she already was.

"You're very pretty." Margaret smiled, tipping her head to one side.

Rebecca pulled the small chair to the bed, sat down, and found Margaret's hand. "You're very pretty too." Her voice shook, but there was no mistaking the joy in her voice. It had to feel good to have her mother recognize her.

Margaret turned to Lydia and Mattie. "Are you friends of *mei dochder*'s?"

Again, the sting of Margaret not knowing them felt oddly uncomfortable. "*Ya*, we are. I'm Lydia, and this is *mei dochder*, Mattie." Lydia pointed to the door. "We can just wait outside."

No one argued with her, and she turned to go. But when she looked over her shoulder at Margaret and Rebecca still holding hands and smiling, she knew things were as they should be.

As she paced outside in the hallway, bouncing Mattie on her hip, Daisy came from around the nurses' station. Another nurse had been there when they arrived. Lydia forced a smile—although she felt like crying, and she wasn't sure why. "Margaret recognizes her daughter, so I'm giving them some time alone."

Daisy put a hand on Lydia's arm, and they shared an all-knowing look. Sighing, the woman said, "Sometimes the good Lord calls us for situations we can't foresee. You looked after Margaret until her daughter could be reunited with her. You did a good thing."

Lydia tried to smile again. "She might not know her tomorrow. She might think I'm her daughter again." A tiny part of Lydia hoped Margaret had a recollection of her and Mattie, although she didn't want to take anything away from Rebecca.

"She might," Daisy said softly. "Now that we know Margaret has family, we had to ask Mrs. Henderson if she'd give us permission to talk to you about her condition. I asked her myself when she called this morning, assuming you'd want to know. Anyway, if I don't get a chance to tell her myself, let her know that several doctors met to discuss Margaret's case. Some of her medications weren't playing well together, so they changed them. She's much more lucid and seems to understand where she is and what's happening." Pausing, she shook her head. "It won't change the outcome. She'll continue to deteriorate, in both mind and body. But for now, it sounds like God blessed her daughter by gifting her this time with Margaret." She patted Lydia's arm again before she returned to her desk.

Rebecca came out of the room about thirty minutes later.

"I'm sorry I was in there so long. She told me stories about her childhood, about swinging on the tire swing, playing at the lake, and making homemade ice cream on the porch, all with her sister." She shook her head. "I heard some of the same stories from my mother, but in each tale, she was an only child."

"Why do you think Delila never brought you to visit your mother?" It seemed heartless to Lydia. "Did she never check on her, see if she was okay? Please don't think I'm being critical, because I'm sure your mother must have had her reasons, but it's confusing because it sounds like they were close when they were girls."

"Apparently, Delila did bring me for visits when I was young." Rebecca looked past her for a moment. "I have the tiniest memories of that, but nothing clear. It explains why the house felt familiar to me when I walked in, though. Delila said that, over time, she grew to believe it would be cruel to keep returning. She knew Margaret wouldn't understand, but she really thought her sister would forget she'd even had a baby. Like I said, Delila sent her cash every month, although she confessed that she never paid taxes on the property. Peter and I will take care of that soon."

They started walking down the hallway toward the exit. "What did she think would become of Margaret?" Lydia was trying to tread lightly, because no matter what, Delila had been Rebecca's mother, biological or not.

"I know Delila must sound like a heartless woman," Rebecca said as she pushed a button to unlock the car. After they had Mattie in the car seat and were both inside, she continued. "She thought she was protecting me, if not from actual harm, then from a life unsuitable for a child. She wrote to several neighbors, asking about Margaret, but no one wrote back. She also mentioned none of them were Amish, though. Delila and Margaret had given up most of the Amish ways, breaking ties with the community, so she didn't think the Amish would still know her sister. If she'd known how horribly my mother was living, though, I'm sure she would have done something."

She paused for a moment, as though reassuring herself that was true.

"Anyway, she told me she left most of the money they had when she took me away—whatever was still left out of the money their parents had saved. Maybe it was just enough for my mother to get that truck and eke out an existence until Delila sent her more."

She started the engine but didn't put the car in gear. Instead, she held the steering wheel and looked down. "I had a wonderful childhood, and I loved my parents very much. But I'm not excusing what Delila did. It was all at Margaret's expense."

Lydia agreed, but she wanted to say something kinder. "I'm sorry for your recent loss of Delila. You must feel overwhelmed."

Rebecca turned to face her and smiled. "How old are you?"

"Seventeen." Lydia glanced at Mattie in the back seat and hoped Rebecca wouldn't put her in a position to explain that Mattie was conceived before marriage. She did have that one thing in common with Margaret. But she wouldn't lie if Rebecca questioned her.

"My daughter is thirty-three." She put the car in gear and backed up. "But you have the wisdom of someone her age."

Lydia smiled. "Thank you for saying so."

After they were on the road, Rebecca said, "Oh. I need to take care of one thing, but I'll take you and Mattie home first. It's a task I'm dreading, though. Someone got my phone number and left a message, saying Margaret's truck is at the police station. I have to do something about it—or at least whatever's in it."

Lydia was quiet for a few moments as she thought about how hard seeing that truck would be for Rebecca, much less going through everything in it. "You don't have to take me home first," she said. "I'll go with you. We can go through her belongings together."

"Wow. God certainly blessed Margaret—and me—when He put you on our path. That would be so nice, if you're sure you don't mind."

"I'm happy to help." *I'm sorry, Gott.* She'd promised not to lie, and she just had. Again, she wished for a time when lying wouldn't be for the good of a cause because, in reality, she knew a person shouldn't lie at all. She could have done without ever seeing that truck again.

Then she remembered what Daisy said. "While you were still in Margaret's room, one of the nurses told me they changed her medications, and they think that's why she's making more sense of things right now. But she'll still become confused as she continues to decline."

Rebecca sighed. "That will be hard to watch. She talked so much about her house, which surprised me, since you said she mostly lived in her truck."

"I honestly don't know how much she went to the house. We saw her sleeping in the truck all over town, but then she would disappear for long periods of time. Maybe she stayed at the house more than we know. And she had to be the one who cleaned the nursery. She might have been waiting for Ben to return, too, secretly hoping to still get married in her home and raise a family with him. But one day she told me he was dead, and then she told me he wasn't, so I don't know if you'll ever know what's true."

Rebecca rubbed her forehead, then sighed. "I don't know if I'll ever try to find him. It's all so sad. If the house was in good shape, I'd ask to take Margaret there so she could see it again. But I don't know how she'd react. Right now, she seems to think it's beautiful inside, as if she's remembering the way it was decorated and clean when she was younger. She might have a huge setback, seeing it like it is."

Lydia asked Rebecca to stop by her mother's house, which was on the way to the police station. Again, she lucked out. Her mother was home and free to babysit Mattie. There was no telling what might be in that truck. It was cool enough to leave Mattie in her car seat with the windows down in Rebecca's car, but she'd fuss if she was in there too long.

As they pulled in front of the station, Rebecca's eyes widened when she saw the blue truck parked to the left of the entrance. "Please tell me that's not it."

"*Ya*, I'm afraid so."

Rebecca pressed her lips together as her eyes grew teary. "I guess I better get it over with." Lydia wondered how much more this woman could take.

They went inside, and after Rebecca filled out the paper-work, the officer told her they could use the dumpster next to the building to get rid of everything they didn't want. Lydia saw several officers milling around within earshot, but when none of them offered to help, she was glad she'd come along.

Outside, Rebecca put her hands on her hips, stared at the truck, then sighed. "Are those nearly dead tomato plants?"

"*Ya.*" Lydia had never been this close to the truck, except the day she found Margaret hunched over the steering wheel.

Rebecca wore black slacks and a black-and-white sweater. She wasn't dressed for this kind of work, but she lowered the tailgate. "How did she even get a driver's license?"

"I don't know. Maybe she doesn't have one." Lydia fought the gag in her throat. The smell was awful, and she worried what they might find. "But if she didn't have a license, I'm sure she would have been arrested a long time ago."

Rebecca lifted herself onto the tailgate and eyed the con-tents. She picked up a small barbecue grill and handed it to Lydia. It was rusted and missing a leg. Lydia carried it to the dumpster and tossed it in.

They found a lawn chair, a fishing pole, a can half filled with gasoline, an old rug that was crusty and rolled up in one cor-ner, and dozens of Coke cans. They also found a box of clean-ing supplies, which seemed odd until Lydia remembered how clean the nursery was. Little by little, Rebecca handed the items to her, and she carried it all to the dumpster.

"What will you do about the truck?" Lydia held her breath as she carried a small bag with rotten apples.

"I don't know. Give it away, I guess." Rebecca lowered an-other bag, larger this time, and even smellier. Lydia didn't look inside. Margaret's daughter didn't seem to have any concerns when it came to money, but the truck was probably worth a few hundred dollars if it was cleaned up.

"What does your husband do for work?" Lydia put a hand to her forehead, blocking the sun, while she waited for Rebecca to give her something else to toss in the trash.

"He's an air traffic controller." Lydia must have looked confused, which she was. "He guides the planes in and out, lets the pilots know when it's safe to land and take off."

"Do you work?" They'd been so consumed with Margaret's life that they hadn't really discussed Rebecca's.

"I just retired from teaching. I'll probably get bored. I'm really too young to retire, but I want to spend as much time as I can with my new grandbaby when she arrives."

Lydia smiled. "It's a girl?"

"Yes." She'd heard the *Englisch* had ways of learning an unborn child's gender. Lydia didn't think she'd want to know ahead of time.

"Oh no." Rebecca covered her mouth with her hand, and Lydia hoped she hadn't found dead dog bones. But she held up a stringer of what used to be fish. "Here's where a lot of the stench is coming from." She held her nose and handed down the offensive item.

After another fifteen minutes, they were done. Rebecca went back inside the police station and asked if Margaret had a driver's license, and the officer behind the desk said she did— as well as a car registration. Both surprised Lydia, but she recalled hearing that mental illness didn't necessarily mean incompetence. And she'd learned that Margaret could read. Then Rebecca asked if someone might benefit from the truck, saying she wanted to give it away, not sell it. The officer told her he'd ask around.

As they headed back to Lydia's parents' house to pick up Mattie, they both seemed lost in thought. Rebecca pulled to a stop when they arrived. "I noticed the name of Margaret's hospice worker on the bulletin board in her room. I wonder how much time they think she has."

"I don't know."

"I'd still love for my mother to see her house before she passes." She shook her head. "But even the best contractor couldn't get it in order in time for Margaret to visit there—not unless he had a hundred people on his crew. I could be wrong, and only God knows for sure, but I don't think Margaret will be here more than a month. A few weeks before she died, my mother looked like Margaret does now."

Lydia caught that Rebecca was still swapping names back and forth. Not surprising. It was surely going to take a while for her to sort through her emotions and land on the names most comfortable for her.

"Would you like to come in and meet my parents?" Lydia felt closer to Rebecca than she probably should, given what a short time they'd known each other. But they seemed to have a strange bond. Maybe that was because Margaret had thought of Lydia as her daughter and now her real daughter was here.

"Oh, wow. I don't know. They'll probably smell me long before I get near them."

Lydia chuckled. "I don't smell any better." She opened the car door. "But I'd like for you to meet them."

Rebecca got out of the car, and they started toward the house. "Yes, I would like to meet the parents of such an amazing young woman."

Lydia's cheeks heated, but her thoughts were elsewhere. She recalled what Beverly said the day they were in Margaret's house.

This haus *is in horrible shape, but the structure looks solid. Maybe the community could come together and help her get the place livable.* If her people could build a barn in a day, they could renovate a whole house in less than a month, couldn't they? Their work crew was in excess of a hundred for sure.

. . .

Samuel listened to Lydia's idea that evening, never prouder of his wife. "I can talk to Bishop Miller and the elders and see what they say about it."

"Do we have to have the bishop's permission? If so, and if he isn't in agreement, the argument would be that no one pushed hard enough to help Margaret. As Christians, everyone should have tried to do more. She lived in squalor in a confused state of mind most of her life. Instead of dealing with her problems, people avoided her." She paused as she gazed into his eyes. "We did too. But now Rebecca wishes Margaret could see the *haus* one last time before she dies. I do too. It will be a double blessing if Margaret gets to meet her granddaughter, a triple blessing if she meets her great-granddaughter."

Samuel nodded. "You also said something about a wedding?"

Lydia chuckled. "I'm glad Joseph is resuming his relationship with Beverly, but I think it's much too soon for a wedding. And I don't know of anyone who's engaged in our community, so we won't be able to fulfill that part of Margaret's wish."

Samuel smiled at his wife before he leaned over and kissed her.

CHAPTER 24

After going home for a day to tell Dawn what was going on and see her husband, Rebecca stayed with Lydia and Samuel for two weeks. And at least a dozen times a day she told them she didn't know how she'd ever repay the kindness she was witnessing.

Samuel had met with the bishop and elders, pled the case to restore Margaret's home, and surprisingly won them over with no opposition. Lydia suspected everyone who agreed to work on the house had turned a blind eye to Margaret at some time during his or her life. Whether or not they were pitching in to clear their consciences, Lydia and Rebecca were thrilled with the way the house was coming together.

Rebecca was packing to spend her first night there when her son-in-law called to say Dawn was in labor. Rebecca headed back to Indianapolis, planning to return in time for their plan.

Lydia, who promised to visit Margaret daily, prayed for Rebecca's family, asking that all would be well. But she also asked God to help Margaret hold on until Rebecca got back.

Lydia hadn't visited Margaret much over the past couple of weeks. She recognized Lydia only as a friend of her daughter's, and Lydia wanted to give Rebecca alone time with her mother for as long as Margaret had left. But she knew Margaret would be heartbroken if no one showed up today and explained where Rebecca was.

Rebecca said Margaret wasn't too confused most days, thanks to the change in medication, but she saw her energy slipping away. On the few days when she had been confused, she'd thrown Rebecca out of her room, so Lydia didn't know what to expect when she opened the door to Margaret's room. But while Rebecca was gone, she would do her best to keep Margaret's spirits up.

"*Wie bischt,*" she said softly as she tiptoed inside with Mattie on her hip. "How are you feeling today?"

Margaret's eyes were barely open, and she'd lost a considerable amount of weight since Lydia had last seen her. A part of her still wanted Margaret to call her Delila, for her to refer to Mattie as Rebecca. It was a selfish thought but there just the same. Lydia owed it to Margaret to be truthful, though.

"Rebecca had to go home for a few days, but she'll be back soon." Lydia held her breath as she braced for a reaction.

"She better hurry." One side of Margaret's mouth curled upward into a smile. "*Gott* is calling *mei* home soon."

Lydia hoped God would wait a little longer. She'd prayed for Him to. So many people had put tons of effort into making Margaret's wishes come true, and Rebecca would be heartbroken if Margaret passed away before they had. She'd be especially distraught if her mother died while she was gone.

Margaret's bottom lip trembled. "I know *mei dochder* has been coming to visit me." She blinked back tears. "But I don't remember her name."

Lydia had just mentioned Rebecca's name, but she'd tell her again. "Her name is Rebecca."

"*Ya, ya.*" Margaret closed her eyes, and Lydia stood by the bed wishing Mary were here right now. Her sister had witnessed her elderly friend, Adeline, die. She might know how close they were to losing Margaret. But Mary had just found out she and Levi were expecting their first child, and she didn't want to deflate her sister's mood. They'd been trying to conceive for a while.

"I'm going to let you sleep." Lydia spoke in a whisper, unsure if Margaret even heard her, especially now that Mattie was making noise. "I just wanted to let you know Rebecca will be back soon."

Lydia was almost out the door when she heard Margaret say, "*Danki*, Delila."

Bringing her free hand to her chest, Lydia slowly turned around and locked eyes with Margaret, praying it wouldn't be for the last time. "You're welcome."

. . .

When Rebecca returned a week later, this time with her husband and the rest of her family, Margaret had grown weaker and less communicative. And she hadn't called Lydia "Delila" or seemed to recognize her as anyone other than a friend of Rebecca's. But she had asked about her daughter daily, even when she didn't remember her name. Every day, Lydia assured her that Rebecca would be returning soon.

Today, Margaret's house was ready. Almost a hundred men had taken turns with the structural work. Windows were replaced, the loose boards on the porch and stairway were repaired, and the outside of the house had a new coat of white, with the porch painted gray.

The ladies in the community had cleaned inside, overhauled furniture, and planted fall foliage in the flower beds out front. Lydia thought fall was the prettiest season in Indiana. She loved the fields of mature corn that lined the roads this time of year, lush green crops that seemed never-ending, and the trees offered a rainbow of fall colors. It was like God's gift before winter settled upon them.

When Lydia and Samuel had visited Rebecca and her family at the house last evening, Lydia had found Peter to be a kind man, and Dawn and Liam were delightful. So was their infant daughter. Rebecca had cried, wondering again how she could ever repay them and the community, but they explained no payment was necessary.

Lydia glanced around the room at the guests. They'd decided to keep the affair small so as not to overwhelm Margaret. Rebecca had already made arrangements for her to pass here, in her own home. A hospice nurse would be coming daily, and Lydia and Rebecca were both grateful to Mary, who had helped Rebecca set up one of the bedrooms with items they'd need to tend to Margaret. She'd also supplied phone numbers they'd need when the time came. The family had decided Margaret would be buried next to Delila and her husband in Indianapolis.

Everyone was eager for Rebecca and Peter to arrive with Margaret. Beverly was aglow, and Joseph couldn't seem to wipe the grin off his face. Lydia's parents, sister, and brother-in-law were all there, and they'd brought Levi's brother, Lucas, and his wife, Natalie. Samuel had picked up his parents earlier in the day.

Dawn was holding her newborn daughter near the front door when they all heard a car pull into the newly paved driveway. It took a few minutes for Peter to get Margaret into her wheelchair, but once they'd pushed her up the temporary ramp on the side of the house and through the door, you could have heard a pin drop. Rebecca carried a small red suitcase,

presumably packed with the few things Margaret had accumu-
lated at the facility.

Please, dear Lord, let this be a good day for Margaret.

Margaret was thin and pale, but as she glanced around the
room, at her restored home and all the people, tears streaked
her cheeks.

Rebecca's daughter was the first to speak. "I'm your granddaughter, Dawn." She leaned down. "And this is your great-
granddaughter. We named her Margaret Delila Witherspoon."
Rebecca beamed.

Margaret could barely lift her hand to touch the baby, but she
said, "So beautiful." Then she found some strength and cupped
Dawn's cheek. "*Mei* granddaughter."

As Rebecca wheeled her through the crowd, Lydia held a
hand over her mouth and watched. Margaret addressed every
single person as if they'd always been in her life in some way
or another.

They finally made their way to Lydia, where beside her stood
Samuel, holding Mattie. Lydia didn't care if Margaret called her
Delila, Rebecca's friend, or anything else. She was just glad to
be sharing this special day with her and all those in attendance.

Margaret reached for Lydia's hand and squeezed. "*Wie
bischt . . .* Lydia?"

It was the first time Margaret had ever called her by her
name, and for fear of choking up, she just nodded.

Samuel, Levi, and Lucas had all offered to carry Margaret
upstairs to visit the nursery, but for now she just toured the
downstairs of her home. Lydia stayed in the front room, but
she could see the delight in Margaret's eyes when she returned.

Then Bishop Miller cleared his throat and asked if everyone
was ready.

Lydia took a tissue from her apron and dabbed at her eyes, determined not to cry now. Samuel handed Mattie to his mother, who was in her wheelchair as usual. Then Lydia took her husband's hand and turned to face him, elated that their family and friends were present to see and hear them exchange wedding vows.

Samuel's parents had been aware of the challenges Lydia and Samuel faced within their marriage, so a renewal of vows didn't surprise them. They loved the idea. But Lydia thought her family would just be excited she and Samuel had chosen to recite their vows again. Then Mary told her they'd all known her marriage wasn't perfect. Lydia was glad it was out in the open. She was tired of hiding her feelings, faking perfection, and being caught up in untruths and lies. And today was a day of celebration and new beginnings.

Renewing their vows had been Samuel's idea, and she'd been speechless when he suggested it. Doing so was a testimonial to the relationship they'd been building over recent months. They were learning about each other's feelings, a process that would continue to help them grow as a couple. And they were in love, truly and deeply.

Margaret was able to see her house the way she'd always wanted to, surrounded by friends and family. Her great-granddaughter would be sleeping upstairs in the nursery Margaret had preserved. And Margaret would get to see a wedding—even if it wasn't her own.

Lydia and Samuel were grateful Bishop Miller had agreed to the wedding on such short notice. He and his wife stood side by side as she and Samuel repeated vows they'd made more than a year ago, but this time the exchange was more than just words. She knew Samuel believed that too. And she could feel

God's blessings pouring down on them as they professed their love for and commitment to each other.

As the bishop gave Samuel a holy kiss on his forehead, his wife placed a holy kiss on Lydia's forehead. Lydia glanced in Margaret's direction. Dawn had squatted next to her, and Margaret had the new baby in her lap. She smiled at Lydia.

At the end of the day, Lydia and Samuel said their goodbyes, and then Lydia held her husband's hand as he carried Mattie to their buggy. She knew they would still experience challenges; that was how a marriage—and life—worked. But for the first time since she'd married Samuel, she felt as one with him, no longer traveling on a separate journey. They were in love, and they'd professed that love to God in front of friends and family. Now it was time to go home and live the life they'd wanted from the beginning.

Everything had been beautifully arranged according to God's will.

EPILOGUE

"W ho's hungry?" Lydia carried a large bowl of chicken salad to the picnic table and set it beside a tray filled with pickles and olives. Beverly was right behind her toting a jar of chow chow, along with two loaves of bread she'd baked that morning.

Lydia put her hands on her hips and chuckled. "Look at those two. You'd think they were twelve again."

Beverly laughed. "At least they're keeping the little ones entertained."

As Lydia watched Samuel and Joseph in their new above-ground pool, she thought about the past ten months. Margaret passed three weeks after Rebecca brought her home, surrounded by her family. And because Rebecca had insisted Lydia was family, she'd seen Margaret take her last breath. Finally, Margaret had gone to be with Delila and her parents, to a place where she was no longer confused. She was perfect now.

Rebecca and her family usually came to Montgomery twice a month, on the weekends. On a whim, once the winter snow had melted, Rebecca went to the spot where Margaret told her money was buried and found it in a can under a rock. The amount was six hundred dollars. Rebecca insisted that Lydia and Samuel take it. She knew Samuel worked hard to take care of his parents.

They refused the money, but then they came home from worship service in late spring to find an aboveground pool set up and ready to use. Rebecca had heard Samuel talk about one more than once. Lydia had trouble getting him out of the pool each evening to come in for supper. But teaching the babies to swim was their excuse for spending so much time in the pool. He'd already taught Mattie how to hold her breath under the surface, and Joseph had taught Susan how to tread water.

Beverly put a hand on her abdomen, then Lydia did the same, and both women laughed. "They'll have two more *bopplis* to start teaching next summer."

Lydia smiled when Samuel held Mattie high above his head. "Wave to *Mamm*!" And Mattie did. It was hard for Lydia to believe their first child was a year and a half old.

Beverly waved too. "Only eight more to go after this one."

"Four more for us," Lydia said. After renewing their vows, she and Samuel had truly found their way to each other and remained hopelessly in love. Joseph and Beverly had married in November. That was only a few months after they met, but neither of them wanted to wait, and their little family was thriving.

Peter honked as he pulled into their driveway with Rebecca. Dawn and Liam, along with their daughter, followed in their car. Liam quickly retrieved ten-month-old Margaret Delila, whom they'd taken to calling Marge, from her car seat. "I hear it's mandatory to teach the babies to swim since the river is nearby," he said before he entered the pool with his daughter, joining the other daddies. Peter was wearing swim trunks too.

"Boys. I'm not sure they ever really grow up," Beverly said as she carried a platter of cookies to the table. She rolled her eyes before she set the goodies down and then hugged Dawn and Rebecca.

Most Saturday afternoons, Levi and Mary showed up with their new baby, and so did Lydia's parents. Samuel picked up his folks if his father was feeling well enough to come. And even Levi's brother, Lucas, and his wife, Natalie, came with Mary and Levi sometimes. Natalie was also pregnant. Soon they would need a bigger pool to accommodate all the daddies and little ones.

Basically, she and Samuel had given everyone a standing invitation to meet at their house on weekends as soon as the pool appeared. Lydia suspected it was a tradition they would carry for years to come.

But at the end of the day, on the weekends Rebecca and her family were visiting and after everyone else had gone home, Samuel, Lydia, Joseph, and Beverly packed up their little ones and traveled to Margaret's former home. Lydia always took a basket to fill with wildflowers, awash in the fields lining the road to the old house. She thought the gorgeous blooms might just be extremely tolerant during the hot months, even without much rain. But maybe God meant them to be a reminder that all things become beautiful under His hand.

Rebecca's family loved the Lord, and today she led them in prayer as they all held hands and stood around Margaret's apple tree. They'd planted it in her honor not long after she died. Even with the right conditions, it might be a while before it produced Margaret's favorite fruit, but sometimes good things were worth waiting for. Until that day, they'd place freshly picked wildflowers around the tree.

Lydia smiled at her husband, then thanked God for His perfect timing.

Acknowledgments

Linda Crane, it is an honor to dedicate this book to you. I cherish the painting you did of me, capturing the first time I went fishing at our cabin. Southern Indiana has become a second home to me, and I think of you as part of my family there.

To Sharon and Sam Hanners, thank you for opening your home and hearts to me. I love and appreciate you both very much.

Natasha Kern, my fabulous agent, I hope we are on this journey together forever. xo

To all the folks at HarperCollins Christian Fiction, thank you for your dedication to each project. Special thanks to my editors on this novel, Kimberly Carlton and Jean Bloom.

Janet Murphy, my dear friend and assistant, you are totally irreplaceable professionally and personally. I love and appreciate you very much.

To Wiseman's Warriors, you gals are the best street team a girl could have! Thank you for all you do to promote my books.

Friends and family—especially my husband, Patrick—thank you for supporting me on this amazing journey that has continued far longer than I could have ever dreamed. And there are still a lot of books bouncing around in my mind, characters shouting to be heard, lol.

And to God, my heavenly Father, thank you for blessing me with stories to tell.

Discussion Questions

1. Lydia and Samuel are both struggling within their marriage. Did you sympathize with one character more than the other? If so, why?

2. Beverly carries a big secret throughout much of the book. Did you agree with her way of thinking? Would things have turned out the same or differently if she'd told Joseph the truth from the beginning?

3. How did you feel when Joseph broke up with Beverly?

4. Margaret is loosely based on someone I don't know, but I see her around town. I always wondered what her story was, and from what I've been told, members of our small town have tried to help this person. Do you know anyone who is homeless? How did they end up that way?

5. There are several tender moments in this story. Which scene was your favorite and why?

6. Samuel and Lydia love each other, but they aren't in love at the beginning of the book. At what point did you notice them starting to fall in love with each other?

7. We don't get to meet Delila in the story, only her daughter, Rebecca. Because of this, we can't fully understand why Delila chose to run away with Rebecca. What might have

been some determining factors as to why Delila left? Or is there no excuse for what Delila did?

8. Lydia feels called to help Margaret. How would the story have ended up if Lydia hadn't followed her calling? What would have become of Margaret? Would Rebecca have ever found out the truth? What about Margaret; would she have been surrounded by loved ones when she passed?

9. Samuel and Lydia have a fight after their lavish date night. The timing was terrible since Margaret chose that as one of the nights to park at the end of Samuel and Lydia's driveway—or was the timing spot-on? Did that need to happen so they would face some of the problems within their marriage?

10. Samuel seems to carry most of the burden about getting Lydia pregnant before they were married. Should he be the one to shoulder the load since he's older? Or, as the saying goes, *it takes two to tango*?

11. If you could change any part of the story, what would it be, and why?

12. Which character could you relate to the most? Who did you feel sorry for, if anyone? Was there someone you rooted for the most?

ABOUT THE AUTHOR

Bestselling and award-winning author Beth Wiseman has sold over two million books. She is the recipient of the coveted Holt Medallion, a two-time Carol Award winner, and has won the Inspirational Reader's Choice Award three times. Her books have been on various bestseller lists, including CBD, CBA, ECPA, and *Publishers Weekly*. Beth and her husband are empty nesters enjoying country life in south central Texas.

Visit her online at BethWiseman.com
Facebook: @AuthorBethWiseman
Twitter: @BethWiseman
Instagram: @bethwisemanauthor

AA# 85FF5D6

Watercan22